T0334218

Also By Abbie Williams

 The Shore Leave Cafe Series

Summer at the Shore Leave Cafe

Second Chances

A Notion of Love

Winter at the White Oaks Lodge

Wild Flower

The First Law of Love

Until Tomorrow

The Way Back

Return to Yesterday

Forbidden

 **The Dove Series**

Heart of a Dove

Soul of a Crow

Grace of a Hawk

a Notion of Love

a

SHORE LEAVE CAFE

novel

Abbie Williams

central
avenue
publishing
2017

Published by Central Avenue Publishing, an imprint of Central Avenue Marketing Ltd.
www.centralavenuepublishing.com

SECOND CHANCES

978-1-77168-107-0 (pbk)
978-1-77168-010-3 (epub)
978-1-77168-056-1 (mobi)

Published in Canada

Printed in United States of America

1. FICTION / Romance   2. FICTION / Family Life

To my sisters, Emily, Marni, Sara, and Kate,
with heaps of love — without all of you,
Jillian would not have been possible.

And to those of you who believe, even a little, in the magic
of the world around you...

Chapter One

Landon, MN - August, 1984

OUR NEW PINK RADIO WAS PLUGGED IN AND POSITIONED on the back of the toilet tank, blaring my current favorite song, "Sunglasses at Night" by Corey Hart. I swayed my hips to the beat as I carefully curled my bangs; last week I hadn't been paying enough attention and burned the crap out of my forehead. Seconds later my older sister, Joelle, flew into the bathroom and slapped her hip against mine, grinning as she effectively bumped me over and then leaned close to the mirror to reapply her new lip gloss. She'd just picked it out yesterday, on her seventeenth birthday. I watched her critically before saying, "It *already* looked fine."

Jo rolled her eyes at me, rubbing her lips together and then miming a kiss in the mirror. Everyone is always saying we look so much alike, and I guess we do, but I always thought Jo, being older, had an edge on me in the looks department. I mean, she's my best friend and I love her like crazy, and I'm happy with how I look—mostly. It's just hard when your older sister is tall and has D-cup boobs, and you aren't tall and yours are still (hopefully) growing. We both have long hair and good tans from being on Flickertail Lake all summer, and I know looks aren't supposed to be important in the long run. Gran is always telling us that it's far better to know how to catch and clean a fish, make a proper margarita, and be a considerate human being. And Great-Aunt Minnie says looks fade but spirit always glows. But *still*.

"Happy birthday," Jo said for the hundredth time today, meeting my eyes in the mirror, a smile crooking her glossy lips. "You look so pretty, Jilly Bean. What time is Chris getting here?"

I couldn't help but grin at the mention of my boyfriend, Chris Henriksen. His sixteenth birthday was back in June and his mom was letting him drive her car until he could afford his own, which would probably be around the time he turned twenty-five or so. I shook out my hair, fluffed my bangs one last time and said, "Pretty soon. How about Jackie?"

"I think I just heard his truck. Here, let me fix your shirt before I go."

She reached and turned my hips so I faced her, then hiked up the bottom of my hot-pink tank top and tied it in a knot, exposing my belly, just like hers. Then she tugged my jean shorts down about two inches and stepped back, satisfied.

"I hate showing my belly button," I grumbled, but Jo slapped my hands from adjusting her handiwork.

"But you have such a cute little belly," she teased. "Now leave it!"

There was no point in arguing. I asked, "Did Mom say anything else about the tattoo?"

Jo rolled her eyes again, complaining, "No, still no. Even though it's all I wanted for my birthday. I mean, it would just be a little daisy, right near my hip. I could cover it up anytime I wanted. I don't get why it's such a big deal."

"Yeah, but what about what Gran said, about when you have a baby someday, and it would get all stretched out?" I reminded, leaning to click off the radio before following her out of the bathroom.

Jo thumped down the stairs, calling over her shoulder, "Believe me, that's something I'm not doing for a *looooong* time! Shit, Jills, can you imagine?"

"No," I said honestly. "Not really."

Outside, the late-afternoon air was clear and mellow, scented by the campfire that Dodge was tending over by the cafe. Jo, spotting her boyfriend, Jackie Gordon, pulling into the parking lot, sprinted ahead. He climbed down from his rusty F-150 and pushed back his sunglasses as she jumped into his arms and they kissed like it was months since they'd seen each other, instead of just a few hours.

"Lookin' good, babe," I heard him say, his hands all over her.

I would have considered this obnoxious except that when Chris got here I planned to cover him in kisses, too. My heart sent a rush through my blood as I thought about Chris, who'd been my boyfriend since last spring. I'd known him forever, of course, like basically everyone in Landon. I hadn't paid any attention to him in middle school, but all of a sudden in tenth grade we had four classes together and he just seemed to be in my mind…a lot. *A lot*, a lot.

I would think of him as I lay in bed with my headphones on, trying to block out Jo, talking incessantly to Jackie on the phone in our room, at least until Gran would get on the extension from the kitchen downstairs and tell her it was time to quit yakking and go to bed. Gran thought that was funny, rather than just sticking her head in our bedroom door. But every song I heard as I lay there in my twin bed somehow reminded me of Chris. His eyes were brown, with a gold sheen and flecks of green sprinkled throughout. It wasn't something you could see unless you looked directly into his irises.

The first time he'd asked me to hang out was last March, after geometry but before lunch. He was with a group of his buddies and I was walking with my good friend Jenny Hull, and he pushed off from the locker he was leaning against and followed behind us.

"Hey, Jills," he said, the nickname just about everyone in school used, but for some reason when Chris spoke it I felt a little extra thud in my heartbeat. I turned and walked backward for a couple of steps so I could look at him, until he laughed and grabbed my elbow, the one not cradling a pile of books, and said, "Don't crash!"

We all stopped, Jenny included, and Chris shot her a slightly flustered look, but then his eyes came back to me and he asked, "Hey, you wanna swing by Dairy Queen with me this weekend?" His voice cracked just a hair on the last word. I found myself studying the face that was so often in my daydreams. He'd grown about six inches between the beginning of the year and March. His hair was chestnut brown, cropped close to his head. He had a square jaw and the kind of laugh that made everyone around him want to laugh, too. His eyes seemed to be sparkling at me as he waited, though I could sense he was really nervous.

"Sure," I heard myself say, and the smile that spread over his face was surely mirrored on mine in the next moment.

"Cool, I'll see you," he said.

And we'd been pretty much inseparable ever since.

"Hi, honey!" Dodge called as I came near. He was one of my favorite people in the world, someone who was such a part of Shore Leave that sometimes, in my most secretly-guarded thoughts, I pretended he was my dad — even though he was married to Marjorie, with two of his own kids, Justin and Liz. Justin was in Jo and Jackie's grade and Liz a year behind me. Dodge ran the filling station and engine repair shop about a quarter-mile around the lake, but he was still here at the cafe all the time, helping out with the things Mom and Aunt Ellen couldn't manage. He stopped in for coffee every morning of the busy season, without fail, sometimes bringing Justin, who helped him in the summers. Dodge's bushy salt-and-pepper hair was held under control only by the aviator sunglasses perched on the top of his head. His full beard and mustache seemed like a continuation of his unruly hair.

"Hi, Dodge," I said, burrowing against him and squeezing tightly. He couldn't hug me back because he held his drinking mug in one big hand and a long, tapered stick in the other, which he used to poke at the blazing fire. Though the sun wouldn't set for a couple hours, the bonfire was already alive and kicking. He kissed the top of my head and I smelled his familiar, comforting scent, a combination of wood smoke, motor oil, tobacco, and Jim Beam.

"Happy birthday!" he said, sounding jovial as always. Truly, I'd never seen him in any other mood. And then he hollered, "Boy! What's taking you so long?"

"Shit, Pa, I'm coming," Justin said, giving us a grin as he staggered up to the fire bearing an enormous armload of wood. "Where do you want this?"

Dodge pointed with the stick and Justin grunted as he deposited the burden on the ground. He stood and brushed debris from his flannel shirt, which flapped open over his tan, bare belly and damp swim trunks.

"Hey, Jilly," he said to me, offering an easy smile. Justin was tall and lean and wiry, with wavy black hair that hung past his shoulders in back, though the sides were shorter, and a face that Gran always said was too pretty for a boy. I was glad she'd never said that directly to him. I'd known Justin forever; the two of us, along with Joelle and Justin's sister Liz, played like siblings every summer as far back as my memory stretched. He treated me like a little sister, teasing me mercilessly when we were kids. Since high school we'd drifted apart, but now he added amiably, "Happy birthday."

"Thanks," I said, and then waved farewell as I practically skipped over to where Mom and Aunt Ellen were busy hanging Christmas lights over the picnic table. I felt a splash of excitement; the cafe was closed for the evening, though people would flock out here in less than an hour to celebrate. Mine and Joelle's birthdays were a day apart, and our party was always the final send-off to summer; school would start next week already, and so I meant to enjoy the weekend to the fullest.

"There's my sweet sixteen," Great-Aunt Minnie said from the porch, where she and Gran sat having a smoke and a couple of beers. "Look at you."

I bounded up the steps and kissed her cheek. Minnie's golden hair hung in a thick braid down her back, nearly to her waist, as she disliked cutting it. My grandma, her younger sister, wore hers in a similar style most days, though Gran let her own hair go white while Minnie kept hers dyed. I was the one who helped her color it; every six weeks or so she'd tip her head back over the tin washtub and I'd use Clairol Natural Palest Blonde to counteract the gray.

"Hi, doll," said Gran, blowing smoke out of the side of her mouth and grinning at me. "You excited?"

"For sure," I said, tingly and happy. I plopped into the chair between them and Gran slid her bottle my direction.

"Just a little one, now," she cautioned. "And for God's sake, don't let your mother see."

I grinned and snagged a sip, the beer cool and with a slight honey flavor. Good thing Gran figured this was the only drinking I'd be doing on my birthday.

"Where's Joelle?" Great-Aunt Minnie asked.

"With that Jackson," Gran said, with a disapproving tone. She always said *that Jackson* instead of just using his name, which drove Joelle crazy. I knew Gran wasn't overly fond of my sister's boyfriend, even though everyone else seemed to love him. Especially Mom. I overheard Mom telling Aunt Ellen once, around last Christmas, that she hoped they'd get married someday. I didn't mind Jackie, but I hated the thought of my sister marrying him and moving across town, and subsequently away from me. I hated the thought of anything that separated us.

Rich Mayes poked his head out the screen door to wish me a happy birthday. He added, "I'll go get Pamela and then we'll be back to celebrate, sweetie."

I hopped up from the chair to hug him. Rich worked at the cafe as a cook, and he and his wife Pam lived just a few miles away. Pam's grown daughter lived in either Texas or Oklahoma, I couldn't remember which; she'd been up to visit once years before, when I was just a kid.

"Oops, there's your fella," Minnie said, indicating Chris's mom's car as it bumped into the parking lot.

"And there she goes," I heard Gran chuckle, but I was too excited to see my boyfriend. I met him just as he climbed out of his car and jumped right into his arms.

"Hey," he said, hugging me hard, my toes lifting from the ground. "My birthday girl. What's your wish?"

"I can't tell," I said, unable to stop grinning at him. He wore his new Van Halen t-shirt, the one with the angel from their latest album cover. I reminded him, "Or it won't come true."

Chris leaned back into the car and reached for a package wrapped in bright pink paper and tied with a silver ribbon. "Well I hope this comes close, anyway," he said, not letting me take it from his hands. When I giggled and grabbed for it, he lofted it above his head, where I hadn't a chance of reaching. I dug my fingertips into his ribs. He yelped and almost dropped it, and finally surrendered it into my grasp.

I shook it gently, then held it to my ear.

"You'll never guess," he said confidently. "And hey, I didn't give you a kiss yet." And so saying he slipped his arms around me and pulled me close. He tasted familiar and sweet, and of Big Red gum. Chris was the only one of our group of friends who didn't smoke, which I admired. He squeezed me tightly and tipped his forehead against mine to whisper, "Love you, Jilly Bean."

"I love you, too," I murmured, and brushed my lips against his one more quick time.

He said, "You taste like beer."

"Gran," I replied, which was all the explanation he needed.

He stroked my hair, wrapping his fingers in it like he always did, before saying, "Let's go celebrate."

An hour later the sun sank like honey spilled on a pale-blue tablecloth. Twinkling lights glowed and lanterns burned, everyone eating, talking, drinking, laughing and dancing. Eddie Sorenson and Jim Olson played their guitar and banjo, like they always did for parties in the Landon area. Rich's wife, Pam, joined them with her accordion; sometimes she used a tambourine. It certainly wasn't Top Forty music like Jo and I normally listened to on the radio, but I couldn't imagine loving what Eddie and Jim played any more than I did; it was the music of my childhood. And no one could sit still. Pam laughed about something as she played, her long brown hair held up in a gold barrette. People crowded the makeshift dance floor, my sister and Jackie locked in each other's arms, even though the song was not a slow one. Everyone came to our birthday bash, and most years the weather was fantastic, like it was tonight, the air calm and Flickertail growing mysterious as the sun disappeared and stole the color from the far shore. Stars began to decorate the darkening sky, and I was sixteen.

Chris and I took a break from the dancing after the next song; I grabbed his hand and we ran down the hill to the glider on the dock, our favorite place to sit and talk. Sometimes we fought my sister and Jackson for the space, though. They thought they were so sneaky, having sex after they'd go skinny-dipping. I couldn't believe they were that brave; at least Chris and I waited until we could be totally alone, and we hadn't even gone all the way yet. I was terrified of getting pregnant, despite Jo's promise to take me to an appointment to get on the pill, like her.

"Here," he said as we claimed our spots on the glider. He'd grabbed his present for me from the stack of gifts on the picnic table. "I can't wait anymore for you to open it."

I was too excited to do anything but rip the paper away. Inside was a white gift box from the local drug store.

"A Precious Moments figurine?" I asked, holding it up and inspecting the side.

"No, silly," Chris said. "I just used the box. Open it."

I did, struggling with the tape he so industriously applied to each edge. But at last I managed and reached inside, extracting a small, blue velvet…ring box? My heart just about stopped, but Chris laughed again, totally at ease. He said, "It's not an engagement ring, Jills. Don't look so freaked out."

I regained my voice and argued, "I'm not *freaked out*. But if it's not…"

"It's a promise ring," he said, and all traces of teasing suddenly vanished. His eyes were serious upon mine in the starlight. My heart punched my breastbone and then began pounding as though I'd just jogged from downtown. He swallowed and caught my free hand between both of his. His hands were big and all knuckles, and I loved them. I loved everything about him, and honestly, if he'd asked me right at the moment to be his wife my answer would have been *yes*.

"A promise ring?" I repeated carefully, cradling the box in my cupped palm.

"Here, open it," he said, and freed my hand so I could.

"Oh," I said, and my eyes stung with tears as the little box opened with a click, revealing a simple gold band set with a heart containing a tiny stone.

"It's a peridot," he explained, and his voice was very soft. "For August. It's hard to tell in the dark."

"I love it," I whispered, my lips trembling. "Oh, Chris…"

He plucked it out and studied my face, before gently taking the third finger of my right hand into the tips of his and sliding the ring over my knuckle. It fit perfectly and he smiled in triumph.

"Joelle helped me with the size," he explained.

"I really love it," I managed to whisper, and tears fell over my cheeks. I felt a shift in my belly when Chris put the ring on my finger, a gut instinct that I'd long ago learned never to ignore. I knew in that moment that he would be my husband someday. Not because of the ring and what it implied, but something much deeper, some instinct that kicked at me sometimes, usually when I was sleeping but occasionally in the waking world, too. And right then, without a doubt, I knew that I would bear his name. And for a split second I felt a third presence, just a flash that disappeared almost instantly.

Chris brought my hand to his lips and kissed it, letting his lips linger. I lunged into his arms and heard the gift box and wrapping paper plop into the lake. But I didn't care; the ring was safe on my finger. Chris gathered me close and kissed me, sweet and tender, like he did just about everything.

"I love you," he said into my hair.

"Oh, Chris," I said, my throat hurting a little, kissing the side of his smooth jaw. "I love you. And I love my ring. It's beautiful."

"Someday it'll be an engagement ring," he whispered. "I promise."

I buried my face in his neck and breathed against him. He slipped his hands around my waist, still bare from Joelle tying my tank into a knot. Sometimes Chris was so hesitant that I helped him along, and reached to slip his palms upward, so that they cupped my breasts. He exhaled in a rush and kissed me, his thumbs moving in careful circles over my nipples. I pressed into his hands and kissed him with all of the emotion that swelled in my heart.

"Hey, kiddos, whatcha doing out here?" came a teasing voice, and Chris withdrew his hands as quickly as if the school principal was headed our way; I kept mine on his shoulders even though Jackie and Jo strolled down the hill from the cafe, holding hands. Jackie sounded half in the bag, despite the early hour and the presence of so many adults. But just about everyone here was probably two-thirds of the way there anyway, and not inclined to notice. Jackie was a local football star, would be Landon High's starting quarterback this fall, and no one really questioned anything he did. He and my sister were giggling about something. Jackie let Jo walk first, as if he actually was a gentleman (which he really wasn't) as they made their way out onto the dock to join us.

"So, do you love it?" Jo asked, tucking her long hair behind her ears and grinning at me. She was flushed and her breath smelled like some kind of fruity wine. She held out her hand for mine.

"I do," I whispered, drawing back from Chris and slipping my right hand into hers. "Thanks for helping with the size."

"Oh, Jilly, it's beautiful," she practically cooed. "I knew it would fit."

"What's this?" Jackie asked incredulously, shoving his way between us. "An engagement ring?"

"A promise ring," Joelle corrected, slapping at his lean belly.

"What's the difference?" he asked, catching her around the waist.

"It's a promise to be engaged," Chris said, giving us all a grin. I couldn't help myself and kissed him again, until Jackie warned, "I'm throwing you two in the lake if you don't quit."

Joelle slapped at him again and he laughed and threatened to pitch her next. She shrieked and wrestled away from him, but in the next moment he stepped back and peeled off his shirt, revealing his muscular chest. Jackie was such a show-off; half the time he was around he was shirtless. He gave us all a wicked grin and then unbuttoned his shorts, doing an Elvis-y thing with his hips as he slipped them down and then cannon-balled off the end of the dock. He surfaced with a roar and began energetically splashing us. We all yelped and Joelle screeched, "We have to do the cake pictures still, dumbass!"

Jackie only laughed, leaning his elbows on the end of the dock; with his dark curls slicked back from his forehead he looked like a handsome, evil merman. He grabbed Jo's ankle.

"Girls!" Gran yelled at us, up on the porch and backlit by the lights. "Get up here for cake!"

"See?" Joelle said to Jackie as he leaped with muscular grace onto the end of the dock and tried to get his arms around her.

She darted away and ran for the cafe, with Jackson dripping in hot pursuit. Chris stood and then surprised me by picking me up like a bride on her wedding night. He said formally, "Happy birthday, Jilly. The first of many to come."

Three hours later most of the guests headed back around Flickertail for home and their beds; just the regulars remained at the fire pit: Mom and Ellen, Gran and Minnie, Rich, Pam, and Dodge. I yet hadn't shown my ring to anyone other than Joelle. In the hubbub of the party no one was aware that I was hiding my right hand from view. I wasn't sure how Mom would react, especially, and wanted to wait until Chris wasn't here so he wouldn't be hurt if she seemed disapproving. No matter if she was; I planned never to remove my new ring.

A big group of us was swimming now, under the intoxicating light of a million stars. The air was so motionless it seemed as though we were characters on a theater stage, spot-lit by the pale glow of the waxing moon. Our words and shrieks and laughter could probably be heard clearly for miles in every direction. I hugged Chris's shoulders as I rode on his back, pleasantly drunk, but not enough that I couldn't hide it from the womenfolk; Jo and I were longtime experts at that.

Jackie and Justin had my sister and Justin's girlfriend, Aubrey Pritchard, on their shoulders. Jo and Aubrey were locked in good-natured combat, trying to knock one another into the water while the guys gripped their thighs and laughed uproariously. A few of our other friends stuck around, too; a bottle of peppermint schnapps made the rounds for shots at least three times. I held my right wrist loosely in my left hand, and Chris reached up every so often to rub his fingers over my palms, or he reached back to caress my legs under the water. I pressed my lips against his chilly neck again and again, or rested my cheek against his back. We watched everyone playing and roughhousing from a safe distance, Chris chest-high in the lukewarm water. My long hair hung in damp snarls over my shoulders.

"I love seeing this on you," he said, holding my ring between two fingers. "I almost picked one with blue to match your eyes."

"Oh, I like the green," I assured him. "I love it."

"I'm glad," he said. And then, softly, "I'm so happy you're mine, Jilly."

Tears wet my eyes again, surprising me. I was so overwhelmed by my feelings for him that my chest literally hurt. In response, I hugged him as hard as I could. He turned his head and I leaned around to kiss him sideways.

"Then I'm the luckiest girl alive," I said back, and he scooted me around with a smooth motion to kiss me much more thoroughly.

Chapter Two

PROM WAS TWO WEEKS AWAY AND I FINALLY CHOSE A DRESS, after much debating. Mom drove Jo and me all the way to Minneapolis to check out the prom shops. The unspoken message was that if we didn't pick something on this extensive excursion, we were up Shit Creek without a paddle, as Gran would say; at least, if we wanted a dress that wasn't from the dime store in Landon. Jo already pictured a specific dress —short, black, and with sequin detailing. Since just about every prom dress on display was either pitch-black or eye-popping teal, there was no problem locating one that could have been made to order. She tried it on with a pair of very high heels, which caused Mom to cluck with disapproval, but Jo brought her own tip money for shoes. I looked at her with complete admiration; I told her Jackie was going to freak out when he saw her.

"That's the idea," she said, too low for Mom to hear as I joined her at the three-way mirror in the dressing room hallway. She pivoted again, asking, "Do you think the heels are too much?"

"No, they look great," I said honestly. "I love the straps up your ankles."

"Thanks, Jills," she said, smoothing the short, tight skirt over her teeny waist and curvy hips. "Now let's find you something to knock Christopher's socks off." And she raised her eyebrows up and down at me; Jo was so naughty. I giggled and felt myself blush, and Jo added, "You're so cute."

"I want something blue," I said as we paced rows of possibilities, Jo clutching the dress-length bag containing her new get-up.

"Indigo, navy, periwinkle," Mom mused, examining fabric colors. "Or what, honey?" Mom followed Jo and me at a small distance, making sure I didn't pass up a good choice. Despite my protests, Mom loaded her arms with about ten options, none exactly the blue I envisioned—sapphire, with a sparkle. Maybe glitter. Or with rhinestones over the front. Long, with a slit up to my thigh.

I tried on every choice, even the non-blue ones, mostly to humor Mom and Jo; one thing I could count on was an honest response from both of them. Jo vetoed the first four, but wolf-whistled at the fifth, a taffeta dress the color of June roses. A deep magenta in color, it fit simply, tight across the breasts and then flaring into a skirt, a basic A-line, but above my knees. I twirled tentatively, trying to see the back.

"Oh, Jilly Bean, this is the one," Jo insisted, turning me by the shoulders to face the mirror again. She gathered my hair and twisted it expertly on top of my head, holding it there to demonstrate the overall look. I met her eyes in our reflection and smiled. She winked at me. Nudging me with her elbow, she teased, "This is it, I feel it in my bones. Don't you?"

"It's not like that," I explained for the millionth time. "And it is pretty. But I wanted blue."

"Not when you have this one," Jo said.

Mom, perched on a chair to wait, agreed, "I like that one, too, Jillian. That is a lovely color on you."

"All right," I relented.

After eating lunch at a fancy (by our standards, anyway) restaurant, we headed back to Landon. Jo elected to drive while Mom dozed in the passenger seat, so we made it home an hour or so sooner, since Jo wasn't afraid to break the speed limit on the interstate. We pulled into the cafe parking lot in the coppery gleam of early evening light; we'd driven out from beneath the thick gray quilt of clouds blanketing the Twin Cities after an hour or so. The sky was currently the mellow blue of early spring, the sunlight slanting auburn over Flickertail as Jo parked and slapped both hands on the steering wheel. I grinned at her from the back seat and then studied our family's business out the front windshield. I loved Shore Leave so much. I couldn't imagine being separated from it for more than a day or so. Jo was different, longing to get away. The thought of that terrified me and so I changed the subject whenever her thoughts veered that direction.

"Jackie's here," I observed, watching as he emerged from the cafe, Justin on his heels. They must have boated over from town, since neither one of their vehicles was in sight. Sure enough, as we climbed out of the car I spotted Dodge's ancient, beat-up dingy tied to our dock, with its outboard motor tilted up out of the water.

"So, you find a dress?" Jackie teased my sister. She made a show of twirling the long plastic bag around her head, but did not let him peek.

"Jackson, *no*," she insisted. "It's a surprise."

He grabbed her for a quick kiss and then said, "We're heading over to Justin's. I'll stop out later."

"Okay," she told him, pulling him back for one more smooch.

I rolled my eyes at Justin, who grinned at me and then grouched, "Come on, dude."

"I can't believe you guys graduate this year," I said, watching the guys jog down the hill and over the dock boards. Justin replaced the motor in the water and Jackie, who'd pulled a white skipper hat over his curls, fired the boat to life. They both waved up at us.

"I know, *finally*," Joelle said, not understanding that I meant this as a lament.

"Thanks for driving," Mom said. She walked up behind us laden with my dress and both of our shoe boxes.

"Jeez, Mom, here," Joelle said, taking her shoes from Mom's arms.

Aunt Ellen stuck her head out the screen door and called, "Joanie! Girls! We could use some help in here."

And so it wasn't until after dinner rush that I was able to call Chris to tell him about my dress. Mom, Gran, Minnie, and Ellen sat in the bar, smoking and rolling silverware for tomorrow, a seemingly endless task. My sister was wiping down her tables out on the porch and I'd just counted my tips.

"I can't wait to see it," Chris said, sounding happy. "Do I have to wait for the dance?"

"Yes," I told him. "At least, according to Jo."

Chris and I celebrated our one year anniversary just last month, in March. I hadn't yet taken the promise ring from my finger, where Chris placed it on my birthday. I loved tipping my hand to and fro in the sunlight, watching the tiny green peridot glint and throw back sparks. Mom hadn't reacted the way I feared; instead she cupped my cheeks and said calmly, "If you promised your right ring finger to Tom and Elaine Henriksen's boy, then I'm happy for you, honey."

Great-Aunt Minnie harrumphed a little, eyeing the ring over the rim of her horn-rimmed glasses, but said, "As long as you finish school first, Jilly Rae."

Gran brought my hand close to her eyes to give the ring a thorough examining. She pronounced, "It's lovely. And Chris is a sweet boy, not like that Jackson."

Thank goodness Jo wasn't there to hear this remark, since Gran would surely have made the same assessment with Joelle present. I said, "Aw, Gran, Jackie's not so bad."

Gran gave me a look that clearly meant, *When you're older, you'll know better.*

"So, what color?" Chris asked, drawing me back to the present.

"Pink," I told him.

"I'll get you roses then," he said.

"Can you come over? I haven't seen you all day," I complained, twisting the phone cord around my finger until the tip turned purple.

"I can't tonight," he apologized. "Dad and I are cleaning the garage. I promised I'd help until it was done."

Chris's parents were older, closer to Gran's age than my mother's; he was an only child, born when Tom and Elaine were in their late forties. And so I understood that when he said his dad needed help, he really meant it.

"I'll see you tomorrow," I told him and kissed the receiver with a loud smack. "There, that's for good-night."

Chris laughed, and my heart felt warm and safe. He said softly, "I wish I was there to really kiss you. Love you."

"Love you, too." And I hung up thinking that someday soon he would be in my arms to kiss me good-night *every* night. He would be my husband and we'd live just across town from Shore Leave. Better yet, we could build a little cabin-sized place on the property. That way I could still see and hear Flickertail on a daily basis, and be here to help Great-Aunt Minnie dye her hair, and work in the cafe, and sit on the dock in the evenings to watch the sun sizzle into the lake as it set.

I was smiling as I helped myself to a glass of root beer. Joelle came through the door from the porch, untying her server apron. Her hair was slung back in a ponytail low on her neck and she looked tired. I was about to ask her if she needed help when the phone on the front counter rang. I caught it up on the second ring, saying cheerfully, "Shore Leave Cafe!"

"Joelle?" asked a voice I didn't recognize, though I felt I should. It was a woman's, vaguely familiar, and she sounded upset.

"No, but she's right here," I said, motioning for my sister.

Jo hurried over at once and frowned at my expression, taking the phone from my grasp and saying, "Hello?"

I watched as her face went from concerned to outright terrified. She said nothing but, "Oh my God," and, "I'll be right there," before hanging up, grabbing her purse from behind the counter and then racing to the parking lot without another word.

"Jo!" I yelled, clacking out the screen door in her footsteps. "Wait!"

She slowed a fraction, digging through her purse for the keys to the station wagon. Tears seeped over her cheeks as I caught up to her, grabbing her arm before she darted away again.

"What's going on?" I demanded.

She said, "It's Jackie, come on, let's go."

We were break-necking to the highway before I heard any more explanation. Jo, wiping tears from her face with one hand, clutching the steering wheel with the other, explained, "That was Jackie's mom. He and Justin are both in the hospital."

"What?" I gasped. "Why?"

"They…somehow they fell off a train!" she wailed, and accelerated.

We drove to Rose Lake, ten minutes away and the next town over, since Landon doesn't have its own hospital. Jo drove seventy-five miles an hour. By the time we pulled into the parking lot, streetlights flooded the space in an eerie white glow, blocking out the glint of stars in the darkening sky. I followed my sister at a jog. Patricia Gordon, Jackie's mother, met us as we bolted through the automatic door that slid soundlessly to accommodate us.

"Oh my God, are they all right? Where is he?" Jo cried, both of her hands plunged into her hair, like she was about to tear it out.

Pat looked more composed than she sounded on the phone, and hugged Joelle close, rubbing her back. She said, "Honey, it's all right, they'll both be all right. Jackie scared us for a minute there, but the doctor says he'll be fine."

"Can I see him?" my sister begged, her eyes still awash with tears.

"Of course, he's up just one floor, room 207," Pat told us.

I followed my sister, feeling useless; probably Mom and everyone was wondering where the hell we'd gone with no word. I figured I better give them a call before they got too worried and called the police or something. Inside the dimly-lit hospital room, Jackie lay on his back in a twin bed, eyes closed. His forehead and one wrist were bandaged, and he appeared unusually pale. Jo made a whimpering noise and raced to the bedside, her hands fluttering over him. I stood in the background, my heart bumping in sympathy for my sister.

"Jackie," she whispered. Even though I meant to keep my distance, I couldn't help but move forward and gently touch her back. Jackson's left cheek was bruised but his eyelids fluttered and he looked up at us, and then attempted to smile.

"Jo," he muttered. "I'm sorry."

She leaned over him and cupped his face. He bent his arm, with a slight grimace, and wrapped it around her hips.

"Don't scare me like this," she murmured, brushing at his curls with gentle fingers.

"Hey, guys," Justin said, coming into the room, and I turned gratefully to him, embarrassed to be witnessing such an intimate scene.

"Hey," I said.

"Just five stitches for me," Justin said, indicating a bandage over his right eyebrow. "I guess that's what I get for being a dumbass. Hope it doesn't scar."

"What happened?" Jo demanded, turning to Justin, who immediately held up his hands like a gunfighter proving he didn't have a weapon.

"We decided it would be fun to hop the train for a free ride. And *smart guy* here slipped and fucking fell off the side, so I had to jump after his ass," Justin said, indicating Jackie.

Jackie groaned, reminding us, "Hey, I said I was sorry."

Jo spun back to him, cheeks flushed, her golden-green eyes flashing with a look I knew well. She snapped, "Dammit, Jackson! You *promised* you wouldn't do this stupid shit anymore! Are you in seventh grade?"

Jackie closed his eyes and even I could tell he was trying to amp up the pitiful look so Jo would quit yelling at him.

"Jills, you need a ride home?" Justin asked. "I was just gonna head out. They discharged me but Jackie's gotta stay the night."

I turned to my sister, who was now smoothing Jackie's hair. I wanted to roll my eyes at this; Jo was too easily manipulated by Jackie. Instead I asked, "You want me to stay, Joey?"

She shook her head. "No, but thanks, Jills. I'll stay here for a while, will you tell Mom?"

I hugged her hard and Justin said, with the kind of affectionate undertone guys use when they care about each other and rely on insults to show it, "Sleep tight, shithead."

Justin and I said good-night to Pat and then walked out into the night together, in silence. The almost-full moon was just rising from the eastern edge of the world. Justin led the way to his truck, and I was surprised when he opened the door for me. But it made sense, because Dodge was a gentleman, always holding the door for ladies.

"Thanks," I said, clambering inside his truck. After he slid behind the wheel and gunned the truck to life, I asked, "Do your parents know you guys are here?"

"Yeah, Mom freaked out a little, but I told her I just got a few stitches," he said, driving us out of the lot. Rose Lake was a pretty town, just a little bigger than Landon.

"So, where did you guys fall off the train?" I asked, studying his profile for a second.

"Shit, somewhere just outside of town, luckily. I told Jackie it was the last time we were hitching a ride the *last* time we did it, but he's gotten all sentimental these last few months, what with school ending and moving away and everything. He wants to do everything we used to do one last time. Especially now that he's been accepted to Northwestern."

This fact frightened me to no end; Jo sobbed for over two hours after Jackie received his acceptance letter, though not in his presence. I was terrified that somehow he would convince her to join him at this college in Chicago, even though Jo hadn't applied there. Just the possibility of her moving that far away made my soul feel like shriveling.

"Then we had to fucking walk back to town to get my truck," Justin was saying, laughing a little. "Jackie was in so much pain that I drove him straight to the hospital and then called Greg and Pat. Greg wasn't home, but Pat rushed right over and then I figured I better call home since there's no way they wouldn't find out anyway. Shit, Dad'll whip my ass for being so dumb."

I giggled a little. "I can't imagine Dodge getting so mad."

"Are you kidding me?" Justin responded easily, driving with his right hand on the bottom of the wheel, the other sticking straight out the open window. It was a gorgeous evening and I rolled mine down all the way, too, letting the spring air rush into the truck. No matter that my hair would be a squirrel's nest when we got back to Shore Leave. He added, with his usual good spirit, "When I was a kid I got spanked all the time. Liz only did once, but she's a quick learner."

"I guess Aubrey *has* mentioned that you like to be spanked," I heard myself say, and felt my cheeks immediately blister, glad suddenly for the darkness. Now why did I say that? Aubrey (who I honestly thought was a gigantic bitch, though I would never confess this to Justin) did love to brag about Justin's prowess, but she'd never actually mentioned spanking.

"What?" he yelped, laughing. "You are so shitting me."

I was laughing then, too, embarrassed but unable to go back on what I'd said now. Maybe a little devil hopped onto my shoulder, maybe I secretly relished being alone with popular Aubrey Pritchard's hunky boyfriend in his truck, getting his attention this way, but I added, "Yeah, she's *really* descriptive, too."

Justin laughed even harder. He angled a look my way and said, "What*ever*, Jillian, you are so pulling my leg." At the same time, he nudged my left thigh with his knuckles, the way you would to emphasize your words, and my heart issued a sudden frenzy of hot, rapid beats.

"I am not," I lied, irritably.

Grinning, this time he mouthed the word *whatever*.

I shrugged as though unconcerned, but found I couldn't quite catch a full breath. There was a tiny part of me that acknowledged how I liked the sound of my name on Justin's lips, but that was far too strange a thought to deal with, so I pushed it away. Immediately I considered the possibility of Justin confronting Aubrey, and then Aubrey angrily confronting me. I imagined this scenario with a hefty dose of anxiety, picturing hiding behind Joelle at school, like a little kid.

We reached Landon no more than a minute later and Justin turned onto Fisherman's and then left around Flickertail, out to Shore Leave. There were still a few customer cars in the lot, probably just people hanging around the bar. Our candle lanterns glimmered on the porch and I could see Gran and Minnie having a smoke at their usual table. Justin sat with his hands hanging over the top of the steering wheel, the truck idling, and I collected my nerves, looked his way, and said, "Thanks for the ride."

His dark eyes held mine as he offered an indulgent grin, the kind you'd give a baby sister. He said, "No problem, kiddo," like I wasn't the same age as his girlfriend. But Aubrey was light-years ahead of me in both confidence and attitude; it was actually better than being called *tomboy*, Justin's perennial nickname for me in the past. One of several.

Not that I cared or anything.

I hopped out of the truck and slammed the door just a little harder than necessary. Justin drove away and I climbed the steps under the shrewd gazes of both my grandma and my great aunt.

"Where's your sister?" Gran asked just as Minnie commented, "You girls took off awfully fast."

I sighed and sank to a chair to join them, suddenly exhausted. I said, "Jackie fell off the train and is in the hospital in Rose Lake."

Mom would have freaked out, despite the fact that my tone didn't exactly suggest a need to panic. Gran squawked a laugh and Minnie casually blew a smoke ring; she'd tried numerous times to teach me, but I had yet to master the art. Gran asked, "How'd you end up with the boy?"

Everyone called Justin *the boy*, like he was still seven years old. He never seemed inclined to mind, and I laughed to myself, hoping he was driving home pondering why Aubrey would tell people that he liked to be spanked.

"Justin was with him at the hospital. He actually brought Jackie there and of course Jo wanted to stay longer, so I hitched a ride," I explained. "Jackie is a little banged up, but otherwise just fine."

Mom stuck her head out the porch door and confirmed, "I just got off the phone with Pat. Seems like the boys were getting into trouble again." She sounded affectionate, as though they'd toilet-papered a yard rather than risked their lives. But that was Jackson, always pushing things and talking everyone around him into doing the same thing.

"You getting excited for the prom?" Minnie asked. She smiled at me around her cigarette, drawing her braid over one shoulder with her free hand and twisting its length. "Joanie showed me your dress, doll. I love that color. Reminds me of a skirt I had once upon a time."

"I wanted blue," I explained. "But this one is pretty. I think I'll wear my hair up in a twist."

"I can help you with that," Minnie said. "We'll get some roses for your hair."

"Why in the hell would Joelle choose a black dress for a school dance?" Gran wondered aloud.

"It's stylish," I replied.

Gran harrumphed and lit a second cigarette with the tail end of the first.

"So what's your fella doing this evening?" Minnie asked, anchoring her smoke between her teeth and beckoning to me. For a split second I thought she meant Justin, but of course she was referring to Christopher. I turned my chair, my face a little hot, so Minnie could have access to the back of my head, and she proceeded to play around with fixing my hair. I kept my eyes anchored on the lake.

"Helping his dad clean out their garage," I said at last, answering her question, little shivers racing over my scalp as she worked. I loved having my hair touched. Chris knew this and often ran his hands through it, wrapping its length around his fingers. He told me once I looked like a mermaid, with her hair trailing all along her waist.

"Chris Henriksen is a kind boy," Minnie said. "He's good for you, Jilly Rae."

I whispered, "I think so, too."

She released my hair and cupped my temples, lightly, her hands going at once still. I sat facing away, so her expression was hidden from me; I tried not to shiver. Instead I studied Flickertail as night descended over its surface, turning the water to ink. Above our heads, silhouetted against the silvering sky, brown bats began to appear, fluttering around in their choppy, erratic flight, feasting on the wealth of mosquitoes. My great-aunt's hands were gentle against my skull; I waited patiently, understanding that she would explain in time. At last she sat back with a small, soft sigh and pronounced, "You'll be all right."

I knew better than to ask her what she meant; if she wanted me to know, she would tell me. Minnie always knew things. The expression she used was *having a Notion*. I always thought of the word with a capital letter and I'd never questioned her statements, because they always proved true. And besides, I experienced Notions, too. Never when I expected, never when I tried to force one; the knowing would hit me with the unexpected nature of a lightning flash in the distance, on a night you thought was only clear. Or, more often, I would have a dream.

The first time it happened I told Minnie, no one else. At age six, I dreamed that a white tree fell onto the cafe, smashing through the roof. Just a nightmare, Mom would have assumed. Except that it wasn't. It was more, and I could only explain that I recognized the difference in my gut. Minnie listened, holding me on her lap, brushing the sweaty hair back from my temples as I described the dream. By morning I'd all but forgotten; Minnie, however, walked around the outside of the cafe with a critical eye and later that day arranged for the ancient birch tree near the north side of the building to be removed.

I curled my hands around my knees as she resumed playing with my hair. She'd said I would be all right, and I trusted that, whatever she meant exactly. But there was a sadness flowing from her fingers that I didn't understand, and again, I knew better than to ask.

Chapter Three

April, 1985

"I'm so glad it's not raining yet," Jo said, scanning the sky. We'd spent over two hours getting ready for prom, crammed into our tiny bathroom while bruise-colored clouds amassed on the western horizon. The air seemed to be holding its breath, and carried the sharp scent of moisture; a fine mist hovered just above Flickertail, beautiful and ghost-like. Birds sang madly in anticipation of the storm. Fine for the birds, I thought, but I would be irritated beyond belief if a downpour ruined my hair before Chris saw it. I studied my reflection with a critical eye as the song on the radio switched from "White Wedding" to "Open Arms." Later we would be dancing to this very song at our first prom; last spring, as sophomores, we hadn't been allowed to attend.

Minnie, as promised, pinned and twisted my hair into what she called a chignon, with small trailing curls picked out to hang along my neck. Jo helped me with my make-up after applying her own, and I zipped into my dress with a sense of giddy delight. I stroked the silky magenta material over my hips, imagining Chris's hands doing the same thing.

"Is my dress too short?" I worried.

"Not at all," Jo assured, applying a last touch of lipstick. I spent a moment admiring my sister, who looked amazing as usual, her long, golden hair combed silken-straight, smoothed to a gloss over her bare shoulders. She'd vamped up her eyeliner more than usual and Ellen helped her with the false eyelashes that no one but Jo could have pulled off. Her dress *just* bordered on slutty, but I would never dream of telling her so, because she looked fantastic and part of me was proud to have a sister who was so sexy. She sat on the edge of the tub to twine the straps of her high heels around her ankles before fastening them.

"You look so pretty, Jilly Bean," she said.

"You, too," I said, and she gave me her naughtiest grin.

"Pretty wasn't *exactly* the look I was going for," she teased. "But thanks."

"Girls, your fellas are here!" Minnie leaned around the stairwell to inform us.

My heart tripped and then took up a pulsing beat.

"Come on, let's go have fun," Joelle said, giving herself one last look in the mirror.

After a thousand pictures and hugs and admonishments to be careful and responsible, the four of us hurried through the parking lot to the guys' respective vehicles. Jackie borrowed his dad's black Buick instead of making Jo ride to the dance in his dirty old truck. We agreed to grab a bite to eat at Landon's only other sit-down restaurant, which was located in the Angler's Inn. It featured fish, just like Shore Leave, but was a step above in atmosphere; most of our classmates would also be dining there this evening, unless they ventured over to Bemidji, the closest big town. Although in this case, big was a relative term.

"We'll catch up with you two after we stop for pictures at Jackie's," Jo said as we parted ways in the parking lot.

Jackie, intimidating in a black tux, came up behind her, wrapped his hands possessively around her waist and bit the side of her neck. He murmured, "Damn, you look fucking good."

"Stop it, you'll mess up my hair," she complained.

Chris squeezed my hand, letting me know without words that he would have expressed the same sentiment about me, but was far too much of a gentleman to put it like that. Jackie's manners were nonexistent, like usual, but Jo never seemed to truly mind.

"We need to stop by my house, too," Chris explained.

"See ya!" they called, scampering into Jackie's dad's car like puppies.

Chris opened the door for me and then hurried around the front of the car. Once inside he grinned sweetly at me, his brown eyes glinting with all of the colors that flashed beneath the surface of his irises, like a woodland pond in the afternoon sun. He looked so handsome, and I loved him so much. In that instant the clouds parted somewhere above, just enough to allow for a radiant beam of red-gold afternoon light to tint the air around us, like a benediction. I leaned over to kiss him, not caring that my carefully-applied lipstick would get smudged. He cupped my jaw and kissed me back, trailing his fingers over my neck. He always touched me like I was made of something so delicate, like porcelain.

"I can't wait until we're dancing at our own wedding," he said. We talked about getting married so often that his parents, especially, took it as a foregone conclusion. At that moment I experienced such a powerful sense of us being truly bound by marriage that I almost shuddered with its force.

"I can't wait, either," I whispered, and pulled him into another kiss.

We caught up with Jo and Jackie two hours later and followed them to the high school, entering the gym to hear a DJ playing "Dancing in the Dark" by Bruce Springsteen.

"Come on!" Jo insisted, and Jackie grumbled but followed her onto the dance floor willingly enough.

Chris and I hung back a little; he kept my hand firmly in his grasp, rubbing the back of it with his thumb.

"You want to join them?" he asked.

"Let's wait for the first slow one," I told him, looking around at the decorations. "So the theme is Midnight in Paris?"

Chris laughed; for whatever reason, our student government thought that this meant a color scheme of pink and black; a wrought-iron Eiffel Tower stood near the punch table, which I knew Laura Henry's father made just for the dance. We were about to grab some punch when the song switched to "Almost Paradise," and Chris said softly, "C'mon," leading us among the other couples and wrapping me into his arms.

I snuggled against him and slipped my arms around his neck while his hands smoothed the material low on my back. Because it was prom they played three slow songs in a row, and when we danced past Jo and Jackie, Jo said, "Chris, I want to dance one with you," so we swapped partners.

Jackie gave me a big-brother sort of grin and said, "Hey there, Dilly Bar."

"Ugh, I hate that nickname," I told him.

Jackie just laughed, of course.

"I can't believe you guys are graduating," I said, gloomy at the prospect.

"God, I can't wait," Jackie said. "Bust out of Landon, finally."

As long as Joelle was safe here, I didn't care if that was his attitude. But then he said, "Maybe Jo and I will settle here eventually. After I come home from college."

"Will you marry her?" I asked, studying him intently.

"That's my plan," he said, with typical confidence, looking over at my sister as Chris spun her around. He smiled and said, "I love her. I'm not ready to get married, but Jo isn't either. It's not like we don't talk about these things, you know."

He sounded serious for once, and I peered up at him, not sure what to make of that, but just then we happened to dance near Justin and Aubrey, and a flash of anxiety rippled over my skin as I recalled the whole spanking thing…me and my big mouth. But Aubrey gave us a big, toothy smile; well, she gave Jackie a smile and ignored me. She seemed pretty tipsy, her arms around Justin, who must have lost his bow-tie somewhere. The top two buttons of his white dress shirt were undone. Aubrey's slinky dress was covered in turquoise sequins.

"Feel this dress, Jack, for real," Justin said, indicating Aubrey's waist.

"It's like sweaty scales," Jackie said, rubbing his hand lightly over the material.

"Justin won't quit bitching about it," Aubrey said, rolling her eyes. "Trade for a minute, you guys," she ordered, moving into Jackie's arms while Justin and I stood looking at each other for a moment of total awkwardness before he gathered himself and drew me into his arms.

He held me as though we were about to begin an old-fashioned sort of waltz, rather than with my arms around his neck.

"So your stitches got removed," I said, the first thing that popped into my mind. Small red marks still faintly criss-crossed his dark eyebrow.

Despite the fact that I'd known him my entire life, Justin seemed oddly self-conscious. He finally cleared his throat and said, "Yeah." And then, "You look real nice, Jilly."

My eyes flashed to his at these unexpected words; I'd been studying the faint stitch marks left behind on his forehead. Justin was taller than me by a good six or seven inches but our faces seemed very close in that moment. His gaze skittered from mine almost instantly and I was mildly confused by this, considering how he was normally at ease with me, and felt free to tease. I found myself all but scrutinizing him, his black hair and eyebrows, his darkly-tanned skin, set off so well by the crisp white of his shirt. He had long, straight eyelashes and lips with a soft, curving shape. I could feel his shoulders shifting as we danced to "Islands in the Stream."

As his eyes came back to mine, it finally dawned on me that he'd complimented how I looked, and I said, "Thanks."

He smiled a little as I spoke, seeming slightly more like himself, and his lips parted as though to ask me a question—but the song ended, thankfully. I mean, I was thankful that it was over…wasn't I? And then Chris found us in the crowd and swept me into his arms, where I went gladly.

"Jilly Bean, let's get some punch," he said, spinning me in a circle before adding, "Hi, Justin."

Justin offered a wan smile before saying, "Hey, Henriksen. Have fun, you two."

"He's being so weird," I noted as Justin disappeared into the crowd, but Chris just shrugged, unconcerned as he gathered me close.

"Can I kiss you?" he asked, smiling down at me, and I went up on tiptoe to kiss him in answer.

We found the punch table and then proceeded to dance the night away. An hour later I was drenched in sweat, though my chignon held out, thanks to Great-Aunt Minnie's zillion bobby pins. I finally took a break to head to the bathroom when Jo caught me, flushed and smelling like wine.

"Oh, Jilly, I was looking for you," she said. "Jackie and I are leaving for a little while."

"Is he okay to drive?" I asked immediately.

Jo nodded with utter assurance, tucking a loose strand of hair behind my ear. She said, "Don't worry, we aren't going far."

"Just all the way," I teased.

"See you later," she told me, with no further comment.

I wish I would have known right then, I *should* have known, just how much things were about to change for my sister.

But this time, a Notion did not warn me.

Chapter Four

October, 1986

"I'D LIKE AN AUTUMN WEDDING," I TOLD CHRIS, BACK IN the summer. We had graduated in June and Chris formally proposed a week later, though I insisted I wanted to keep my peridot promise ring rather than wear a new and unfamiliar one; I did consent to switch its placement from my right hand to my left.

Maybe we were too young to be married, maybe we should have thought more about college. But we were so happy together and delighted to be free to make decisions for ourselves. Chris worked every day with his father at their cabinetry business, and would continue to do so; I planned to keep my job at Shore Leave, mostly since I couldn't bear the thought of not seeing my family on a daily basis. We decided to move in with Elaine and Tom for the time being, as their basement was equipped with a small kitchen and we could live there inexpensively until we managed to save enough for a place of our own. I knew Chris wanted to build us a house with his own hands, from the ground up; we talked about it and planned, drew pictures and cut images from magazines. Of course we called it our dream house, and Chris vowed someday he would build it for me.

The Thursday before our wedding, Jo and Jackie, along with their daughter, flew in from Chicago. They drove up to Landon in a rental car and I was whole-heartedly glad to see my sister, from whom I'd been parted for almost two years now. For many months after her absence,

I was utterly despondent; Chris was the only person able to cast away the gloom. And it still made my heart ache; a part of my body severed with my sister so far away, a part of my soul. I'd never been without Jo for more than a day or two in a row, and for a time I hated Jackie with a white-hot intensity, blaming him for taking her from Landon. I hated that she'd been irresponsible enough to get pregnant on prom night, forcing their marriage only a few months later; I was all set to hate their baby, but the moment I held Camille and put my nose to her tiny, sweet-scented head, I realized how foolish I'd been.

It was evening now at Shore Leave, the trees in their full autumn splendor of scarlets and oranges, here and there a splash of molten yellow; by contrast, the lake shone a somber indigo, no longer the enchanting, sun-kissed blue of summer. The air had a bite, and I was bundled in a big white sweater and jeans, waiting with zero patience for them to arrive. When the rental car pulled into the lot, I raced and practically dragged my sister from the passenger seat. She was laughing and crying at once as we rocked together, hugging. Jackie leaned into the backseat to unbuckle Camille from her car seat and bounced her on his arm; she was adorable, with thick brown curls and Jo's golden-green eyes.

"Hi, Milla!" I said brightly, but she hooked a finger in her mouth and pressed her forehead against Jackie's jaw, hiding her face.

He laughed, reaching to hug me with his free arm.

Jackie looked exactly the same, as though he didn't have a care in the wide world, but my sister appeared changed since her venture into wife- and motherhood; though she seemed otherwise content, I noticed hints of smudgy shadows under her eyes and her silky hair was cut short these days, just long enough to tuck behind her ears. She hugged me again and murmured, "It's so damn good to be home."

"Here, Milla, go to Mommy," Jackie said, but she clung to him.

Jo rolled her eyes, with affection, saying, "She's such a daddy's girl."

Chris bounded down the steps, hugging everyone, smiling and exuding happiness, as always. The womenfolk crowded out onto the porch and Jo ran up to greet them while Chris unloaded their luggage and

Jackie carried Camille up the porch steps, where she was yet too shy to allow anyone but him to hold her.

Much later Jo and I found a moment to sneak out to the dock, though sitting under a mid-October evening sky was vastly different than a July one; the air crackled with a dry sort of chill, none of the stroking humidity of just a few weeks earlier. The stars appeared brilliant and jagged-edged on the black backdrop of the sky, and I toted the afghan down from the house to drape around my shoulders while Jo wrapped up in Jackie's thick jean jacket.

"I'm so happy for you, Jilly," Joelle said as we shared the glider and a cigarette, our elbows bumping. For a moment I imagined us back in middle school, pre-boyfriends, when Jo belonged only to me. She went on, "And Chris is adorable. He can't keep from smiling. You guys are just so meant to be."

I rested my head on her shoulder for a couple of beats and then asked, "How are you guys doing, really? How's Chicago?"

Jo sighed and took a long drag on the smoke. Exhaling, she admitted, "I still miss it here. I thought that would go away, but it hasn't yet. And Jackie is so busy finishing school I barely ever see him."

"Stay here," I pestered. "Just move home."

"Jackie loves it in Chicago," she said quietly, as though talking to herself. "He loves the city, and the glamour and the bustle. We used to talk about moving back up here, but I don't believe that's a possibility anymore."

My heart constricted, squeezed in a scalding iron clamp. Hearing the petulance in my voice and hoping it overrode the fear, I whispered, "Then *you* move home."

Jo laughed a little and said, "Yeah, right. Like I could do that." She sounded so defeated, and said immediately, "God, I'm sorry Jills, this is your wedding weekend and I'm acting this way. I'm sorry. Forget I said anything."

I echoed her words, "Yeah, right, I'm just gonna forget. Think about it, Jo, please. You and Milla could move back in here."

She shuddered lightly. "Back in with Mom, no thanks."

"With Chris and me, then," I insisted, provoking another huff of laughter from my sister.

"With you two as newlyweds? Thanks, but I can't handle hearing that much sex when I'm not getting any."

I giggled in spite of myself, holding out my hand for the cigarette, which Jo passed over, as though it was a joint. I'd hijacked a smoke from Minnie's pack on the windowsill and she preferred menthols, prompting us to share just one. In a more serious tone Jo continued, "Besides, after Saturday you'll be a married woman and you won't miss me so much then. You'll probably have ten kids before you know it. Chris can barely keep his eyes off of you, so I would imagine his hands aren't far behind."

My cheeks heated up and I shifted my head so that my long hair partially sheltered my face. Jo knew me far too well to be fooled and bumped her shoulder against mine. I admitted, "Chris wants a ton of kids. He's always hated being an only child. And Elaine drops hints about grandchildren all the time."

"See, you'll be busy with your babies. God, it's weird to imagine you having a kid. I can barely keep up with my own."

"She's beautiful," I said.

"But exhausting," Jo said. "That would be one great thing about moving back home…the womenfolk would be around to help me take care of her."

Up on the porch the screen door creaked open and Jackie called, "Jo, you coming to bed?"

Jo lowered her voice and whispered, "He's thinking sex since Milla is sleeping with Mom."

I teased, "Yeah, I'm sure it's been *ages* for you two horn-dogs."

"You'd be surprised," she muttered, turning over her shoulder to call, "I'll be right up, honey!"

"Go and make some love, and I'll see you in the morning," I said, and we hugged hard before she climbed up the incline to Jackson.

Minutes later Chris found me, pulling me onto his lap and snuggling me against his chest, resettling the afghan around us. He said for the millionth time, "I'm so happy, Jilly Bean."

I twisted around to kiss his chin, murmuring, "No one would ever have guessed."

He kissed my left ear and then tightened his arms. "I've only wanted to marry you since the fifth grade, you know."

"Really?" I thought I knew everything about him, but this was a new one.

"Yeah, Mrs. Beasley's class, you sat two seats ahead of me. All I could think about that year was how much I liked you."

"And you waited until tenth grade to ask me out?" I badgered, lining his forearms with my own. "What about all of middle school?"

"I was too chicken," he admitted. His voice was husky with sincerity as he added, lips against my temple, "But now we've got our whole lives to spend together, Jilly Bean."

I turned and expertly straddled him, smiling into his eyes. My heart thumped hard as he clutched my hips and held me close. I smoothed my palms over the sides of his face and ran my fingernails through his hair, which I knew he loved. Words couldn't express what I wanted to say, what was in my heart, so instead I tipped my forehead against his and forced the strength of my feelings directly into his eyes. Chris's crinkled at the corners as he smiled and his hands moved up over my waist, to my neck and at last my face, which he tilted to the right to kiss me properly.

Our wedding service was small, held at the local church, where the Henriksens, and indeed most of Landon, had been members since long before my birth. I truly wanted our ceremony to be on the porch at Shore Leave, under the sunset sky, but I kept that desire quiet, knowing Chris would be torn; it was important to his parents for us to marry in the same chapel where they were wed, many years ago.

Jo was my attendant and Chris's best friend Neil Gorman would walk her down the aisle. I wore a satin dress; the color wasn't quite white, but instead a glimmering shade called *candlelight* and it was singularly the most beautiful gown I'd ever owned. I never felt more gorgeous or fairy-like in my life. Jo was in charge of my make-up, Minnie my hair, into which she pinned two seed-pearl combs that once belonged to her mother, Myrtle Jean Davis, founder of Shore Leave. My dress fit like a slim sheath, with cap sleeves and an open back decorated by delicate strings of pearls. And my shoes…they added over two inches to my height, made of matching candlelight satin, with straps that wound up my calves. I clung tightly to Dodge, fearful of tripping on my way down the aisle.

Dodge tucked my elbow securely against his bulky side, suspiciously red-eyed, and kept clearing his throat as we waited together in the vestibule. The little chapel was filled to the fifth row of pews and my heart beat hot and fast, though we'd rehearsed everything seamlessly last night, before the groom's dinner; that particular event was held at Shore Leave, loud and boisterous, with barbecue chicken and ribs, baked beans and steak fries, apple fritters and chocolate cake, all of Chris's favorites. The party lasted well into the night.

Justin, who came solo since Aubrey was out of town (which was preferable to me, though I wouldn't have admitted that) teased me about the less-than-gourmet menu and made sure to ask if our ceremony was going to be held in a barn and feature square dancing; he also asked if I planned to wear a checkered dress. Justin and Aubrey's wedding occurred just a few months earlier and Aubrey, as expected, had insisted on top-of-the-line and pretentious everything (Dodge's words, in private, to Aunt Ellen). I caught Justin's eye for just a second, as he sat in the front pew between his little sister, Liz, and Jackie, everyone peeking back to see when the wedding march would begin, and battled the urge to stick out my tongue at him.

See, I look fantastic, I wanted to say. *Nothing like a square dancer or a tomboy.*

But then the music swelled and Chris entered the chapel from a door in the front, to take his place near the altar. My heart moved from double to triple-time, seeing my man up there in his tuxedo, his hands folded and eyes fixed on the back of the church. This was it, my wedding. After today Chris and I would truly belong together in every sense of the word.

Dodge tightened his grip on my arm and cleared his throat again, asking gruffly, "You ready, little one?"

I watched as Jo, on Neil's arm, walked gracefully along the aisle in the indigo gown she purchased in Chicago; I hadn't been picky on anything but color. She carried a bouquet of asters, tied with azure ribbons, to match mine. Next was our turn, and everyone stood in anticipation. I gulped a little, clinging to Dodge's arm, but kept my gaze fixed on Christopher, who grinned like a giddy little boy. To my almost-father I whispered, "I sure am."

The dance was held at Rose Lake Lodge, one of the most beautiful lodges in the vicinity, and much larger than Shore Leave. Considering that I planned to dance until I dropped with all of the people I loved, we needed the extra floor space. Eddie Sorenson's nephew played in a band and we'd hired them for the evening; by the time Chris and I arrived at the Lodge, most of the guests were already there, drinking and enjoying the spectacular view of Rose Lake, the gleaming body of water for which the town was named, out the wide front windows.

Neil took Chris and me, along with his own girlfriend Sarah, on the "scenic route," which meant Neil drove the back roads while Chris, Sarah, and I passed a bottle of champagne and then did a few shots of coconut rum. The downfall of only being nineteen at your own wedding—no drinking in public. Chris and I didn't stop kissing until Sarah threatened to pour rum over our heads. I kept my hand tucked around Chris's arm as we entered the main room of the Lodge, still in disbelief that he was mine, that I was a married woman.

The guys in the band were setting up on the wooden dais in the far corner. The windows allowed for a panoramic, utterly breathtaking view of Rose Lake, slightly larger than Flickertail, glittering under the late-afternoon sun. The far shore burst with radiant autumn colors, predominantly deep reds and brilliant flame-oranges, with birch trees scattered here and there like spilled golden coins. I sighed in complete contentment, tugging on Chris and insisting, "See? If we had a July wedding the view would have been different."

Chris was flushed and grinning; he almost looked stoned and I giggled, my own cheeks likewise broiling. He bent and kissed me flush on the lips, then said, "Whatever you say, Mrs. Henriksen."

I remained a little stunned that my last name was no longer Davis. Although, being a Davis was in my blood, bones, and heart; it mattered little that my surname changed. And I was so delighted and proud to be Jillian Rae Henriksen. My own grin stretched as wide as a dinner plate.

Jo came and caught me in the growing crowd, hugging me close and saying, "Come on, little married lady, we have to get your train buttoned up so you can dance."

Dance we did. Eddie's nephew's band, called Uprising, was fantastic and catered to the numerous shouted requests. They started the evening with more mellow numbers, but then picked up the beat as the night, and the drinking, progressed. Even the most reluctant guests were drawn to the dance floor when they played "I Knew the Bride," during which I was passed from one set of arms to another, in a continuous whirlwind of motion. I ended up with Justin and he gave me an extra spin as the music ended and Uprising slid seamlessly into "Wonderful Tonight."

"How about it, tomboy?" he asked, giving me his old teasing grin.

"Sure," I managed to say, out of breath and sweaty, my face hot from exertion and a pretty damn strong buzz. I'd discarded my high heels hours earlier, but still stumbled a little as Justin drew me into his embrace; though he probably would have kept us in a waltzing stance, I slid my arms up around his neck for stability. My thumbs came to rest on his collarbones. His hands moved more slowly to my waist and over the thin, smooth fabric of my candlelight dress.

"Well, congratulations," he said softly, no longer grinning, dark eyes serious on mine. Though Justin was much taller than me, especially since I wasn't wearing shoes, I still found myself slightly disconcerted by how close our dancing embrace put our eyes; but that was ridiculous, since I'd danced this way with every other male guest all evening. Chris was equally in demand with the women; other than our first two dances, I'd hardly seen my husband.

"Thank you," I said automatically, and my voice emerged unnaturally reedy, certainly from drinking too much. I felt drunker than ever, now that I'd slowed down. I heard myself say, "And I don't look like a square dancer."

Just a hint of his grin this time. I caught the scent of whiskey on his breath as he agreed, "No, nothing like a square dancer."

I realized that I wanted him to compliment me and for a strange, unexpected moment my heart beat a heated rhythm against my breast-bone. Justin swayed us to the music, but so slowly that our feet scarcely moved. Our eyes held—I couldn't think of looking away from him. His hands were very warm on either side of my waist and I felt that he was attempting to span it with his palms. He swallowed. I could hardly breathe, feeling his gaze all the way to my tailbone. For a split second, his grip on my waist tightened.

The song ended.

"There's the little bride!" Dodge was saying, jovial and red-faced, his shirt collar open and the scent of booze preceding him like a trumpet section. But then again, it was a day of celebration. He insisted, "Next dance is mine, little Jilly."

I blinked and moved into Dodge's arms, and he swept me away as the next song started.

It would be more than a decade and a half before I allowed myself to remember my wedding-day dance with Justin Miller.

Chapter Five

November, 1987

"Jilly Bean, look at our little baby," Chris said, tucking his chin on my shoulder and cupping a wide palm about our son's small round cheek. He enthused, "Look at his little nose, it's so perfect. And his fingers. They're all there, all ten."

I kissed the soft, fuzzy little head and adorable smushy face of our boy. I said, "Of course they're all there. He's just perfect, isn't he?"

"His toes!" Chris said, sounding a little frantic. "I didn't check!"

"Same as his fingers, don't worry."

Chris cupped the back of my neck and kissed my temple; with his other hand he gently nudged at the baby's fist, which opened and then clung to his daddy's finger. I giggled, watching, while beside me Chris gulped a little and I didn't have to look to know that tears were building in his eyes. My throat thickened immediately.

"Hey, buddy," Chris crooned. "Hey, little man. What should we call you?"

"I was thinking Danny," I said, after Dodge, who I loved just as much as I could have loved a real father, and wanted to honor with my son's name. Chris and I had talked about Daniel, or Thomas, after Chris's dad. I speculated, "Or does he look like a Tommy?"

Chris rubbed his tears on one shoulder rather than relinquish his hold on either me or the baby. He pursed his lips in serious consideration and said, "You know, I don't think he looks like either. You know I like Clint, what about that?"

I said, "Christopher, we are not naming our baby after Dirty Harry."

"But it's such a cool name," Chris insisted, warming to this opinion. "I think it suits him."

It was so rare for my husband to insist on anything. I kissed our baby's soft forehead and tried it out, murmuring, "Hi there, Clint."

"Look at that!" Chris crowed in triumph, as the little one opened both eyes and blinked solemnly at us, just as I spoke his name.

"All right, you sold me," I relented, and Chris bent his head to kiss both me and our new son.

"Clint Daniel, how's that?" he said. "Or something else?"

"No, that has a nice ring to it," I agreed, drawing my husband back for another kiss.

He caressed my cheek and said, "I didn't think I could be happier than when we got married, but I am right now."

"Oh, honey," I said. "I know."

"I love you so much, Jillian," he told me. "Promise me we'll have a whole pack of kids."

I rolled my eyes, teasing, "Give me a minute here. I just forced this one out after nine months."

At that moment Mom, Elaine, and Aunt Ellen bustled in, all of them wanting to get their hands on the baby. I grinned at them and said, "Hi, you guys. Meet Clint."

August, 1990

"Can I take this off yet?" I asked, my fingers going again to the bandana tied over my eyes. Unable to remove it yet, I gathered my long braid over one shoulder and twisted it in my right hand. Chris was driving us somewhere, while Clint stayed home with Elaine and Tom; now that I thought about it, I remembered both of Chris's parents smiling as we left, obviously privy to some secret that I was not. Even with my eyes covered, I could sense my husband's quivering anticipation. I slapped at his direction, demanding, "Tell me, Christopher!"

"Okay, here we are," he said, and the excitement in his voice proved contagious. Before he gave me permission, I ripped away the blindfold and then stared out of the windshield in surprise. Chris parked in a clearing a few miles outside of Landon, a roughly-circular area, probably about an acre, ringed with towering pines. I asked, "You want to have sex in the car like in the old days?"

Chris laughed and pulled me close for a quick kiss before saying, "Come on," and bounding out of the car, hurrying around the hood to haul my much slower ass from the passenger seat. He took my hand and tugged me along to a For Sale sign; across its yellow length was stretched a SOLD banner. I studied this for a minute before the truth dawned, and then my gaze flashed over to my husband, who was practically hopping from one foot to the other in giddiness.

"Sold?" I asked.

"To us!" he said triumphantly. "I just put the down payment on it yesterday. I'll build you our house here, Jilly Bean."

I was a little dumbfounded that Chris would do such a momentous thing without consulting me…but then I turned in a slow circle, really observing the place. I squinted my eyes and pictured our house, the one that Chris and I spent so many hours envisioning and planning in our little bedroom in his parent's basement. Our house, which would have a wraparound porch, and a huge laundry room, one in which I would never bump my hip on the dryer trying to navigate my way clutching a basket of clothes. There would be a flower garden and Clinty would have bunk beds…and there would be rooms enough for at least nine more kids. Tears spilled down my cheeks and I absolutely leaped into my husband's arms.

"Sweetie, isn't it great?" Chris said, holding me close to his heart and swaying us side to side.

"I'm just so happy," I told him, pressing my face against his chest to stave off more tears. "Chris, when did you…I didn't even know you were looking."

"I wasn't *exactly* looking, but I found the ad for this place just a few weeks ago. It's been for sale for a long time, so they were willing to lower the price and Dad and Ma helped me with the down payment money. We won't be able to break ground until next spring, but we can maybe camp out here in the meantime, bring the tents, have a fire…"

More tears gushed over my face and Chris thumbed them away, looking down at me with so much tenderness and love. I gulped a little and then kissed him, pulling his face to mine. Though I wanted him to lay me down right here in the soft grass, I could tell he was too excited to show me our new property. It was so like him to radiate enthusiasm this way; nothing brought him down and I loved that.

"Come on, there's a couple of birch trees over here," he said, pulling me along behind him.

"Hey," I said to his familiar back, and he peered over one shoulder, not breaking stride, eyebrows raised. "I love you," I said and my throat hurt with the force of it.

He said, "I love you too, honey. And I promise I'll build you the most beautiful house you've ever imagined."

And at that moment I really believed he would.

February, 1991

Wrong. Something was so very wrong.

It was as though a hockey buzzer was going off in my head as I floundered from bed, pulled directly from deep sleep, and I wavered to my feet, utterly disoriented and dizzy. I leaned over to the mattress, my hands seeking at once for Chris, but he was out snowmobiling with Neil and a couple other guys, not yet home.

Clint.

I raced across the basement to my son's room, clicking on the overhead light, heart slamming my breastbone like an angry fist. I saw at once that he was fine; he drew up his knees and shifted under the unexpected glare, but went on sleeping. I allowed a breath, but the hockey buzzer hadn't quit. My heart still throbbed inside of me, frantic and dissatisfied.

Dammit. Something was terribly off, chilling me to the bone. Right then I longed for Minnie so much that I felt faint; she would know, she would be able to tell me what ripped me out of my bed and flung me into this panic. But she was gone; she'd passed away only this past autumn, along with Chris's father, both just before Clint's third birthday.

Calm down, I commanded. *You aren't solving anything this way.*

I turned out the light in Clinty's room and proceeded back to my own, but couldn't get into bed with this sort of agitation rushing through my veins. I tugged on my long braid, twisting it as I did when anxious, and then trooped up to the main floor kitchen, debating waking Elaine or calling Gran, or Joelle. But it was nearing midnight. I hated when Chris stayed out so late; we'd fought about it just two weeks ago, when I discovered that they'd been drinking. He felt bad, I knew, but loved these occasional nights out with his buddies. They had all snowmobiled this way together since they were teenagers.

A storm coming, maybe? I parted the curtains and peered out into the winter night to find a gorgeous ivory moon staring back, unblinking. The world appeared peaceful, if frozen in crystals, not a breath of wind to stir the bare black branches. I exhaled slowly, moving on silent feet to put on the kettle for a cup of tea. Since Chris's dad's death, Elaine slept poorly and I didn't want to cause her unnecessary alarm. But if I wasn't drowsy within fifteen minutes, I would call Jo, late or not.

I was unsure how much time passed when I realized the phone was ringing. Pulled from a restless doze, bent over my forearms on the table, I lifted my head and knew with absolute certainty that I should not answer that sound. I'd been in the midst of a nightmare, this time one in which birds were trying to pull out my hair, screeching, and the noise they made in the dream suddenly became the phone in the dark kitchen. I stumbled to my feet and picked it up, only to hear the drone of the dial tone. And then I realized that it wasn't the phone at all but the doorbell, and that someone was now knocking with a forceful thump. My knees rattled and if we owned a dog it would have been going apeshit. I felt as though I was about to vomit, but forced my feet to the front door, my fingertips so numb I tried the knob three times before the door swung open.

"Dodge?" I said in confusion. He was bundled in his down jacket and a green hunting hat, cheeks red from the cold.

Before I said anything else he made a noise I'd never heard him make, as though he was choking. He stepped into my entryway and pulled me against him, hard and tight. I heard another sound then, a high-pitched keening. I didn't realize at first that it came from my throat.

"Jillian, sweetheart," Dodge said against my hair, his deep voice gruff and terrible.

At that second, I knew.

I started crying, fighting to get away from him. He didn't let me, holding me so close, finally saying, "They tried everything, oh God, they tried to…"

Chris. Oh God, Christopher.

Sobs overwhelmed me, ripping through me as I gave up struggling to get away, clinging now to the only father I'd ever known, who'd come with a message he'd certainly rather have died than tell me.

"What…" I sobbed. "What…"

"He went through the ice on Rose Lake," Dodge said roughly. I clung to his jacket, smelling snow and tobacco in its puffy folds. "They tried to get him, Jillian, they tried. But he…but he…"

I screamed then, hitting him with both fists, ineffectual as that was. He was lying, this was a joke. Any moment he'd laugh and tell me who put him up to this. And then Chris would pop in behind him.

From upstairs, the hall light preceded Elaine's terrified voice calling, "Jillian? What in the world?"

"Mama?" came another voice at the same moment, a small voice full of uncertainty.

I froze, would have doubled over if not for Dodge's presence. He gently led me to the couch, calling to Clinty, "It's all right, little one. Your mama is just fine."

But your daddy isn't, I wanted to shriek. *Your daddy isn't.*
Oh God, oh God.

My fault.

How could I have failed to see this? Minnie would have seen it; Minnie would have had a Notion and warned me. I'd have stopped Christopher from ever leaving the house.

You'll be all right, Minnie said long ago. Inside my head an unending scream rippled in response. *I will never fucking be all right again! How could you let this happen?* I didn't know if I intended to blame Minnie, or myself.

I rolled forward, curling around my midsection, scarcely able to breathe past the sobs shredding my insides. I saw Dodge move swiftly to Clint, standing at the top of the steps leading back down to the basement. Dodge scooped my boy into his embrace. He spoke to Clinty in a soft voice, carrying him into the kitchen. A distant, detached part of me, who seemed to be hovering near the ceiling to silently watch events unfold, was ashamed that I didn't move to comfort my son.

Mom and Gran and Ellen were in my living room next. It was sometime later, I wasn't sure how many minutes since Dodge arrived. Time lost all meaning as I huddled on the couch, wrapping my head in both arms, unable to move. Gran managed to unfold me, her eyes dark with concern as she pulled me into her arms, holding me to her bosom. She rocked me and smoothed my hair, murmuring words I wouldn't later recall. Mom and Ellen clutched Elaine, whose sobs destroyed me anew, while Dodge did everything Gran ordered, including talking with Charlie Evans and Dave Jensen, the cops who came to the house.

"Joelle will be here in the morning," Mom said at one point.

Dawn broke, morning came, sunlight sparkling over the fresh snow, despite the fact that my husband was gone forever. It would be months before I could manage to say the word *dead*. I felt hollow, and would, for a long, long time after. But that first morning was the most horrible, surreal and sickening. I would have done about anything for its permanent banishment from my memory.

"I want to see him," I insisted later that day, despite Mom's gentle suggestion that I remember Chris as he'd been. Elaine went to the funeral home with Gran and picked out a coffin at my request, taking along the suit in which her only child would be buried. I spent most of the day wrapped in a blanket on the couch. Neil, Chris's best friend and the one who'd pulled him from the frozen lake, came to the house to see me, but I couldn't manage it and left Jo to explain.

"I'll bring you there, Jilly," Jo said as the afternoon drifted away.

I was numb, heavy, as though made of concrete. Jo drove me across town to the Price's funeral home, both of us wordless with grief. I rode with my forehead pressed to my knuckles and required help from the car. Oddly, I'd climbed these same steps twice in the last few months, for both Minnie's and Tom's funerals. Never in all my imaginings would I have suspected that next I'd be climbing them to view my husband's body.

Oh God, oh God.

I wasn't warned. A Notion hadn't alerted me, flashing into my mind to save my husband.

Why?

"Why, Jo?" I asked, as she helped me up the stone steps. My voice was weak as a kitten's, and I hated that.

"I don't know, sweetheart," Jo said, holding me close. I knew she didn't understand the question I actually asked.

Later, I was glad that I insisted upon seeing him. But nothing, not one thing, could have prepared me for the rending in my soul. He had drowned. It was too unbelievable to be true; my Christopher, who spent probably a third of his life swimming, who had just been dancing around the bedroom with me, night before last, teasing me that it was time to have another baby—or at least keep trying. I would remember him like that, not like this. But I needed to see to believe that he had actually left me forever.

I touched him, my fingers tentative and my heart like ice, tracing my fingers over his inert, waxen face, his hair that still felt soft. His same face that I had kissed a million times, the same hands that held me with more love than probably anyone deserved in this life. Terror was too thick in my throat to allow for sobs, disbelief too rampant in my veins. The coldness beneath my fingertips was shocking. I wanted to see his eyes, was suddenly overwhelmed with a terrible and perverse need to see them open, because the last time I saw them open he'd been alive and was kissing me good-bye wearing his snowmobile face mask, the silver one that covered every part of his face but his mouth and eyes. He'd said, "See you later, honey." And now his eyes were closed.

A panic attack hit me so hard I went to my knees.

The door banged against the wall as Jo flew into the viewing room.

Later, I didn't remember anything about her getting me to the car and out of there.

More cars clustered at my house like a herd of ugly metal animals, more people offering sympathy. I wanted to tell them all to fuck off.

Jo parked the car. I climbed out and tried to walk up to the house, but instead I sank to the snow drifted on the side of the driveway. All of the sobs that hadn't emerged when I touched my husband's embalmed body came ripping out, with a vengeance. Jo knelt at my side, also sobbing, trying to help me up, but like a petulant, inconsolable child I curled in the snow, wrapping my arms around my head. I didn't know if the horrible, choking sounds came from my throat or from my sister's. The snow froze my body, but I welcomed it, wanted it. I wanted to freeze to death in that moment. The early evening cast long, blue-gray shadows all across the driveway.

"Help me," my sister pleaded.

Strong arms curled me close, lifting me up.

Dodge, I thought. I tried to fight away, but there was no strength left. I buried my face behind my forearms and felt as though something had broken inside of me, cracked or split, releasing a hellacious floodgate of sobs. *My heart*, I realized.

"Bring her to her room," Gran murmured, holding open the front door.

He carried me down the basement steps, where the roar of voices in the living room was blessedly muted. I was deposited with great care onto my bed, the room dim in the encroaching evening. Blindly I reached for my husband's pillow and pulled it against my face. Seconds later Jo lay down behind me, curling her arms around my waist, fitting her body to mine. I didn't know how much time passed before I calmed. Jo stroked my hair and murmured to me until drowsiness began to weight my eyelids. I whispered, "Where's Clint?" through a throat that felt lacerated.

"He's at the cafe with Mom," Jo whispered. "She took him over there earlier today. He's just fine."

I rested my forearms over hers, clinging to my sister. Jo pressed her face against my back. I experienced the irrational sensation that if she let go, I would die. I whispered, "Thank you for bringing me down here. I'm sorry…I'm so sorry I freaked out."

"Don't apologize," she whispered. "Jilly, don't. And Justin carried you down here, not me. I couldn't get you out of the snowdrift. Thank goodness he was here."

But I'd exhausted all of my words. With Jo holding me, I slept.

Chris's service was the next day, a Sunday, two days after he drowned. Early that morning I stood before the mirror in our tiny basement bathroom and spread my long hair over my cold, bare shoulders. Joelle, who was staying with me, lay asleep in my bed; I couldn't sleep unless her arms were locked around me. I ran my fingers through its golden length, imagining Chris doing the same. I brushed it slowly, carefully, to a gloss before neatly braiding it and drawing the thick braid over my left shoulder. It was so long these days; I hadn't cut it since our wedding.

The scissors on the counter were the sharpest in the house, wickedly long-bladed. I clutched my braid in one fist and lifted the shears in the other. For a moment, looking into my own eyes, which resembled burn holes in a white sheet, I considered jamming the blades into my wrist and tearing a long wound. I'd watch the blood rise up and then cover the bathroom floor in a crimson gush. I fantasized about it for a little while. Maybe I could jam them into my neck, my soft, pale neck. Then this misery would end, and I wouldn't have to think about facing the rest of my life alone.

But I wasn't alone. I was a mother. It was selfish and cowardly to even imagine killing myself. But I did imagine it, in vivid detail. When the scissors snipped I shuddered a little, but they cut through my hair with ease. What remained was shaggy and the back of my neck too exposed, raw without the usual length of my hair. I tied off the sheared end of the braid as though it was an umbilical cord, making it neat and then laying it carefully on the counter. Almost a foot and a half of golden hair, which would now spend eternity in Chris's hands.

No one questioned what I'd done. When Jo got up, she helped me to even out the hair that was left, tears streaming quietly over her cheeks. At the church I clung to her and Gran; Elaine held Clint, who was silent and pale, watching everything with solemn eyes. Jackson brought Camille, Tish, and tiny Ruthann to his mother's house. I was vaguely aware of the faces of everyone we knew, people from Landon here to pay respects, but I felt surrounded by strangers. I felt a thousand years old and probably looked it, with my shorn hair. I didn't speak, though I thought, much later, that I should have said a few words at the service. I was too overcome; it took all of my strength to walk up to the open casket and place my braid into my husband's folded hands. Jo walked at my side, supporting me. On the way back to our pew, the waves of crying seemed to flood my ears like icy rain.

"I want Daddy," Clint begged, as my knees gave out and I sank to the wooden seat beside my son.

I curled my arms around him and he clung to my neck. I thought, *I want your daddy, too, baby, all I want in the whole world is your daddy.*

Joelle stayed for another week, though Jackson flew home on Monday. She and little Ruthann stayed with me in the house, the two older girls bouncing between my place and Shore Leave.

"I'll never love again," I vowed in my kitchen late one night. My voice was sandpaper grating over gravel. I whispered, "It's like Minnie said, Jo, she was right. Our family is cursed. We're *fucking cursed.* Davis women lose the men they love."

Jo, opposite me at the table, didn't contradict anything I said. Her face was ravaged with the pain of my words, but she did not try to stop me from talking.

"Chris was doomed the moment I married him…"

"Stop it," Jo finally insisted, unable to continue sitting there in accepting silence, her face stark and white. Her voice conveyed her horror. She whispered, "That isn't true, Jillian. The curse is not real. You know this."

"How can I keep going?" I whispered.

"You will," she told me, her voice soft and certain, holding my hand too tightly. "You will, Jillian."

"But how?" I insisted. I wanted answers.

"Because you will," she said, the kind of non-answer you'd give a child.

"I'm a widow," I said. And then, "Our house. He was going to build it for us this spring, Jo, this spring. He already bought the land. It was going to happen."

Again Jo said nothing, simply kept hold of my hand on the tabletop.

"Jo, why didn't I see? Why didn't I stop him before he went? I should have known…why didn't I know?" My voice was a tortured whisper.

"Because you're not superhuman," my sister told me, and her voice was edged with anger now, that I would blame myself for something of this magnitude. She insisted, "You can't predict everything. If I ever hear you say such a thing again, I am going to be really mad."

"Move home," I said, which was a pretty lowdown tactic.

Jo's eyes were bordered with shadows of exhaustion. Her shoulders drooped and she looked agonized. She whispered, "I wish I could, Jilly. I so wish I could. We've talked about it before. But Jackie wouldn't make near the money back here."

"So?" I pressed. "Please, Jo, I'm begging you."

"Jilly," she moaned. "Maybe someday."

Chapter Six

July, 1995

"Hey, you need help with that?" asked a voice behind me, and I turned to see Justin, who momentarily abandoned his shopping cart to jog over to us.

"Yeah, actually, thanks," I told him, grateful for the help; I'd been trying to load the Rug Doctor I just rented from the co-op into the back of the station wagon, while Clinty watched with interest, and zero help, from the backseat. Though, at seven years old he wouldn't have provided much assistance.

"No problem," Justin said, and I felt his gaze on my face. I swiped self-consciously at the sweat trickling over my temples.

In the years since Chris's death, Justin had become a friend…a different sort than the teasing boy of our youth. He was always at Shore Leave for coffee with Dodge on summer mornings; that first June, four years ago now, when I could barely force myself out of bed to face another day, he took to treating me like a cross between a mental patient and a beloved little sister, with quiet kindness. He asked me if I still had teeth and when I stared up at him in an uncomprehending fog, he said, "You haven't smiled in so long I couldn't remember, tomboy." And at his words, I'd actually giggled.

"Hi, Justin!" my son said brightly, on his knees in the third row of seats, which were vinyl and hot as hell under the broiling summer sun.

Justin ducked to peer into the wagon and said, "Hey there, buddy. You make a mess on the carpet, or what?"

Clinty laughed, his blue eyes sparkling. He said, "No, Grandma's dogs are potty-training."

I laughed a little, adding, "You know those pups Eddie had for sale? Mom took two."

"The retrievers? God, they were cute as hell," Justin said, loading the cumbersome machine swiftly and easily. He'd grown a goatee this summer, making him seem almost like a stranger—the tall, dark, and insanely handsome one that a fortune teller might warn you about. I looked quickly away, tugging my thoughts to safer territory. Justin went on, "I almost took one myself. Eddie had them in a cardboard box in the bar for a couple of nights."

"Yeah, that's where Mom and Ellen spied them," I confirmed, shading my eyes, the better to see him, conveniently forgetting my intent to keep my gaze away from him altogether.

He grinned effortlessly, bracing one wrist on the edge of the open hatchback. He speculated, "Those two out on the town?"

I felt a smile play over my lips at this question, replying, "They wanted to hear the music last Friday. So they *said*, anyway. They drove the golf cart and came back a little tipsy, actually."

Justin laughed and shook his head.

"And Elaine's house is on the market," I told him, a momentary shadow passing across my heart. "I told her I'd get in there and clean the carpets this week."

Justin's black eyebrows knitted together as he regarded me solemnly, his smile gone. He asked, "She moved up to International Falls to live with her cousin, right? I thought Dad said that."

I nodded and at that moment a horn honked from somewhere behind us.

He said, "Guess that's my cue to get my ass moving."

I still had trouble disguising my dislike for his wife, and commented, "She can't just come over and say hello, too?"

Justin's brows lifted this time, perhaps amused by my tone, but he said only, "Nah, we're heading over to Bemidji tonight, and she wants to get going."

Oh, I mouthed. It was absolutely none of my business. I added, "Well, thanks again, Justin."

"Anytime," he said easily and jogged back in the direction of Aubrey the bitch. I inhaled a small, tight breath and then turned to my son, forcing a bright smile.

July, 1998

Dodge was running across the parking lot.

I noticed this from my vantage point on the porch, where I stood, in the middle of taking orders from a six-top. Not only was such a pace unusual for him, but he'd just been mowing the lawn, and now suddenly his every movement suggested panic. I dropped my order pad on the table, to the surprise of my customers, and darted into the cafe, calling, "Mom!"

Mom met me halfway across the floor and caught me in a hug; before I could draw a breath, bile rose up the back of my throat, unwittingly pitched back to that horrible February night more than seven years ago. Shaking, I pulled away and asked, "What?"

"It's Justin," she said, and her throat sounded raw. "I don't know…"

My heart sliced along a jagged plane. Justin had been in the cafe only a few hours ago for coffee with Dodge, and I focused on that image of him, hale and whole. What in the hell could have happened in the intervening hours?

In a voice I barely recognized I asked, "What do you mean?"

Mom shook her head and I turned to watch as Dodge's car burned rubber getting out of the parking lot; the Charger roared away and left us standing in shock.

This time I demanded, "What's going on?"

Mom said, "Aubrey just called from the hospital," and the blood froze in my veins. "Justin's there, in Rose Lake. Something happened at the station."

"But what? What could happen there?" I turned in a panicky circle, reminding myself that it wasn't my place to race at once to the hospital and see what was wrong; undoubtedly Justin's wife would dislike that. But I felt tense and twitchy, my limbs ready to dash outside and follow Dodge as fast as I could.

One of the customers from my six-top poked his head inside and inquired, "Is everything all right?"

Mom cupped my arm firmly, her touch conveying the need to calm down, and said in her authoritative tone, "Jilly, we'll find out what's going on soon enough. You head back out there and finish up, all right, honey?"

I couldn't concentrate on shit, and it was two agonizing hours before Dodge finally called us; he got Ellen and we all crowded around as she spoke with him. I could tell nothing from her one-sided conversation and my thumbnails were just about nonexistent by the time Ellen replaced the receiver.

Her lips compressed briefly before she said, "He got burned with battery acid. He was never in danger of dying."

"Which someone could have told us!" I couldn't help but interject.

"But he's hurt pretty bad," Ellen continued, folding her hands together and pressing them against her belly. She added, "His face got the worst of it."

"When can we see him?" I demanded, wanting to grip my aunt's shoulders and shake answers free.

Ellen's eyes swam with tears and she said, "Honey, he doesn't want to see anyone right now."

That night I curled in my bed, unable to get the image of Justin's face from my mind. I pictured him as a ten-year-old, just younger than Clint was this summer, Justin with his dark eyes always full of mischief, just like Dodge. I saw him as a wild teenager, his lips that always seemed to be smiling or about to laugh. All the past summers I'd taken for granted the fact that I saw him almost every morning when he and Dodge came in for coffee; Shore Leave was convenient stop, just around Flickertail from the filling station and shore shop where both of them worked repairing things, mainly boat and car engines. I considered Justin a dear friend and if a hint of something more than that ever dared flicker into my mind, if I found myself enjoying his company perhaps a bit more than I should, I stomped it out, at once and with real determination. He was a married man and I was so lonely, and those two things could be a potentially dangerous combination.

I turned the other direction, restless and hot and fearful, all at once, pressing my cheek into the pillow, wondering now when I'd see him again.

August, 2000

"Aubrey's left him," Dodge told Ellen around the bonfire that night.

Just across the leaping flames from the two of them, about to take a sip from my beer bottle, my stomach went cold with sympathy, my arm drifting slowly to my lap. Though the rumors were flying in Landon I purposely blocked out what I'd heard, determined to find out the truth without asking; which of course meant waiting for Dodge to elaborate.

For the past two years Justin's stops at the cafe remained infrequent. He preferred to do his drinking after work and I knew Dodge was worried as hell about his son. I worried too, though quietly, knowing that Justin would despise any hint of concern or pity directed his way. He was a changed man since his accident and it hurt all of us to see it; we were all equally helpless to do anything.

"Oh no," Ellen said, her voice low with concern. "Damn."

Dodge inhaled a slow, deep breath and directed his gaze over to me, saying, "Jillian, don't let on that you know, honey."

"I won't," I promised. "When…"

"This morning she was gone," Dodge said. "I hated to leave the boy today, but he was…"

My heart constricted further; Dodge was teary-eyed. Ellen put her hand on his knee and squeezed, and he covered her hand with his own, returning the gentle pressure. It was just them and me, and I felt restless and uncomfortable, not because they were touching (I had long known that Dodge and my aunt liked each other more than either would admit), but because I wanted to find Justin and it would be the worst possible mistake I could make, at least tonight.

"Where is he now?" I asked, unable to help it, my throat dry and hoarse.

"Probably passed out over his kitchen table," Dodge said. "Liz was going to go over there this evening, she's the only one who I thought he might possibly be willing to see right now. I'll call her in a little bit."

"I think I'll take a walk," I whispered, leaving my beer in the cup holder of my lawn chair.

I ambled for over an hour and would surely be pockmarked with mosquito bites by the time I returned home. But I was too upset to remain around the fire, stewing in my worry over Justin; I could just as easily walk the lake path and let my thoughts turn to him, too. Flicker Trail was so familiar to me that the pitch blackness was no deterrent; though a milky half-moon glimmered through the treetops, the dense foliage along both sides of the road obscured most of the appreciable celestial light. I walked the mile into Landon, but didn't angle onto Fisherman's Street as I'd originally intended. I was about to turn and make my way back to Shore Leave when I felt a little jolt, a hint of gut instinct, telling me to continue onward instead, around the lake to the far side, along the gravel road that led to the old state park campsites where Jo and me and all of our friends used to hang out on long summer nights.

And so I did.

I reached the public boat landing, which was shadowed and silent this time of night, the lake lapping the moorings with a constant, soothing murmur. I paused, looking across the water at the cafe, our porch lights glinting into the night in a welcoming array, like the deck of a ship. The bonfire was just a speck from over here, where Dodge and Ellen were certainly still sitting and chatting. I hoped that Liz managed to talk to her brother today, and that he was at least partially all right. I debated stopping by Justin's house, but immediately vetoed what would surely prove a poor decision. Probably he was all but passed out over his kitchen table and therefore in no mood for visitors.

Aubrey's leaving was a long time coming, though I realized that the knowledge made the reality no easier to bear. Aubrey couldn't put up with her husband's bitterness, which a small part of me was able to understand; I found room to empathize, despite the fact that as a grown woman Aubrey was no less snobbish and bitchy than she'd been as a teenager, definitely not a kindred spirit of any kind. I long wondered what Justin saw in her, other than the fact that she was pretty. But all the beauty in the world couldn't constantly mask a nasty spirit, a spiteful personality. I believed from the bottom of my heart that he was better off without her. But convincing him of this was not my place; like every other realization in life, he'd have to recognize it on his own.

I sighed and stretched both arms above my head, inhaling the familiar scents of the lakeshore, when my eyes fell upon a shape at the very end of the boat landing dock, on the L-shaped extension that jutted out over the water, parallel to the shore. All at once I understood that I'd stumbled upon Justin, however unwittingly. Somehow I knew it was him sitting alone out there; he'd obviously walked over here, as his house wasn't more than a few blocks from Fisherman's. I pondered just leaving him alone, but my feet wouldn't obey. The wisdom of approaching him was perhaps questionable…but I'd wanted to find him and now I had. And I wouldn't walk away.

Just above a whisper, I hissed, "Hey, Justin!"

He shifted and turned immediately in the direction of my voice, calling, "Jillian?" The surprise was apparent in his tone.

Instead of replying I made my way out onto the dock, studying him as I walked along the familiar old boards, still slightly warm under my bare feet from the wood's retention of the long evening sun. Justin sat with both knees bent, forearms braced over them, his wide shoulders slightly hunched in a defensive-looking posture. In the inky darkness he wasn't more than a silhouette against the silvery sheen of the lake, watching silently as I approached.

I reached him and sat without invitation, folding my legs crosswise without a word, not looking over at him, though suddenly I ached to clasp his face in both of my hands and touch every inch of his scars, let my fingers trail over his skin. I was certain that no one had touched him that way in probably two years. But I kept both hands safely in my own lap.

"Is Dad still over at Shore Leave?" he asked, not questioning how I'd found him here. He kept his face turned away now that I was close, though because I sat on his left side, his scars were not visible. He looked exactly as he always had—handsome as hell, his profile clearly defined against the backdrop of night sky.

"Yeah," I whispered.

I offered no explanation for my presence, and for long minutes we sat in total silence, though not the companionable kind of old. The air between us was charged with tension on his part and uncertainty on mine; I was so scared to say the wrong thing and set him off. But, dammit, I wanted him to know that I cared and that I wasn't about to be put off by his shit attitude. When at last he spoke, I startled a little, my belly jumping.

"Jillian, I swear to God, if you tell me you're fucking sorry for me, I will come unglued right here," he said, and his voice was so taut with venom that I almost got up and left him sitting there. Though I understood clearly that it was not me he was so furious with. Aubrey, fate, life…any of these could be candidates for his wrath.

For another protracted moment I said nothing. I bent one knee and caught my chin on it, my gaze directed out over the darkness of the lake, same as his. I sensed that he wanted me to snap back, give him an excuse to unleash his anger. Finally I said, softly, "I'm not, and I won't tell you that."

He exhaled in a shuddering rush, and then from the corner of my eye I saw him tip his forehead against his bent arms. It was a gesture that tore at my heart; it was the way a child hid his face when life was too much to handle. He remained utterly still. I turned and studied him fully, realizing I'd never understood how sad total stillness could seem. Again I longed to touch him, at least rest my hand on his back, but sensed deeply that would be the wrong move. It was like sitting near a wild animal—one mistaken gesture and I may end up with teeth marks… at least, metaphorical ones. I laced my fingers together and kept quiet.

After a time he gathered himself enough to lift his face. His voice rough and with a note of despair, he said, "I'm sorry. You don't deserve that. I'm acting like a monster. I look like a fucking monster so maybe it makes sense."

"Dammit, you *do not*," I whispered, angry now, but also terrified by the defeat in his voice. His lips pressed into a thin line and he shook his head.

He said bitterly, "No matter what you or anyone says it doesn't change the truth."

"Justin," I said firmly, facing him. "You *do not*. Please listen to me."

He laughed, humorlessly. "Thanks for saying so, but I can see myself in the mirror. You think I couldn't see how disgusted she was?"

Fucking Aubrey. I wanted to say that, but it would only feed the flames. Instead I sat in silence, knowing anything I said would be wrong. I wanted to know if it was true that Aubrey actually ran off with a fisherman-tourist. But never in a million years would I dare ask. Besides, it would only make me hate her even more than I already did, to the point where I might have to track her down and chop off her long auburn hair, then maybe a couple of fingers.

"Look at me," he said, unnecessarily, as I was already gazing directly at him.

His eyes appeared black in the dimness. Though part of him surely wanted me to look away first, prove his feelings justifiable, I stared back unflinchingly, with a carefully blank expression.

"I'm a fucking freak show," he whispered.

"Justin!" I bitched, no longer able to retain a calm voice. If he vented on me after this, maybe I was asking for it anyway. I sat up straighter and railed at him, "Stop it! Do you want to spend the rest of your life feeling sorry for yourself?"

So much for keeping my opinions to myself.

Shit, I was on a roll; the next thing I heard out of my mouth was, "She's a *fucking bitch* and always has been! Jesus Christ, you mean to tell me you *never noticed* in all of these years? Good riddance, seriously!"

Oh, Jillian. Holy shit.

I snapped my mouth shut.

Justin stared at me in what appeared to be stun; his lips actually dropped slightly open. I braced myself for the onslaught of defensive anger that was sure to follow, but it didn't come. Finally he blinked and then observed, "I have never heard you get so angry before."

I exhaled in a semi-relieved rush, contradicting, "You have so, when we were kids."

"You really think my conceited, cheating wife is a fucking bitch?" he asked, and I detected what could possibly be a hint of humor in his tone, though dark and cuttingly cynical.

"Yes!" I yelled, and it was refreshing to be so honest. "You know it's true! I know you do! Goddammit, Justin, I was trying to make you *feel better!*" I didn't know where all of this anger was flowing from. But my face glowed hot with its energy.

He studied me in silence; his surprise hovered like a third presence on the dock. At last he said, "I get that you're trying to make me feel better, tomboy, even if it's in a totally fucked up way. Thanks for that, truly." And then he wondered, "What's with the smile?"

"That name," I told him. "You haven't called me that in years."

"Old habit," he said, and sighed deeply, resuming his defensive pose, forearms on knees, shoulders curled forward.

"Justin…" My anger suddenly arced away like an arrow I'd released. I stared into his dark, fierce eyes and wanted to say so many things.

"What?" he asked, seeming to soften just a little.

"Come have coffee again in the mornings," I said, and because I couldn't resist touching him for just a second, I put my hand on his upper arm. His muscle was like a curve of warm, solid stone under my palm, so very strong. I almost shivered, and discreetly removed my touch. I implored, "Please."

And then I stood and forced myself to walk away, leaving him sitting alone in the night.

Chapter Seven

April, 2003

"RICH'S GRANDSON?" I ASKED MOM, LEANING ON MY ELbows over the counter.

Mom flung a bar towel over her shoulder and then clicked the start button on the coffee maker, clarifying, "His stepdaughter Christy Tilson's son, you remember Christy, don't you? Her son is named Blythe, and he's looking for a job."

"In Minnesota?" I pressed.

Mom turned to face me, bracing her palms on the counter just opposite. Undoubtedly hoping to startle me a little, she commented, "He's been in jail. Two years ago he apparently stole a car."

"You're hiring a car thief? A jail bird?" I teased. "In the Old West he'd have been hung from the nearest tree!"

"When did you become so judgmental?" Mom asked, pretending shock, though her eyes held amusement. She assured me, "Rich insists that he's a good kid. He must have had a good reason for stealing a car, and you know we can trust Rich."

I twisted up my mouth in a skeptical knot, at last conceding, "Yeah, that's true. But promise me that if he seems in any way shady you'll send him packing for Oklahoma."

Mom rolled her eyes. "Oh for the love, Jillian."

Ellen came out of the bar and caught the tail end. As she headed into the kitchen she added, "Honey, your gran has already insisted that she have the final say. You know how she gets. We can all rest assured that Ma won't let any calamities befall the cafe."

Mom snickered but I felt doubly reassured; I maintained total trust in Gran. If Gran thought this ex-con grandson with the strange name was all right, I would trust that.

"Does Joelle know?" I asked next, anticipation surging through me at the thought of my sister coming home next month. And this time perhaps for good, now that Jackie finally proved false.

"No, I haven't said a thing, not with what she's going through," Mom said. "She's got enough on her plate right now."

"Good riddance," I said firmly, and watched Mom's lips draw up as though she'd just bitten into a lemon wedge.

"Jillian, that's a terrible, flippant thing to say," she admonished. "Jo and Jackson need to work on their marriage, not throw it away."

Oh, Joelle would throw her crappy marriage away if I had anything to do with it; I wasn't totally heartless… maybe just a little selfish, as I finally saw my chance to keep Jo here in Landon where she belonged, after all these years. Jackson sank so low as to screw around on Joelle, simultaneously giving her the perfect excuse to leave him, though I did hate the fact that she was so devastated in the wake of his cheating; she'd walked in on Jackie last Christmas, going at it with a slutty co-worker named Lanny, right smack on his office desk. Jackie was my sister's first and only love, after all, not to mention the father of her girls. And shit, Mom would use both of those things to work on convincing Jo to forgive the hound dog.

"Mom, you can't mean—" But I stopped mid-word as footsteps sounded on the porch, turning just as Justin came through the door.

"Morning, ladies," he said. "It smells great in here."

Mom beamed at him. "Caramel rolls will be done any second."

Justin straddled the stool to my right and my heart seemed to find this an invitation to beat a little harder. This sort of thing happened to me lately whenever he appeared, and it rattled the hell out of me. To cover it, I moved around the counter and snagged the coffee decanter, as Mom disappeared into the kitchen.

"Thanks, Jilly," Justin said as I filled up his stainless travel mug.

From a few feet away I regarded him in the early morning light. He had such beautiful eyes, with long spiky lashes. Almost five years had passed since his accident, and more than two and a half since our midnight chat on the boat landing dock, after which he began to rejoin Dodge for breakfast, to my considerable relief. I was so used to how his face looked that I didn't even notice his scarring anymore. Just his eyes, which flashed into my thoughts at odd moments.

"Why are you being weird?" he asked, knowing me well enough to wonder why I stood in silence, staring at him. He appeared amused.

"I'm not," I said, irritated, which of course just emphasized the fact that I was being weird. On sudden inspiration I said, "I was just thinking about how Mom and Ellen are hiring Rich's grandson from Oklahoma."

Justin set down his mug and stretched his torso, bending his elbows, fists near his ears. He did this with no regard for how his muscles bulged as his work shirt stretched taut across his powerful biceps and chest. Justin was a mechanic. I'd heard all of my adult life how he was good with his hands; it was common knowledge in Landon. And suddenly I wanted to know just how true this was. I watched, almost transfixed, but then snapped my gaze away as he resumed his earlier pose and picked up his coffee.

He was saying, "Yeah, Dad mentioned something about that. The kid's been in jail, but Rich seems to think he's all right. When does he get here?"

"Um, this week," I said, and cleared my throat.

Justin shot me another amused look.

Fine, I admitted to myself. I was attracted to him. I was very fucking much attracted to him, and I had known this for a long time. Fat lot of good that knowledge did me.

Mom breezed out of the kitchen carrying a tray of caramel rolls. She plunked these on the counter and Justin helped himself. He finished his coffee while I tried to appear preoccupied, stirring sugar into my own mug.

"You trying to make the spoon stand straight up?" he asked. He rose to his full height, forcing me to lift my chin to continue looking at him. I suddenly wanted to ask if he still missed Aubrey, or if they still talked. Justin tipped his head to the side for a second, as though trying to determine my thoughts from my expression. My heart thumped almost painfully. At that moment Dodge clacked through the screen and we looked instantly away from each other, as if guilty of something.

"Morning, kids!" Dodge said, and I moved to get him some coffee.

"Dad, I'm heading out. Have a good day, Jilly," Justin said over his shoulder. I found myself watching the back pockets of his jeans, and swallowed hard.

I remained edgy for the rest of the day.

That evening, sitting on the dock in the sunset light, I wallowed in a contemplative mood. For a long while, I thought about years. Thirty-four years I'd known Justin, from the time I was born. Twelve years since my husband died. Five years since Justin's accident. Two years since his divorce from Aubrey was final.

Long ago I remembered thinking that Dodge and Ellen liked each other perhaps more than prudent; had I overheard a conversation between Minnie and Gran, maybe? I struggled to remember any sort of history I might have eavesdropped upon, however inadvertently. Back then it was just a passing thought, more pronounced after Marjorie Miller, Justin and Liz's mother, divorced Dodge and moved back to her own hometown, somewhere in Iowa. I never found a reason to suspect that Dodge and Ellen acted on anything, but there was an undercurrent there. And now one had sprung up between Justin and me, forcefully. Or maybe just me. Maybe he couldn't care less about me in that way; more likely, he still regarded me as the tomboy tagalong from his childhood. A little sister. I thought back to our summers as kids; Justin called me 'Jill the pill' when I was six, tormenting me endlessly. I spent my eighth summer with an enormous crush on him, which, oddly, I never even confessed to Jo. Maybe somewhere in the back of my mind that had always lingered. I pictured him as he'd been back then, a skinny kid who'd grown tall in his early teens, lanky and always suntanned. His effortless smile, his easy way of making everything a joke.

When Justin married Aubrey, only a few months before I married Chris, Dodge told Ellen it was a mistake; Ellen hadn't mentioned this fact to me until the past year, though I could have guessed. Aubrey, the Homecoming Queen. Aubrey with her endless need for attention, her long auburn hair which she loved to flick over her shoulders, her spiteful little eyes; how had Justin put up with her for as long as he did? If I was honest, I had to admit that I still hated her, still felt everything I'd yelled about her to Justin that night on the boat landing dock. She hadn't returned to Landon since their divorce and he never mentioned her since, at least not in my hearing. I knew the past years hadn't been easy for him—and that was a severe understatement—though in the last year or so he seemed slightly more like his old, teasing self.

And his old self made me seriously crazy these days.

I called Joelle a little later, once the sun set, excited for her to get home. I craved seeing her so badly that it manifested as a physical ache in my gut. It would only be a month now, as soon as Milla, Tish, and Ruthie finished the school year. I wanted to tell Jo all about Rich's grandson, and get her opinion on the matter, but my poor sister was so full of her own sorrow and stress that instead I let her talk. And by the time we said good-night, I forgot all about what I planned to tell her.

The next Saturday night we gathered on the porch to welcome Blythe Tilson, who called at dusk to tell Rich he was approaching the interstate exit to Landon. Rich was almost dancing with anticipation as he went outside onto the porch. I followed and hooked an arm around his elbow, my second surrogate father, who winked at me, patting my forearm. Rich was older than Dodge, with fine white hair and bushy, caterpillar-like eyebrows. He'd aged markedly since his wife Pamela's death, but this evening he looked positively giddy.

I smiled up at him and asked, "So, what's the kiddo's name again?"

Rich laughed and said, "Well, he's not exactly a kiddo," and just as he spoke a black truck rumbled slowly into the lot. Mom, Ellen, Gran, and

Clinty all came outside in the next instant, our eyes fixed on the new arrival. I felt a pang of sympathy for the poor guy, having to walk up to a
porch of strangers, all of whom were curious as hell about him and doing
a poor job of hiding this fact.

"Do you think he'll be all tattooed? Maybe have one of those ankle
cuffs?" Clint asked in a stage whisper, and I giggled as Rich hurried
down the steps to hug his grandson.

And then I fell abruptly silent. The "boy" emerging from the truck
and bear-hugging Rich was no boy at all, but a tall, broad-shouldered
man with a long ponytail. I'd been expecting someone seedy I admitted
it, a kid with greasy hair and grungy black clothes. I should have known
better and trusted Rich, though he failed to mention just one *rather* sig-
nificant detail. Mom met my gaze and raised her eyebrows as Rich led
him up to the porch; no matter what we'd all been subconsciously picturing, it certainly wasn't the man before us at the moment.

Holy Moses, I thought. *Oh, my goodness.*

He was unbelievably good-looking. Even Gran appeared slightly
stunned; if she were anyone else, her mouth would be hanging open. The
grandson smiled almost shyly and extended a hand to Gran first.

"Blythe Tilson," he said in a warm, deep voice. "You can call me Bly."

Gran gathered herself together and shook his hand, with vigor.

"Bend down," she ordered imperiously, and I bit the insides of my
cheeks to keep a smile at bay. *Only Gran.* She added, "I want to look in
your eyes."

Blythe tipped forward without hesitation while my gran glared at
him for a long moment, then sat back with a satisfied air. "You'll do,"
she affirmed, and another smile, perhaps tinged with relief, passed over
his face.

"Bly, this is Louisa Davis, and her daughters, Ellen and Joan," Rich
said and Blythe shook everyone's hand. Rich went on, "And this is Jillian
Henriksen, Joan's youngest, and her son, Clint."

"Hi," I beamed at him, couldn't help but do so. Blythe smiled back and
shook my hand, and as he did I was fisted in the midsection with such
a strong image of him and Joelle that my vision momentarily clouded.

He shook Clint's hand next, and my son speculated, "Hey, maybe you can help me hang up the basketball hoop on the garage."

Blythe said, "Sure thing," and Clint grinned.

"We'll have you start first thing tomorrow," Mom said. "I'm sure you're hungry."

"Famished," he said easily.

"Well, you've come to the right place," Rich said, and I could sense his relief; Rich knew the womenfolk well enough to sense their acceptance of his grandson.

Joelle remained in my mind, clear as a sunrise on a cloudless day. This boy—*this man*, I corrected myself—was somehow connected to her, before they even knew one another existed. I shook my head, peering in the front windows, sticking around outside with Gran as Mom seated Blythe at the counter and served him a heaping platter of fried fish and boiled red potatoes. Though Clint had eaten already, he felt free to take advantage of a second supper.

"Well," said Gran, and I turned to see her grinning; she squinted one eye to light a smoke.

I giggled a little. "You can say that again."

An hour later we were still at the cafe. Mom dragged out a pile of photo albums to show Blythe what Shore Leave looked like over the years, and in different seasons. Blythe wouldn't have known it, but this was a major set of points in his favor. The womenfolk liked him, and not just because he could have been a Greek god come to life. He exuded a sort of gentle kindness that was very appealing. At the moment he was laughing over a couple of photos from around 1975 or so, featuring Jo, Liz, Justin and me swimming in the lake.

"What a great place to grow up," he kept saying.

I happened to be watching as he looked at one of Joelle from senior year, in which she rode piggyback on Jackson, her head flung back with laughter. He studied it closely before asking me, "This is your sister?"

"Yeah, that's Joelle."

"Does she live around here?" he asked, his voice casually offhand.

Good, I thought, recognizing that this question meant Rich hadn't told him much about Joelle's situation. I planned to tread very carefully here; I hadn't experienced such a strong Notion in a long time and the last thing Joelle needed was to get home and walk into a whole new set of complications.

"No, she lives in Chicago," I told him.

"She'll be here in a few weeks though," Clint said, with excitement; he adored his cousins. And then, "Gran, can I have some more of that blackberry pie?"

"Sure, honey," Gran said; Clint was the only person on the face of the earth to whom Gran was never, ever sarcastic.

Blythe perked up at Clint's statement about Joelle getting here soon, looking over at me as though for confirmation; he'd already ascertained the best way to learn more about her was to question me.

I said, "She and her girls will be here in May."

He nodded, not seeming to want to ask the obvious, but I supplied, "Jo brings her daughters up every summer."

"That's her husband, Uncle Jackie," Clint said next, indicating the photo that Blythe still held, using his fork to point out Jackson.

Blythe nodded more slowly this time, still studying Jo. I could almost hear his thoughts, but before he could ask any more questions, Mom observed, "Clinty, it's getting late."

My son groaned, eating his pie in double-time, as though Mom planned to snatch it away.

"Yeah, time for bed," I agreed, and all but dragged Clint home, the Notion concerning Blythe Tilson and my sister at the forefront of my thoughts, heavy and unavoidable as a heat wave. I lay awake for hours, pondering what it might mean, before at last drifting into a restless doze. And just before dawn, I had a dream.

In it, I swam lazily in Flickertail, under a sky tinted the hue of a June rose. The air smelled likewise sweet and the water lapped silvery and silken around me, pleasantly warm. I floated on my back, naked, which wasn't a first; I'd skinny-dipped in the lake more times than I could even count. I was enjoying the sensation, the caress of the water and the magenta sky, when I felt a hand glide over my belly. Somehow it didn't startle me; in fact, just the opposite—I anticipated it. Justin, his black hair wet and hanging almost to his shoulders, just as it would in real life, surfaced near my breasts, water purling off his strong, wide shoulders where they broke through the water.

My heart thrashed my ribs as he ducked under again, touching me beneath the water, hot and sleek. When he resurfaced, I righted myself so that I could pull him against me, his long, wet length. I touched his face, running my hands over his scars as I'd wanted to do so many times. His dark eyes burned into mine. I slipped my hand down his torso and caught hold of him under the water. He was so hard in my grip; my entire body pulsated at the feel of his swollen flesh. He pulled me roughly against him, bringing my mouth to his...

And I woke with a gasp, my heart going like a jackhammer.

The sheets twisted between my legs. I tried to draw a deep breath and could not, too revved up. I closed my eyes and pressed my face into the pillow, wanting Justin so much that I thought I might die. I hadn't wanted someone like this in over a decade. I knew that wasn't natural, but it was true. Suddenly the dearth was catching up with me, catching me terribly off guard. Especially since it was...

"Justin," I breathed, just to speak his name.

At breakfast I remained shaken. I remembered Minnie saying once, years ago, that when you dreamed about someone you knew, chances were you appeared in that person's dreams the same night. I'd never given it much thought, except when my dreams would include Christopher, and I would wake to wonder if he was somehow thinking of me from heaven. Today, however, my cheeks burned hot as coals imagining such a thing. Justin and Dodge came in for coffee, as per usual, and to meet Blythe. Justin wore his work shirt, which was undone just enough that I could see a little of his hairy chest. My fingertips literally tingled to touch him, picturing how he'd looked at me in my dream. How I'd touched him under the water. I'd seen his bare chest a million times in my youth, though not so much in the past years of adulthood. And here I was, imagining myself undoing—no, ripping—the rest of those buttons free and then...

In the bustle of everyone talking and eating, I didn't actually have to a chance to speak to Justin, an enormous relief at the moment. Though I kept shooting sidelong gazes at him, I didn't know if I'd be able to meet his eyes directly without pushing everything from between us, forcibly, leaping into his arms and commandeering his lips. Just before he and Dodge left for the filling station, he caught me as my back was turned. I jumped a little when, from behind me, he said, "Hey, Jills, can you refill me quick?"

I stood messing with the coffeepot, and when I turned around it was with a smooth, calm expression. But then I saw that he leaned over the counter, grinning at me as though he knew a secret, and all the air in my lungs instantly solidified.

"Time to switch to decaf," he teased, holding out his travel mug for me to splash full. His black eyebrows quirked as I hesitated, staring wordlessly at him.

Jillian, I scolded. *Pull it together.*

His thick black hair was always disheveled, like he tried to brush through it but never quite found time to finish. It was wavy, not curly, and practically begged for me to sink my hands into it. Clearly he'd just shaved this morning, but retained a hint of five o'clock shadow no matter what time of day; I found this so appealing, so goddamn sexy, that I could hardly stand still.

"Here, I'll help," he said, sounding amused. And to my chagrin, he put his hand around mine on the handle of the coffeepot and filled his mug.

My heart wanted to beat through my chest. And Justin, damn him, gave me a little half-grin, saying, "Thanks, Jilly," before heading after Dodge to go to work.

I almost put my head in my arms on the counter.

Much later that evening I sat on the dock, overwhelmed by a gloom that I envisioned hovering over me and trailing streaky rain wherever I went. My thoughts swirled around in a semi-panic; I was thinking of my motives for convincing Jo to stay in Landon—that her marriage wasn't worth fighting for. Jackson had cheated on her, proving utterly untrustworthy. If that wasn't enough to end a relationship, what was?

But Mom's words made me second-guess my intentions. Besides, what if Jo didn't want to stay here? Was it selfish for me to hope that she would? Realistically I knew that I couldn't make my happiness dependent on what my sister chose to do. I braced my forehead against my fingertips. Goddammit, I was so lonely. Somewhere in the back of my mind I was also thinking about my son, who mentioned something about college just a few days ago. God, Clint would be gone from Landon before I knew it. That's what this was really about, the loneliness punching me in the stomach lately.

When footsteps reverberated behind me I didn't turn around, assuming Mom was taking pity on me, maybe bringing me a beer. At the last second I realized that Mom would have a much lighter tread and looked up just as Justin stopped and regarded me with a somber expression that matched my own. My heart flared desperately to life as I stared up at him, suddenly terribly self-conscious of my grease-spattered jean shorts and limp tank top I'd worn all day under my work shirt. Undoubtedly I smelled just like the fry vat.

"What are you doing out here?" he asked, his gaze holding steady on mine.

"Feeling sorry for myself," I admitted.

Exactly as I had that August night on the boat landing, Justin moved behind me and then sat on the edge of the dock to my left, though he kept a good twelve inches of acceptable, proper distance between us. He said quietly, "I thought I had the market cornered on that."

The air was soft, motionless all about us, and I was so conscious of him beside me that my entire body felt wired. He sat with his long legs bent, forearms draped over his knees, staring off over Flickertail in the same direction as me. His hair was even wilder than this morning, his shirt stained with motor oil and sweat. But he was more appealing to me than I could even admit to myself. Because it was equal parts terrifying and exhilarating.

I said, "No, God no."

"So what was up this morning?" His voice held just a hint of teasing, despite everything.

I swished my bare feet in the water, buying a moment. Justin looked my way when I didn't immediately answer, and I felt the heat of his gaze as potently as a touch. I wracked my mind, considering how to make him look at me that way all the time. But when I dared to meet his eyes, he hid away anything but polite interest.

"Nothing," I said, trying to sound casual. "Just tired."

"So why are you feeling sorry for yourself, Jilly-Anne?" he asked. The nickname came out of the ancient past; the summer I'd crushed so much on him, it was one of many he invented, making my first name into two. He asked, "Do I need to start yelling at you, or what?"

I said, "I was just missing Jo. And thinking about Clint moving away to go to college. I can't bear the thought."

"He got to be a teenager so quick," Justin said. "I remember seeing you around town with him when he was small, seems like yesterday."

"Yeah, it does seem like yesterday," I agreed. It felt so good to talk with him; his voice stroked my skin, warm and caressing. I realized I was hugging myself around the midsection and casually let my hands drift back to my lap.

"He reminds me so much of Chris," Justin said, catching me off guard. "I can't imagine how that must be for you."

My throat was a little thick, but I said, "He's very much like Chris."

"You're lucky to have him," Justin said.

I nodded agreement, not trusting my voice.

"I always wondered what it would be like to have a couple kids," Justin went on.

"Didn't…you guys didn't…" I started to say and then trailed off, not sure what I was asking.

But Justin seemed unruffled. "We tried. Aubrey wasn't entirely sold on the whole having kids thing. Now, though, I'm relieved. She would have taken the kids with her, probably, and that would have killed me."

Before I could consider the wisdom of it, I heard myself say, "You'd be such a good dad. Like Dodge."

Justin laughed a little and from the corner of my eye I saw him shake his head. "Well thanks. But I'm glad Aubrey and I didn't have any. I wouldn't want kids to have to go through a divorce. And I know from experience how much it sucks. Even as an adult."

"Do you hear from your mom very often?" I asked. His voice was uncharacteristically gentle and I realized he hadn't sworn once, totally unusual for him. I wished I was brave enough to curl the fingers of my left hand around his right, which was closest to me.

"At Christmas," he said, though there was no trace of self-pity in his tone. "Liz misses her a lot more, especially since she and Wordo have kids. But at least Dad is here in Landon. And he's a great grandpa."

"I love him so much," I said sincerely. "He's more like a dad to me than anyone I've ever known. Thanks for sharing him with Jo and me, truly."

Justin shifted a little. His gaze came to rest on me as he said softly, "Dad loves you, too. You know it, Jillian."

Our gazes clung and I was overwhelmed with pure, simple want. I wanted him to pull me close, I wanted to kiss him, I wanted to breathe against his neck. He looked hard at me for a moment, deeply, before inhaling an unhurried breath and sending his gaze back out over the lake. I was crushed with disappointment, but said, to keep him here with me a little longer, "Do you wish your parents were still together?"

"All kids want their parents together," Justin said, matter-of-factly. "Even when it's the worst decision in the world."

"I always wondered if I'd feel that way if I'd ever known Mick," I said, referring to my father, Mick Douglas, refusing to believe that he left our family for any reason other than simple immaturity. Not because he dared to love a cursed Davis woman. I explained, "I mean if he'd been around long enough to allow for a few memories. But it's always just been the womenfolk."

"Do you think he's still alive out there?" Justin asked.

"Probably, but I don't know that it would matter anymore. He's a stranger to us."

"Still, I'd like to thank him," Justin said.

"What are you talking about?" I asked.

"For being around long enough to get Joanie pregnant with you,"

Justin said guilelessly, his eyes holding fast to my face. He sensed my outright surprise and added hastily, "I mean it. I can't imagine not having you here," and I could hear the undertone in his voice, as though he was also struggling to keep it casual. This knowledge made me swell with hope.

"Thank you," I whispered, and wondered what he would do if I dared to straddle him right here, right now, dig my fingers into his hair and kiss him like tomorrow didn't exist.

But I remained motionless. I was too chicken.

"So…" he said after a moment of silence.

At the same second I asked, "Doesn't that just make the whole evening worth it?"

I pointed to a ribbon of sunset light that suddenly broke free of the purple clouds grouped low on the horizon, striking the tops of the budding trees on the far side of Flickertail. It was the kind of thing that made my throat ache a little, no matter how many incredible sunsets I'd watched from this exact spot.

"Yes," he said, soft and slightly hoarse. But right then he was looking only at me.

Chapter Eight

May, 2003

TWO WEEKS PASSED AND I DIDN'T GET ANOTHER MOMENT alone with Justin. But I kept my disappointment hidden away, concentrating on the fact that in just over a week Joelle would be home and then I could start testing my plan to keep her here forever; the problem was, Blythe Tilson inadvertently threw a wrench into the whole deal with his very presence.

After working with him in the cafe nearly every day, I'd grown incredibly fond of him. He was sweet, with a good sense of humor; he treated Clint like a little brother, shooting hoops with him and his friends some evenings after the cafe was closed and everything cleaned up for another night. He joked around with me all the time; in that way, he almost seemed like my own little brother, the one I'd never gotten, even after begging Mom for an entire winter, until she threatened to sell me to the gypsies. He asked me about Joelle, a lot. At first I could tell he tried to be casual, but then he seemed to realize that there wasn't really a good way to remain casual when constantly and transparently asking about someone you'd never met; besides, he didn't know my powers of observation, with just a hint of precognition thrown into the mix.

"So your sister likes Billy Idol?" This after Clint dug out a wire basket full of old tapes that belonged to Jo.

"When is her birthday?"

"How long has she been married?"

"Do you two talk very often?"

"Does she like it in Chicago?"

"How long is she staying in Landon?"

"Joelle's husband cheated on her?" This he at least managed the presence of mind to ask me when we were relatively alone, cleaning up the dining room after a busy Thursday dinner rush. Now that May was advancing, business would steadily grow busier. Upon seeing my surprise, he admitted, "Sorry, I asked Gramps about it."

I pondered several options before admitting, "Yeah, he did. But don't let on that you know, okay? Jo would hate that." I kept my eyes on the table I was wiping down but could almost hear his thoughts anyway.

He said, "Of course. That's so shitty. Who does that to his wife?"

"Yeah, but if you knew Jackie you'd understand how it happened," I said. "Everyone saw this coming a long time ago, except Jo."

I could tell he was dying for me to elaborate, but I couldn't continue, not with Joelle's personal business. I concluded, "But she'll be all right, if I know her."

Clint burst through the door just then, with a breathless demand, "Mom, I need those pictures for school tomorrow!"

I reminded him, "The shoebox above the fridge," and he darted away, to reemerge minutes later toting the box of loose photos, which he set on the counter to dig through. Finding two, he said, "Thanks, Mom," and then took off again, a perpetual whirlwind.

Unable to help myself, I lifted one from the top of the pile. *Junior prom.* I smiled, though my heart formed an involuntary fist as I looked at Chris and me, posing right here in the cafe on that long ago April afternoon, along with Jo and Jackie. We'd been so happy that night. I traced Chris's face with my index finger just as Blythe came up beside me.

"Lemme see," he commanded, again like a little brother. "More pictures?"

"Clinty needed one of me and his dad," I explained, passing it into his big hands.

"Wow, your hair was so long then. And that's Clint's dad, huh? He looks just like him," Bly said, tipping the photo this way and that. And then he touched its surface, just as lightly as I had moments ago. He said softly, "And that's Joelle."

He sounded reverent, there was no denying.

"Yeah, that's her. And that's Jackie, her husband. Well, boyfriend in those days."

He studied the photo intently.

"How many days until she gets here?" he asked quietly.

"Not fast enough!" I replied, choosing for the moment to ignore the tone in his voice, holding out my hand for the picture. Blythe seemed to gather himself and surrendered it to me.

"You miss her a lot, don't you?" he asked, settling onto a stool at the counter and pulling the bandana from his forehead.

"Hell yes," I said, sitting near him. Without asking permission he leaned over and began riffling through the shoebox of photos. I shoved it his direction, confessing, "God, I hope she stays here, for good. But don't tell anyone I said that. Mom would shit a ring around herself."

Blythe regarded me with amusement. He said, his voice with its hint of an Oklahoma accent, "It's so funny to hear you swear. Why would Joan do that?"

"Because Mom adores Jackson," I said, not questioning why I spilled these things to him; certainly because I considered Rich family, and Blythe was Rich's grandson. He probably knew half this stuff anyway. Besides, Blythe struck me as a good listener.

"Joan adores him even after he treated his wife that way?" Blythe wondered aloud, finding a wallet-sized senior picture of Joelle, the only pose in which she wasn't offering her glowing smile to the camera. Instead she sat on the dock, staring across the lake, knees bent, arms draped over them. We always laughed about how fake-serious she looked in this one, like a model reacting to a photographer coaching, "Now, let's see 'contemplative!' That's it!"

"Mom has always loved Jackson," I explained. "She thinks he made a mistake. She thinks Jo should forgive him."

"That's a pretty goddamn serious mistake," Blythe commented, his eyes still locked on Joelle.

"See, *you* understand," I said, finding a shot of Jo and me jumping off the dock, probably around 1975 or so. Gran and Minnie had floated in the canoe, out on the water, to snap this one.

"So, you think Joelle might stay around here?" he asked next. I thought for a second that he was actually going to put the picture of her in his shirt pocket; I experienced the sense that if I wasn't in the room he would have. But he blinked and then looked over at me.

"I hope so," I whispered. "I've missed her every single day since she left, way back in the summer after she and Jackie graduated."

"And they got married that same summer, right?"

"Yes," I said, exhaling slowly at the memory. "God, I was so sad that day. I couldn't believe Jackie was taking her away from me. But they didn't know what else to do, since she was pregnant." Blythe nodded, so very serious, and I elaborated, "I hated Jackie for that, and Jo a little too, if you want to know the truth. She got pregnant on prom night, how's that for cliché? But it wasn't even that she was going to have a baby, it was that they moved so far away. I felt like a piece of my soul got torn away. It was totally selfish of me."

"No, I get how you felt," Blythe said, and I believed he really did, somehow. "You're lucky to have each other."

"We are," I murmured, noticing all over again how very attractive he was, so muscular he appeared chiseled, with the broadest shoulders I'd ever seen in real life. His hair was long and wavy, his lips beautifully sculpted, his blue eyes very intense. And he was far more mature than his age would suggest.

Shit, shit, shithole. Warning lights flared to life in my mind as I imagined how Joelle would react to him; he was certainly smitten with her, despite the fact that he'd never even met her. I wondered again how I could keep my sister from being inadvertently hurt; I recognized that Blythe would never dream of hurting her—the pain would come from her end, as I'd already sensed. *Joelle,* I mourned. *How can I help you? What if it's too late already?*

Out of nowhere, I noticed Justin's silver truck pull into the parking lot. My heart sizzled instantly to life. I demanded, "What's *he* doing here?"

Blythe turned and followed my gaze, "Oh, Justin? This morning he asked if I wanted to grab a drink after work."

I watched in silence, slightly spellbound by the sight of Justin climbing from his truck and striding across the parking lot. I thought of what he'd said on the dock, about wanting to thank my father—I'd thought of little else. I heard him call hello to Mom and Ellen, both out on the dock, before taking the porch steps two at a time and banging through the screen door, same as always.

"Hey guys, you in the mood for a drink or three?" he asked, catching sight of us.

"Yeah, that sounds good, actually," Bly said, replacing the photographs in the shoebox. But not before touching a fingertip to Joelle's face.

Justin, in his dirty faded jeans, came right over and leaned beside me, checking out the array of pictures; having him so close made me literally squirm with desire. His work shirt was unbuttoned two past the collar, allowing for a glimpse of his dark chest hair. He smelled like motor oil, the outdoors, and a trace of cologne or maybe aftershave from this morning. I felt a keen, itching urge to lean near his bare neck and inhale. But of course I didn't. I shifted on my seat, my nipples pressing against my bra, round and tingling. I would not—*would not*—allow myself to imagine clutching Justin's hair as his lips opened over them…

"Shit, the good old days," he laughed, unaware of my wildly inappropriate thoughts, finding one of all four of us kids posing with a stringer of fish. I couldn't remember that day from a thousand others like it, but Justin said, "This was the afternoon Jo got a leech on her leg, remember that? That was so funny. See, you've got on that yellow unicorn swimsuit, that's what made me think of it," he elaborated, indicating my image in the picture.

"Oh yeah, it got all muddy after I tried to hold Jo's leg still for your dad," and I laughed at the memory. My unicorn swimwear appeared clean in the photo, so the leech incident hadn't yet happened. I giggled, "God, I *loved* that bathing suit."

"Dad tried to get her to keep still so he could burn it off," Justin explained to Bly, whose forehead wrinkled in confusion.

"Burn it?" he asked.

"Yeah, if you try to pull them out they just stretch and don't unlatch, but if you use a lighter the little fuckers fall right off," Justin explained, giving me a sideways grin.

"But Jo wouldn't hold still, even with me clutching her ankle. She was screaming and kicking her leg like it was some kind of new dance," I added.

"And then—" Justin began, but I interrupted, saying, "And then Justin here, sensitive guy that he is, finally managed to get her to calm down and pulled the leech out, longer and longer, like a black rubber band." I shuddered a little.

"But then I felt bad since she started to cry," Justin said.

"I thought she was going to faint when you let go and its stretched-out body flopped against her leg," I said, laughing hard now. "You did that on purpose."

"God, you guys are mean," Bly said, leaning on his forearms and watching us with amusement.

"Aw, shit, everybody gets a leech now and then," Justin said, slapping his palms against the edge of the counter. "You joining us, Jills?"

I looked up and over at him. He finally let his gaze hold mine without hiding anything and heat absolutely flared between us. My heart attacked my ribcage. His eyes caused a sizzling ripple across my belly; my nipples were round as pearls, aching for his touch. But I said with impressive casualness, "Sure, why not?"

"Eddie's?" Justin asked. "You guys can ride with me if you want."

"You're not going to clean up first?" I teased, and he laughed.

"What about you, server girl?" he teased right back, leaning near like I'd just been fantasizing about leaning into him, and smelling my hair. He confirmed, "Yeah, fresh fried fish. Try saying that five times fast."

"Ugh, get *away*," I complained, shoving at him.

"I'll drive my truck, you guys," Bly said as we reached the parking lot. "I'll head home afterwards anyway."

"We'll see you there!" I called. Justin did pause to open the door for me and I climbed inside, running my fingertips lightly over the leather seat beneath my bare legs. I was in his truck, alone with him. Though it wasn't the same vehicle, I recalled the last time I'd been, the night he and Jackson fell off the train.

"So, Jo's gonna be here next week?" Justin asked, sliding behind the wheel and firing his ride to life. From this direction his scars were more vivid than ever. I suppressed the desire to reach over and touch them. In nearly three years I hadn't yet been brave enough to try. Surely he would self-consciously turn away from my touch. He added, "I haven't seen her in ages."

"I know, I feel like I haven't either." I rolled down my window and inhaled the night air. "I miss her so much it hurts."

"I know you do," he said. "And I'm sorry it hurts you."

"Jackie *cheated* on her. Not just once, either, and she actually walked in on him and this woman he works with." As much as I hated that Jackson would do such a thing to my sister, not to mention the repercussions on their family, a large part of me was glad, so glad, because it meant she finally had a valid reason to leave his ass behind. *And come home to stay, Jo, please oh please.*

"Yeah, Dad told me he cheated, but not that she *saw* it. That fucking sucks," Justin sympathized. "But is anyone really surprised? I mean, come on. It's Jackie. Shit, he probably started messing around way back in college."

It was so good to talk with someone who knew, who shared our collective history and didn't require explanations for every other thing. I said, "That wouldn't surprise me a bit. But he hurt her so much. She would've done just about anything for him. You know."

Justin parked in front of Eddie's, Blythe just behind us, where the usual crowd was assembled, recognizable by their vehicles. Inside, the place was familiar as always—the wide, irregular planks of the wooden floor, the long bar to the left, polished to a glossy sheen, an ancient Pabst Blue Ribbon mirror with speckled glass hanging on the wall behind. In the far corner near the lone pool table, Eddie sat strumming his guitar in accompaniment to the jukebox, which crooned an old Johnny Cash tune. Jim Olson and Del Christianson were elbowed up to the bar, mugs in hand. They both turned to acknowledge us, Eddie calling, "Hey there, kids! Jilly, good to see you, hon."

Justin headed to the counter, clapping both of the older men on the back. Blythe continued more slowly, ducking his head just a little in a shy way, still getting used to everyone. I felt a rush of almost maternal affection and hung back with him, saying, "They're harmless, I promise."

He gave me a grin and claimed a seat near Justin, leaving a stool between them, which I took to be mine. I settled there and smiled at Eddie as he moved behind the bar.

"The usual?" he questioned, and Justin and I nodded. Eddie poured two tall drafts of Schell for us, and then raised his eyebrows at Blythe.

"Ah...same as these guys," he said.

"So, Jillian, you getting excited for your sister to get home?" asked Jim, leaning around Justin and regarding me with kind, if bloodshot, blue eyes.

"Hell yes," I said for the second time this evening.

"Jackie coming with her?" The interrogation continued, this time with Del asking the question.

"Maybe later this summer," I hedged without missing a beat. No way could I let these guys think anything otherwise. "He's so busy with his law firm these days, you know."

"They have three kids now, or four?" asked Jim.

"Three girls," I said.

"Imagine that," Del said, draining his mug.

"Well, bring her over the minute she gets to town," Eddie said.

"I will," I promised. The three older men headed to the pool table, leaving Justin, Blythe, and me leaning on our elbows against the bar.

I was acutely aware of Justin on my right, angled so that his knee was just a few inches from mine. He said, "Don't worry, I won't tell anyone about Jackie cheating. It's no one's business."

"It seems like everyone knows anyway, at least at Shore Leave," I said.

"I know how she feels," Justin said. "I'll talk with her when she gets here. I know how bad it fucking hurts."

Blythe said, "Yeah, you don't exactly get over that kind of thing."

Justin muttered, "Especially when it's your wife."

Blythe didn't ask any more questions, but again I was struck with the sense that he was a good listener. Justin must have subconsciously reached the same conclusion, because he added, "Aubrey and I were married for a long time. And we dated in high school, too. Shit, I stuck around here to wait for her."

I curled my hands around my beer mug and studied Justin's reflection in the mirror; he was looking up and to the right, back into time. Finally Bly followed up with a quiet, "What happened?"

"This," Justin said, indicating his scars, with no drama; it was just a matter of fact. "This happened, and Aubrey couldn't live with it."

Blythe narrowed his eyes as though in speculation and said, "You know what's funny?" When neither Justin nor I responded, he added, "I don't even notice your scars unless you talk about them."

It was the best thing he could have said. Justin, who'd appeared just a wee bit confrontational, laughed a little and turned back to his beer. I gave Blythe a small, sidelong smile, letting him know he'd said the right thing. I totally agreed with him.

An hour later the mood lightened considerably, perhaps because I was fairly drunk, Eddie's partner for a round of pool. Justin and Jim were taking us on while Blythe hunkered on a stool and watched. He insisted that he was not a pool player, and would rather relax with a beer and be our audience.

"Those pool cues feel like toothpicks in my hand," he explained in his deep voice, his Oklahoma accent more pronounced the longer he continued drinking. "I can't handle 'em right."

Though I doubted Blythe ever had trouble handling anything in those big hands, I left him alone, concentrating instead on beating Justin. Jim was the lesser of the two evils on their team. Justin, though, was canny. He was also drunk, but that was no impairment to him; in fact, it even seemed to sharpen his focus. I was a good pool player myself, and determined to beat Justin; the competition between us reached a peak by this point. It was no-holds-barred between him and me now, though Eddie and Jim were still hanging around the table, laughing and heckling us, by turns. I still had the two and the three, Justin just the fourteen, and the table was currently mine.

"Come on, honey," Eddie coached as I leaned over the table and muttered, "Two in the corner," nodding at the pocket.

I was fixated on my shot, knowing I must sink this one or lose for sure, my fingers perfectly poised over the end of the cue, when Justin commented wryly, "You know, Jillian, some people might consider that cheating."

I knew he was trying to distract me but my traitorous gaze flickered over to him anyway. He stood just across the table, his cue balanced on the floor, both of his hands wrapped around the top of it, chin tipped just slightly down. His eyes skewered me, directed straight down my shirt, which, from the angle I was currently in, allowed for a pretty deep glimpse of cleavage. Sitting just behind him, Blythe made a choked sound, like he was trying not to laugh, and actually flushed a little.

Jim and Eddie both laughed heartily, though Eddie said, "One more word like that about my partner and I'll kick your ass, boy."

Although I was flustered as hell, I refused to give Justin the satisfaction of acting embarrassed. Probably four beers had something to do with it. I squared my shoulders, offering even better viewing access to say *so there*, and from the corner of my eye was terribly pleased to see Justin's lips twist up in a crooked little smile. A hank of black hair fell over his forehead, causing him to look even more disreputable, and admittedly, sexy as hell.

I returned my gaze to the ball, concentrating on my shot with real effort (a trickle of sweat actually skimmed over my temple), and sank the two in the corner. Eddie howled while Jim slapped Justin's back and Justin gave me a knowing grin.

I stood straight and blew a lock of my hair from my eye. I needed to stand right where Justin currently was to make my last shot before the eight. I moved his way, pinning him with my eyes. He lifted his eyebrows at me as though in challenge, but then moved to the side so I could have access. I was incredibly self-conscious of having to bend forward over the table again, in my jean shorts that were probably a little shorter than they should be, but shit, I liked showing off my legs. I zoned in on the three, murmuring, "Three in the side," while Eddie ordered in a mock-strict tone, "Eyes off my partner, Miller."

But I couldn't pay attention to them, knowing this was it; I had to sink this ball or Justin would nail me. *In the game*, I hastily corrected myself, but my heart was already going triple-time just thinking about the other context of that thought. I inhaled and held it, drew a bead, and lightly tapped the cue ball, gently as I could manage. Time seemed to crawl as I stayed bent over, watching it roll along smooth as butter and click against the three, and...sink it. I exhaled in a burst of air, feeling a smile flow across my face.

Eddie whooped and Justin shook his head, raising his mug of beer in a silent salute. I gave him my most sugary smile and sank the eight ball with no pressure this time, winning the game. Blythe grinned, clapping proudly. I sauntered over to Justin, who stood his ground and regarded me with amusement and something else...something that made my heart blast off into my throat. But I didn't let him see any of my discomposure, instead saying sweetly, "I believe you owe us a round of drinks."

"You got it, Jilly-Anne," he teased.

"I think I'm in the mood for a shot," I said, though I should have known way better. Did I think I was still in high school? This tigress attitude was a direct result of four beers in quick succession, certainly not because Justin seemed tethered to me by an invisible thread, following in my wake and straddling the barstool beside mine, leaning over on one elbow and regarding me with his eyes slightly hooded and a smile playing over his sexy mouth. Eddie appeared behind the bar and asked, "What'll it be?"

I kept my eyes on Justin's as I requested, "Your most expensive shot of tequila."

Justin narrowed his eyes even further, but said gamely, "Make it two."

Blythe ambled up and patted my back. "Good game, Jills. I'll see you guys tomorrow."

I managed to look away from Justin and asked, "Aw, you're going already?"

Bly nodded, glancing between Justin and me. He winked and said, "Have a good night, you two."

"See ya, buddy," Justin added as Eddie lined up three shot glasses and proceeded to fill them with golden liquid from a square glass bottle.

"Here's to my partner," Eddie said, bumping his shot glass against mine. Eddie never had to be asked twice to toast with his customers.

"Thank you," I said, batting my lashes at him.

"I'm only buying the two, Ed," Justin teased as he chimed his glass against Eddie's.

I held my breath, poised with my glass in the air; Justin tapped our shots, lightly, and we all drained the round.

"Another!" I pronounced, though Eddie shook his head at me and moved to rejoin Jim at the pool table.

"Jilly, you'll be sick," Justin said.

"I'm fine," I insisted. I teased, "Let's go dancing."

Justin rolled his eyes and suggested, "How about I get your ass home."

I wasn't about to relinquish this unexpected time with him. "No, I'm not ready yet."

"Jillian," he said then, and there was something in his voice that made my heart kick-start. But in the next second he stood and said, quietly, "Come on."

"Should you be driving?" I asked.

"Shit, I'm fine," Justin said, plunging a hand through his hair. "But you're in for a hell of a hangover, I'm afraid."

I couldn't read him at all. During the entire pool game until just a few seconds ago, a vibration of heat burned between us. And now it was as though he'd purposely stomped on it, becoming friendly but business-like all of a sudden, as if we were nothing more than acquaintances. Confused as hell, I studied him as he pretended not to feel the weight of my gaze, finding his keys and then a twenty-dollar bill to put on the bar.

"G'night, kids!" Eddie called over as Justin held the outer door open for me, and we waved good-night to him and Jim.

Outside, the late-night air was still mid-spring chilly and I shivered a little. Justin clicked the automatic locks on his truck and opened the door for me, while I climbed inside and tried to reconcile what I felt with what was happening. My insides were jittery and as Justin slid behind the wheel I felt the stinging prickle of tears. But I wouldn't dream of letting him suspect that I wanted to cry.

"Shit, are you cold? It's cold out here," he muttered, starting the engine and messing with the controls. "Here, I'll get the heat going, sorry, Jills…"

"I'm fine," I said shortly. The buzz I'd been enjoying fizzled fast under a wave of sudden gloom. I wanted him to pull me against his warm side. I wanted it so much, and so fiercely, that I could hardly even look at him. He drove to Shore Leave in silence; when we got to the parking lot just a minute later I finally braved it and looked his way.

He held my gaze, though the rest of him remained motionless, both hands hanging over the top of the steering wheel, like always. My belly jumped and everything was so tangled up inside of me that I needed to get out of his truck. Or I would embarrass myself by surrendering to my desperate urge to straddle him and make him forget all about his scars, and his bitterness, and Aubrey…

He seemed about to speak, and I lost my nerve all at once, saying, "Thanks for the ride," before hurrying out of the truck. He stayed there, engine idling, until he made sure I was safely up my steps and inside my apartment. Once out of sight, I leaned against my door, palms braced behind me, and listened to him drive away.

Chapter Nine

Two nights later I hadn't seen a wink of him, even in the mornings for coffee.

I missed him so much that it had grown to a physical ache behind my breastbone. This may have been why I'd also consumed three margaritas during our Davis women summer-Saturday ritual just a few hours earlier, all of us joyously celebrating the fact that by next Saturday, Joelle would be here to join the festivities. But now hours had passed since everyone went to bed and I was alone in the dark, out on the dock, with no more convenient distractions available. The night air felt soft as a lover's hands on my bare shoulders. I raked my fingers through my hair and then crunched up the handful of TicTacs in my mouth. I usually loved sitting down here in the wee hours, letting my thoughts drift a little as I studied the stars. Sometimes I thought about Chris; how could I not, with so many memories of us built into these plank boards, this very air? But tonight I thought only of Justin.

Dammit.

He lingered in my thoughts all the time, though especially after I lay down at night, longing for sleep, hearing my son snoring in the next room. Justin and his way of coming into the cafe and making me feel whole. A way that I hadn't felt in over a decade. Just the sight of his eyes—there was something about the darkness of his irises that made him all the more appealing, so full of heat, like embers of a campfire, smoldering for hours. I rubbed my shoulders roughly, arms crossed over my chest. I'd slid off my bra hours earlier, but it didn't matter since no one was here at this time of night, nothing stirring except the mosqui-toes. I was irritated that my nipples were as stiff as peaks of meringue under my t-shirt at just the thought of Justin. And he came to me in my dreams almost every night. I hadn't wanted a man this way since Chris. Justin was the opposite of my husband in so many ways, but that was fine with me; where Chris had been tender and sweet, Justin was blunt and temperamental, with an enormous chip on his shoulder. But such wide shoulders, such powerful arms. How I wanted those arms around me.

"Damn you," I whispered to the night, uncertain whether I addressed Justin or myself.

I wished desperately that Joelle was already here. Fuck, I missed her and she would be such a distraction when these kinds of thoughts came creeping at my door. I knew Mom had left a pack of smokes on the windowsill and headed over the dock boards to find them, chin tipped down. With real effort I dragged my mind from Justin, and was instead thinking that maybe I should repaint my toenails pretty soon, and when Justin suddenly said, "I knew you'd be out here," I startled so hard that I almost fell into the lake. My head jerked upward to see him walking down the incline from the cafe; I watched with my jaw all but hanging open, my heart slamming wildly.

He's here, he's here! Oh my God, he's here!

I knew if I tried to speak I would sound embarrassingly nervous. I crossed my arms over my breasts and, despite the joy that tidal-waved through me at the sight of him, mustered up a glare. He wore a pale t-shirt and his faded jeans, and was barefoot, of all things. He offered no explanation for why he was here at Shore Leave at this time of night, scaring the shit out of people. For a second I wondered if I'd consumed more alcohol than I thought and my intense longing conjured up his image. But he was absolutely really here. And some part of me knew he would be, sooner than later. He reached the dock but said not a word and continued right past me, moving to sit on the glider. I turned slowly, my face burning and my pulse refusing to calm. He leaned back as though to study the silvery, starry view in leisure.

Finally he asked, without looking at me, "You care to join me?"

"What are you doing here? You're barefoot! Are you drunk?" I demanded, abruptly finding my voice. I moved to stand near him, keeping my arms tightly crossed. I probably appeared angry with my current stance. But I was a little angry, and though I hated to admit it with him so close, totally and completely aroused.

He said, "I'm not drunk, Jilly. I just knew you'd be out here."

"So?" I asked, and the word emerged sounding more irate than I intended. After he brought me home so rapidly the other night, I was still a little stung. He bent forward and rested his forearms on his thighs, keeping his eyes on mine.

"Because," he said, his voice uncharacteristically soft, offering no other explanation. Maintaining total politeness, he invited, "You want to sit?"

I sat, keeping inches between us. I heard myself say, "Remember how we all used to skinny dip out here?"

He laughed a little. "Of course. Is that an invitation?"

My heart tried to leap out of my chest. Without thinking, I flew to my feet and Justin caught my arm.

"Wait," he said. "Please, Jilly, don't go…"

We studied each other through a crackling net of tension. And then Justin stood and with no hesitation took my upper arms in his strong hands. I made a small sound, deep in my throat, and my arms went way up around his neck. In the next moment I was crushed against his powerful chest, being kissed like this was Justin's last night before shipping out to war in the morning. I moaned again, tilting my head the other way to deepen our hungry kiss, as I'd been dreaming about for weeks now.

No…for much, much longer than that.

"Jillian," he murmured against my mouth, his hands all over me.

I went way up on tiptoe and dug my fingers into his thick black hair, greedy to touch him. He glided his palms beneath my ragged old t-shirt, cupping my breasts, our lips parting with a soft suckling sound as he broke the kiss only to free me from its confines. I yanked off his shirt, curling my fingers through the dark hair on his powerful chest, impatient, dying for more. I went to my knees, following the narrow line of hair on his hard, lean belly, unzipping his fly and tearing down his jeans, taking him into my mouth before I even knew what I was doing. A red-hot haze descended over my vision.

"*Jillian*," he gasped, cupping my head with one hand as I took him deep, and then deeper, stroking my tongue over his rigid cock, teasing the firm ridge around the tip, taking him straight down my throat and loving every moan and muted cry that I elicited from him. I would have swallowed every drop, I was that into it, but he shifted suddenly and knelt beside me, gathering me into his arms and tipping his forehead against mine.

"Oh my God, woman, you're incredible," he said, sounding like he'd just swum across the lake at sixty miles an hour. He worked quickly, spreading his t-shirt on the dock boards while I watched, moved at this gesture and loving the sight of his broad, muscular back shifting as he made a space there for us. He kicked out of his jeans, then caught me close to his naked body. I was shaking, incredibly wet, as his mouth plundered mine, so urgently and with such skill. I didn't break the kiss as I shimmied out of my shorts and pulled him over me, lying back on the dock on the t-shirt he'd spread with such care. I curved my thighs around his hips.

He held himself poised over me, looking down into my eyes with an expression I couldn't quite read. His breath came fast and I was sure that if I pressed my palm to his chest his heart would be generating enough energy to illuminate the whole state, same as mine.

"Justin," I breathed, reverently, my voice hoarse, and his eyes lit with joy as kissed me again, taking my lower lip between his teeth. I bucked in adamant invitation, feeling his hard length against my thigh, needing him inside. I needed it so much I was a little afraid of myself. I grasped firm hold and he groaned like I'd plunged a knife into him, gliding his hands over my hips and then driving deep. I cried out, trying to muffle the sounds against his neck. He beat into me like nobody's business, but I needed that, meeting his thrusts and then some. No condom, nothing. But I knew neither of us had made love in so long we were practically insane from the deprivation. It wasn't like I was getting pregnant, not since I took the pill to keep my periods regular.

"*Oh my God, Jilly...*" he groaned harsh and hoarse, and would have pulled out if I hadn't clung with both arms and legs.

"It's all right," I murmured minutes later, cradling him against me. He was still deep in my body and still hard, though he'd just come about a milk truck's worth. "I'm on the pill."

"Jillian," he murmured against my cheek, kissing me there before lifting his head, bracing above me on one forearm. He traced the side of my face with the backs of his fingertips, studying me, rapt and wordless. When I reached to him he understood my intent and whispered faintly, "No..." but I refused to let him shy away.

"Let me," I implored, and touched his damaged face at long last, caressing every last ridge and deformation.

He shuddered a little and closed his eyes, whispering, "That feels so good."

"I've wanted to touch you for such a long time," I whispered, almost shy. His eyes opened at these words, as though he thought I might not be serious, and I curved my fingers around his ear, brushing a thumb along the scar that tugged his right eye slightly downward, his beautiful brown eyes that I had known all my life; the damage to his face was heartbreaking, but it did not put me off, had never. It was part of him now. Tears welling, I whispered, "I have, you know."

He kissed me with so much feeling that a small but intense orgasm ricocheted through me. Justin groaned, low and husky, in response, feeling the way my body tightened around his, grasping my ass firmly in his hands, rolling me to my back as I lifted in urgent welcome. He bit my earlobes, my throat, my lower lip, took my nipples between his teeth. I shivered and melted by turns as he played with me, running his tongue between my breasts, placing suckling kisses all over my skin. Sweat beaded, fine as mist, as I came again, gasping against his neck. And still he didn't stop.

"Justin, oh God, *Justin*," I moaned, panting in between intense rushes of pleasure. He slowed his pace but deepened his thrusts, as though reading my mind.

He grinned at me, sweat trickling over his temples and down his chest, taking my chin between his teeth. My nails raked against the dock boards, as though seeking sheets to clench in my fists. I clutched his shoulders instead, pressing my face against his collarbones and inhaling his scent, and though I'd never been so close to him, it was utterly familiar to me. I marveled at finding this passion with Justin, whose easy laughter and bright, teasing spirit had diminished so much in the past difficult years that Dodge worried his boy would never regain those things; just as my family feared for me. And in that moment I was struck forcefully by the knowledge that I loved him, was so in love with him that it had surely been building for years, just waiting for the moment of recognition. It burst like firebombs through my mind, sending trailers across my soul.

But I couldn't tell him, I couldn't risk that. Not yet.

"I knew...you'd be like this," I managed to say instead, though my breath was shallow. I twined my fingers into his wild thick hair, caressed his face, his chin scratchy with stubble. The edge of my thumb brushed his mouth and he bit it, before my hands continued their course over his neck, his shoulders. He was as sensual as I'd imagined in my most secretly-guarded thoughts. He claimed my mouth for one last kiss before he came again, flooding me, and I moaned against his lips, stroking his tongue with mine, quivering along my entire length. I noticed that the stars had rotated across the sky, studying them with a sense of stunned wonder; I curved my arms more even snugly around Justin's satisfied weight, nearly crushed beneath him.

"You're still so hard," I observed, my body so hungry for his that I wanted to beg him to stay inside me until morning.

I felt him grin against my neck, like a naughty boy. Experimentally, I shifted, spreading my thighs a little farther, and he muttered, "Jilly, you're gonna kill me," but he slanted his head over mine while I dug my fingernails into his tough shoulders, returning kiss for kiss.

"Let me..." I said, nudging with my hips, and he allowed me to roll him to his back. I braced myself on his chest, remembering how my long hair used to swing wildly in this position, like a golden curtain. I felt free, uninhibited now, with no such restraint. His head bowed back as I worked over him, sweat beading between my breasts and on my temples. The muscles in my thighs quivered, my breath coming in hot bursts, again pretty damn proud of myself for the sounds I caused him to make. I ordered, "Not…yet…" liking him beneath me this way, as though subject to my every desirous demand.

"Holy…*shit*…" he gasped, clutching my hips, and I fell over him as he came hard, shuddering and muffling a groaning cry against my neck. When I caught my breath, he took my face between his hands and said, "Holy *Jesus*, woman. I knew you'd be like this, too."

We were naked and sweating and probably quite mosquito-bitten, down here on the dock, Flickertail lapping the moorings, murmuring like an old friend. A beaming smile overtook my face and I kissed him flush on the lips, whispering, "I won't be able to walk back to the house unless I find a towel somewhere."

He laughed out loud, startling a couple of birds from a nearby tree, both of us laughing then and trying to muffle it, as terrified of getting caught as if we were still in high school.

His eyes glinted with naughty teasing as he said, "I think I'm keeping things in check right now," and this provoked more laughter, to the point that our bodies almost uncoupled anyway; I pressed closer, to prevent this. Even in stillness he filled me up, and I loved it; tingling, jolting aftershocks of the force of our lovemaking kept rippling through me. He ran a hand down my side, coming to rest on my hip. He kissed my cheek, then traced the same spot with the tip of his tongue.

He whispered, "You're so beautiful and soft, Jilly, oh God, like hot silk."

I shivered and giggled delightedly, murmuring, "Hot silk, hmm? And do you always stay so hard?"

He laughed heartily, tickling my skin, finally saying, "Fuck, it's been so long since I've made love that I think I'll be hard until sunrise."

"*Yes*," I whispered, tugging his lips back to mine, kissing him open-mouthed. He made a sound like a low growl, hauling me firmly against his body. I gasped a little and knew I would be sore later today, but I didn't give a fuck. I craved it. I wanted to feel him inside of me even after he'd gone home and this moment was just a memory.

Much later, probably just minutes from the sun cresting the far shore, Justin cuddled me on his chest and inhaled against my hair. He murmured, "You smell so damn good."

"Like fresh fried fish?" I murmured, and he laughed, a rumble that vibrated through his chest.

"You know how long I've wanted to make love to you?" he asked, and then kissed my hair. "You drive me crazy, Jillian Davis, and you smell fucking amazing."

"Such a sweet talker," I added, thrilled at his words, my cheek pressed to his heartbeat as he stroked rhythmically along my spine, like he was playing a harpsichord.

My eyes could barely stay open and the parts of me not glued to him were freezing, but I hated to move before forced. But the womenfolk would head to the cafe very shortly to get the first pot of coffee perking. What a sight we'd make down here in our nakedness. Gran would probably call out some heartfelt congratulations. Dodge would surely give his son the whipping we'd talked about once, long ago in another life, in Justin's old truck.

"We better get moving," I said at long last, a gaping hole of reluctance already beginning to open in my chest.

He kissed my forehead, then lifted my chin and studied me with the same intensity with which he'd made love to me, all night long.

"You've got the most beautiful eyes I've ever seen," he said.

"Thank you, Justin," I whispered—and why did my voice grow shaky now, as dawn began to tint the day—as if I already knew that he was saying good-bye just as we'd said hello.

He drew me gently to my feet and we hurried into our clothes, probably covered in bug bites. No, surely covered. My ankles were itching even as I thought about it. The air grew rapidly silver now, objects taking on depth and texture. And with everything in me, I did not want daylight to arrive. I feared that what we'd shared would suddenly evaporate with the dawn, like a midnight spell. I threw my arms around him once more and clung, and he drew a deep breath and held me just as fiercely. Against my temple he whispered, "Thank you for last night."

Later, in my own bed, I considered those words. When I thought about what we'd spent the better part of the night doing, my stomach soared and my heart pitched against my chest, over and over. I hugged myself around the middle and bent my head against my forearms, drowning in my feelings. I was indeed sore, but it was so magnificent. So incredibly worth it, the best sex of my life, if I wanted to be honest about it. And not just because it had been too long. Justin discovered an untouched place in my soul, one I hadn't realized was there.

But what, exactly, did he mean by *thank you?*

I fell asleep with this unresolved question in my mind. By the time I woke again it was nearly eleven and I knew I needed to hustle to get ready in time for lunch. I showered, though reluctantly, as Justin's scent still clung to my body. Had he stopped out with Dodge for coffee this morning, like usual? My belly fluttered again at the thought and I was disappointed I may have missed him. Surely I'd missed him by now, since he started his day at the filling station by nine. I jogged over the lake path, my heart and feet both light, happiness lingering on my lips despite the slight twinges of pain I was experiencing below, a reaction to the wealth of sex after years of none. Gran would guess in an instant if I wasn't careful. Inside, Mom sat talking to Rich at one of the booths, both of them holding their coffee mugs, while Blythe brushed down the grill in the kitchen. I waved to everyone and found my cup on the shelf, filling it to the brim.

Ellen popped her head around from the bar to say good morning; no one seemed inclined to question why I was so late and obviously just out of bed, so my stomach relaxed a little. I found myself scanning the parking lot for signs of Justin's silver truck, even though there was no way he'd be out here before evening, if then. Would he call? Should I call him? I wanted to hear his voice. My heart gained momentum just thinking about it. If I was honest, I didn't want to just talk to him. I felt like a dam that burst open and was currently flooding its gates. I almost giggled at the thought.

"Hey, Jills," said Bly from behind me. "You want a couple eggs or anything?"

He was so tall necessity dictated that he duck his head to look at me through the ticket window and as he did I was blindsided by a vivid image of him and my sister—dammit, that was irritating. I stared at Blythe in semi-consternation, which was hardly fair, considering, but I meant to keep an eye on this potential situation. Jo was in no position to be falling for Blythe, as much as I truly liked him—we *all* liked him, every last one of us at Shore Leave. But he needed to be off limits to her. Blythe was so young, and not planning to stick around Landon, and Joelle was a mother and hadn't even yet decided to divorce Jackson.

But I couldn't shake the sense that Blythe was on a collision course with her.

Bly tilted his head, brows raised; he cupped both hands around his mouth and called, "Earth to Jillian!"

I blinked and refocused; I'd been staring like a crazy woman. I muttered, "Sorry, late night."

"You want breakfast, Jilly-billy?" he asked, having fashioned his own nickname for me, which I admittedly found endearing.

"No, but thanks," I said, a smile tugging at my lips.

"All right," he said agreeably, shaking his head. I sensed he thought I was a little nuts, but in an affectionate way. Affectionately nutty. And I giggled at the thought, thinking that if this kept up I would have to slap myself; I hated gigglers.

"Jilly, can you grab the bleach bucket for me?" Ellen called from the bar, and it was off to the races for another day.

By evening Justin hadn't appeared at Shore Leave, nor had he called. I was flustered and irritable, and when I mixed up an order (which I never, ever did), I knew I needed to find him. I rolled silverware with my fingers flying, deciding what to do and how to do it…should I call? Driving to his house seemed too desperate somehow, but I was this close to desperate anyway. I just wanted to see him. No, I wanted to see him and then jump into his arms and tell him I was in love with him.

Dammit, Jillian. Dammit.

I was alone on the porch, sitting at a four-top, when his truck suddenly rolled into the parking lot and I dropped the trio of silverware I held, my heart reacting like a trip wire suddenly sprung. I watched, breath jammed up in my chest, as he parked in his usual place, stepped down from the cab and started for the cafe. Not seeing me yet, I observed with a sinking heart; he looked upset. Worse, he looked resigned. His hands were in his pockets, chin tipped down, the last rays of sun slanting over his black hair and broad shoulders and long legs in faded jeans. He should have been running, skipping, leaping…like I'd been restraining myself from doing all day.

Before he got another step closer I rose and made my way down the porch steps, untying my apron and pitching it over the railing as I walked. In jean shorts and a pale-yellow tank top, my cheeks scalding with what was perhaps becoming anger, I stopped him in his tracks with just a look. He saw me and his feet stalled. I watched him swallow and his eyes grow even darker with longing. I knew it, but then he steeled himself; I saw that, too. He said, his voice husky, "You look so beautiful, Jills."

Instead of thanking him, I asked, "But?" I didn't allow the tremble in my throat to escape with that word.

"Walk with me," he requested.

We walked along Flicker Trail in silence until the cafe fell away behind us. He might have been a million miles away from me, and dread built inside my chest. That, and anger. Just as I was about to let loose he said quietly, "I just want you to know you don't owe me anything."

I stopped and studied the ground at my feet, feeling like I could hit him. Like crying. Like screaming at him for doing this, for acting like me choosing to make mind-blowing, earth-shattering love with him was something I'd done out of pity. I was too riled up to reply, and he went on, "I just don't want you to feel like…like you have to…" He faltered to silence and out of the corner of my eye I saw him cup his forehead with one hand, gripping hard.

This time the tremble in my voice was overt, despite my best efforts, as I asked, "Is that what you think?"

Silence.

I faced him now, fists to hips, my voice rising in both volume and pitch, "You think I did what we did last night out of the *goodness of my heart?!*"

"That's not what I mean," he said, sounding like there was a husk in his throat. "Last night was incredible. The best night I've ever had."

"Me, too," I whispered truthfully, staring up into his tortured eyes, thinking, *Take me in your arms, Justin, just do it. Don't be like this.*

His eyes begged me to understand. He said, his tone bordering on harsh, "But I think we made a mistake."

He might as well have backhanded my face. I stared up at him, furious and so hurt, even if a part of me understood exactly what he was doing. I glared at him, his familiar face, his dark eyes and black hair, his long lashes, his lips that I wanted everywhere on my skin…his livid scars that he allowed me to touch last night, almost more intimate than making repeated love.

Though I didn't truly think it was about her, I demanded, "This is about Aubrey, isn't it?"

His chin jerked, as though I'd struck him. There was true surprise in his voice as he said, "Of course not." He looked at me intently, as though to read my thoughts, and added softly, "I just…I don't expect you to…"

But I was not about to hear it. I shoved aside his hand, heart beating wildly, and cried, "If that's what you think then *fuck you!*"

I was even more furious when my voice didn't emerge as the angry shriek I intended. I whirled away and headed back to the cafe.

He yelled, "*Jilly!*" but I didn't look back, knowing that if I disappeared inside he wouldn't dare follow and make a scene in front of everyone. Once in the parking lot, I switched course and flew to my apartment, knowing I was about to give into full-scale weeping and sure as hell didn't want to explain why to anyone.

I sobbed for a long time, huddled around myself in my bed as evening faded to night. My head ached, my thoughts snarling all over themselves, but it was nothing compared to my heart. I thought about Chris and what we'd shared together. I thought about the peridot ring that remained tucked safely in my jewelry box, where it would be treasured for always. I thought about how I hadn't actually made love since my husband died. That wasn't normal, I knew this, but I'd never felt ready, not until last night. Last night I felt as though all of the unresolved parts of my soul were at last brought together. Justin was who I'd been waiting for. God, how could I have only just realized this?

I rolled to my other side, clutching my midsection. A part of me had always loved Justin, I knew that now. I traced back through my memories, combing and teasing out every last picture of him from the past. Our childhood and teenage years, our marriages to other people, and then the accident and his scars dominated his life. I thought about Aubrey leaving him and the way he basically shut down. In some ways, like I shut down after Chris. A question hit me like a wrecking ball—did he still long for Aubrey; did he still love her, wish they were married? I hugged myself harder and understood he intended to protect me by pushing me away. He was afraid because of his face, his scars, trying to reconcile his bitterness with the strength of his feelings.

He was terrified of being hurt, and even if he wouldn't admit it, this *was* about Aubrey, to some extent. She left him vulnerable, which I understood as I lay in my bed vacillating between fury and hurt, understanding his motives but wanting to shove him in the chest because of them. And, I could not deny, because I'd longed all day to make love with him tonight. I thought about it every other second, and my body ached for goddamn Justin Miller right now. With a soft moan I flopped to my other side and pressed my face into the pillow, slipping a hand over my belly and touching myself lightly, still feeling him within me. There were burns on my neck and breasts from his stubble, pale-blue bruising on my hips from his fingers. But these were the marks of intensity, and I only knew I wanted more, and then more of him.

Joelle would be here soon, and I comforted myself with this knowledge. I wouldn't tell her about Justin. Not yet. Everything was too raw. And it wasn't over. I *knew* this. I clung to this truth for even deeper comfort. I must be patient, wait for him to find the courage to tell me how he felt. In the meantime I would act as though everything was fine. I could be chipper and perky and hide the real me deep inside, for now.

Chapter Ten

A week passed and Justin avoided the cafe. Dodge still came out every morning, and I forcibly restrained myself from begging him to tell me what Justin was doing, how he looked, if he was as miserable as me. Gran noticed his absence, and made a point of asking me, which clued me in to the fact that she hadn't missed anything. I wouldn't go so far as to say she knew we'd made love…but she knew something was up. She was Louisa Davis, the most observant woman I'd ever known, other than Minnie. And myself.

"The boy hasn't been out with you all week," she said to Dodge just this morning, with a distinctly accusatory tone, and he shrugged with characteristic ease.

"He's been out of sorts," Dodge allowed, finishing his coffee while Gran trained her suspicious gaze on me; I hurried to look the other way, fiddling over refilling the coffee maker, shamelessly eavesdropping.

"Out of sorts, huh?" my grandmother responded, while I cringed and tried harder to appear busy.

"Yeah," Dodge said, and I heard the note of worry in his voice. I'd been a wreck all week. Clinty hadn't noticed; he was finishing up the last two weeks of his freshman year of high school, oblivious to anything other than the fact that summer vacation loomed on the horizon like an oasis of unimaginable beauty. Mom and Aunt Ellen hadn't seemed to realize—a result of my stellar ability to act as though everything was fine; but of course I wasn't fooling Gran. If Great-Aunt Minnie was still alive she'd take one look over the upper rim of her tortoiseshell frames, pin me with those Davis eyes, and I'd crack apart like a hollow eggshell, all over the floor of the cafe.

Aunt Minnie, I despaired, briefly closing my eyes, wishing for the countless time that I could speak to her; that somehow she'd respond. I'd counted on her advice so very much; when it came down to it, Minnie was the only other person who knew how it felt to experience a Notion. I thought, *Even a dream. Couldn't you at least manage to talk to me in a dream? I see Chris sometimes, why not you? What would you think about everything between me and Justin Miller?*

I'd almost called him a dozen times now, clutching my phone and imagining what I would say when he answered, *if* he answered; I climbed behind the wheel of my car last night, intending to drive to his house, the house he'd shared with Aubrey for all of their marriage and where he now lived alone, and had for the past three years. *Justin, Justin.* Stubbornness and pride prevented me from driving over and beating down his door. The only thing that kept me going this week was the thought that Jo and the girls would be here tonight. I couldn't wait to see her. At that moment my cell buzzed and I plucked it from my apron pocket, noticing that it was my sister, as though sensing my need for her presence.

"We just left Milwaukee," Joelle said as I answered. She sounded exhausted, her familiar voice huskier than normal.

"Yay!" I said in response, not even having to force cheer into my tone—I was that glad they were already on the second leg of their journey. "Drive safe and we'll leave the lights on for you."

She giggled a little; I could hear the girls in the car, bickering about something, and the radio in the background. She said, "I can't wait, Jilly Bean."

"Me, either," I told her. I looked over and saw Gran beckoning for the phone. "Gran wants to say hi." I handed over my phone, glad that Gran would be occupied and therefore unable to grill me about Justin.

Dodge finished his coffee and ruffled my hair. Justin looked more like his mother than Dodge, but Dodge reminded me of Justin enough that my heart absolutely ached. I wanted to burrow against his warm, comforting side and confess that I loved his boy with all of my heart and most of my soul. I was astounded by the strength of my feelings, now that I'd finally acknowledged them. Surely I was resonating at some perceptible level, like a tuning fork.

"See you later, honey," Dodge said. And then to Gran, "See you, Lou!"

Gran waved, still on the phone with Jo, and I went back to work, determined to make the day pass quickly and get my sister home where she belonged.

Evening came and went; Clint rode his bike into town for a ballgame, arriving back at Shore Leave in time for a late supper. The Saturday dinner traffic was still light this time of year, since the tourist season wasn't yet in full swing, and by nine Shore Leave was empty but for us. Rich and Bly had the kitchen spotless, but they were both lingering; Rich to greet Jo and Blythe for the same reason, though no one but me was aware. Blythe was uncharacteristically silent all evening, taut with nervous energy, checking the clock every five minutes or so. After he broke a glass I took pity on him and ordered, "Why don't you go grab a beer? I'll get the garbage out." Seeing the question in his eyes, I added quietly, "They'll be here any minute."

Anticipation lit his face anew; he nodded gratefully. Dammit, I didn't want him to hurt my sister, however inadvertently. But he was so sweet in his own way, and I absolutely adored him. Maybe Jo would be too distracted by Jackson's cheating ass and her own problems to take notice of him. My eyes skimmed over Blythe's huge shoulders as he headed for the bar, where Aunt Ellen was restocking the beer fridge.

Fat fucking chance she won't notice, I thought grimly.

"Ma, where's Clinty?" I asked, coming out of the kitchen bearing a heaping bag of garbage.

"He and Gran went up to bed," she told me. "Poor kid could barely keep his eyes open."

"Shit, he'll be disappointed," I said, clacking out the screen door. I walked over behind the garage and was stuffing the bag into the dumpster when headlights beamed across the parking lot. My heart thudded in pure joy and I shrieked, "Mom! Aunt Ellen, everybody, they're here!"

Jo parked and the girls tumbled out and raced at me, hooting and laughing. They caught me at the edge of the parking lot and we tumbled over and into a heap. Chester and Chief bounded down from the porch, going apeshit, leaping on us; Chester caught hold of Tish's shorts and began tugging her. She laughed and shoved at his big wet nose as Mom, Rich, and Aunt Ellen flooded outside to wrap Joelle into their arms. I noticed that Blythe wasn't bold enough to venture after them. I hugged my nieces tightly, loving the scent of their perfume and flowery hair products; they smelled like Jo and me, once upon a time. I managed to extract my body from their exuberant grip and then bolted across the parking lot and launched myself at my sister.

Joelle hugged me tightly, still taller than me by a good three inches. I clung to her, inhaling her particular scent, familiar to me as my own, or my son's. The girls were passed around for hugs, everyone chattering at once. I drew back from Jo and studied her; she was so beautiful, even if she wouldn't believe me if I said so anymore. She'd been spurned, and Jackie had taken up with a younger woman, and no one could convince Jo that this was anything but commentary on her desirability. But as she stood there and regarded me with her golden-green eyes, her soft lips with a fond smile, I knew what would happen when Blythe saw her.

Shit. Trouble, that's what that was, and she was about to walk right into it, totally unknowing. Jo let her hair grow long since last year, making her look more like her teenage self than ever. It was soft and golden, falling over her shoulders. She wore a faded blue t-shirt with what was probably a coffee stain on the lower front, along with faded jeans; her feet were bare. I knew she thought she looked terrible, but all I could see was what Blythe would—a lovely woman with a knock-out bod, whose husband had cheated. Someone who might possibly need a little convincing that she was still sexy.

Tish was asking, "Aunt Jilly, where's Clint?"

To silence my worried mind, I grabbed Tish in a headlock and gave her scalp a thorough knuckling. I told her, "Not here, punk. He must not care that you guys were coming." Of course she knew this was a total lie.

Minutes later Ellen hustled the kids inside and Rich took his leave. I joined Jo at the porch rail, where she leaned, drinking in the familiar sights to comfort her soul. I knew the feeling. I leaned on my elbows beside her and she tipped her head to my shoulder.

"You okay?" I murmured. I knew we'd have a good talk after everyone else went to bed.

She lifted her head and sighed, but then asked, "Rich's grandson? Rich doesn't have any kids, does he?"

Here we go.

I said, "Actually it's his stepdaughter Christy's son. You remember her, don't you? Pam's daughter who lives in Oklahoma?"

"Yeah, I guess, vaguely." She considered for a second. "Teeny bikini and big hair, like 1978, right?"

"Yeah, that's her. She stayed with him and Pam that summer. Crap, it seems like a million years ago now," I said, and sighed a little, too. "Anyway, she had a kid, and now he's staying with Rich in his trailer, even though Pam's gone. Mom hired him to help in the kitchen this summer." And finally, "He's actually here now, having a beer."

"Dammit," my sister muttered, and I could sense her annoyance at him infringing on her homecoming. Her eyebrows drew together and she demanded, "Is he even old enough to drink?"

"Yeah, he's in his twenties," I told her. And then, because she needed to know, "And he was in jail."

Jo's head snapped around and she stared at me with her eyebrows now raised in shock. She demanded, "What?"

"Seriously, I freaked a little bit, too, but Rich insists that he's a good kid," I said, purposely using that word, though Bly was the furthest thing from a kid I'd ever seen. I didn't tell her how sweet he was, or gorgeous, or how much we all liked him. Maybe she wouldn't notice these things. I saw then that she was truly upset and said quickly, "He stole a car and some cash in Oklahoma, two years ago."

I watched as Jo looked back at the cafe and could almost hear her thoughts churning. She whispered, "Jilly, what was she thinking?"

At that I couldn't help but laugh, so glad to have her here beside me on the porch again. I intended to do everything in my power to keep her here forever. I ran my hands through my hair and squeezed her arm, teasing, "It's not like you have to whisper, Jo. I don't think he has super-hero senses."

Mom climbed the porch steps now, and Jo wasted no time rounding on her, snapping, "Mom, how could you?"

Mom didn't immediately answer, reaching into the front pocket of her overalls to extract her smokes. She passed one to me, lit her own, and then handed over the lighter. I lit it and blew smoke over the railing, ready to referee. Finally she said, "Honestly, Jo, he's a good kid. Do you think Ellen or I would've hired him if we didn't think so?"

"Because of Rich," Jo bitched at our mother. "You couldn't say *no* to him, you know it."

Mom shook her head and I elbowed Jo, telling her to cool it. Mom bitched back, "Rich wouldn't have taken him in, even in honor of Pamela's memory, if he thought Bly was dangerous. Crimeny, Joelle."

Jo turned to me and asked, "Bly?"

"His name is Blythe," I supplied, blowing smoke through my nostrils. Mom went inside without responding further, annoyed at Jo within the first fifteen minutes of her being here. Well, that was expected. I was dreading the moment when Mom would start to trot out the whole 'why you should still be with your husband' argument. As the screen door clacked shut, I couldn't resist teasing my sister, saying, "And she's wrong, he *is* dangerous."

Jo glared at me but I just smiled around the filter in my lips. I heard the girls chattering with excitement and followed after Mom, informing Jo over my shoulder, "The girls are meeting him right now."

Jo hotfooted it after me. I heard Ellen saying, "Girls, this is Rich's grandson," as I popped around the arch into the bar. Blythe's eyes flashed immediately to me, his Adam's apple bobbing as he swallowed nervously. I would have bet his hands were sweating. He realized it was me and I could almost hear his thoughts—*No, that's not who I was waiting for.*

And then Jo came around the corner, her cheeks flushed, and I continued to watch Blythe; wonderment took him hard in the gut—the woman he had been dying to meet at last here in the cafe and no more than ten feet away from him. Jo stopped as though she'd come up against a glass wall. I watched several things pass over her features before she looked away, fast, her cheeks flaming even brighter. Camille, Tish, and Ruthie chattered, vying for Blythe's attention, and Mom was telling him something, so he looked back at her, though I could tell he was hyper-aware of Joelle from the corner of his gaze. I hoped that no one else noticed the flush creeping over his cheekbones. *Fuck, that was fast.* But what did I expect?

Aunt Ellen took charge, saying, "Honey, this is Rich's grandson, Blythe Tilson. Bly, dear, meet my niece, Joelle Gordon. She's just in from Chicago."

Blythe's eyes were drawn back to Jo's face like a magnet to metal. He said, "Hi," and reached to shake her hand. I had the distinct impression he would have shoved everyone out of the way to get to her, though he played it cool.

"Hi," my sister responded, her voice low and throaty. She added, "Nice to meet you."

"Likewise," he said, sounding so polite, and yet I could hear the notes of awe in his tone. He seemed to gather himself together and said, still looking at Jo, "Well, Joan, Ellen, I better head home, let you have some family time."

Joelle stared after him wordlessly as everyone else trailed him to the door. I perched on a bar stool; seconds later Jo sank to the seat beside mine. Bly called back to us, "Have a good night, ladies. Good to meet you, Joelle."

I inched my own seat closer to her and said, totally resigned, "*Told you so.*"

By the time I went to bed that night, in the smallest of the wee hours, I wanted Justin so much I could hardly even bear the thought of lying in my bed alone. I listened to Clint snoring like a lumberjack; I knew if I were to peek in on him, he'd be positioned on his back, right arm flung up over his head, exactly like Chris used to sleep. And just like his father, all I needed to do to quiet the snores was lower that arm, but I didn't bother my son. Instead I went to my tiny kitchen and poured a vodka and lemonade, light on the lemonade, then sat at the table and proceeded to caress my cell phone and debate calling Justin.

Damn him. He was stubborn as hell doing this to me, keeping away in a long-distance equivalent of the silent treatment. But then again, I could leap from the high dive and tell him how I felt. I indulged in a fantasy for a moment, in the darkness of my apartment, lit only by the dim green glow of the microwave clock, picturing driving over to his house and telling him the truth. I played out what would happen next, from his stunned face to his own words of love, and then he'd pull me into his arms and I'd tear off every stitch of clothing he was wearing, which probably wasn't much since I doubted he slept in anything but boxers in this weather...*oh my God, I wanted to rip those from his body with my teeth...*and then we'd make love on every horizontal surface in his house. I gulped my drink and then pressed the back of my knuckles against my lips. My heart was thundering and my belly pulsing at just the thought of him that way.

Jillian, I reprimanded sternly and bit down on my knuckle, hoping to restore my senses.

But...oh my God. His body seemed made for mine. I still couldn't believe I was having these thoughts, realizing these things. I knew in my heart that I wasn't betraying Chris. He was gone, and Justin was here, had always been here. Trouble was, he was farther away than ever.

The next few weeks passed and I saw nothing of Justin until the night Jo and I drove the golf cart over to Eddie's for a beer, the first I'd managed to get my sister off of Shore Leave property. Despite my deep desire, I hadn't confessed anything about what happened with Justin, or what I was feeling for him, to Joelle. I hated keeping secrets from her, and rarely did, but I was determined to wait until I found a chance to confront Justin first. And it was getting ridiculous. If he thought I was going to let him go, to give up on him that easily, he had another thing coming. But it hurt, I admitted, it hurt me deeply that he continued to avoid me. He was being such a chicken.

The nights that passed since we'd made love only served to increase my longing for him. Unfortunately both my nerves and my resolve to let him make the first move were also growing thin. And then, as I pulled the golf cart into the parking lot at the cafe that Monday night, I noticed that Dodge, Ellen, Tish, Clint…and Justin all sat around the fire pit, gazing into the leaping orange flames. Tish and Clinty slowly turned marshmallows over the flames, everyone besides Justin chattering. He sat meditatively; no one noticed Jo and me on the golf cart, since I drove it around behind the garage, its small engine inaudible over the radio, which was anchored to an outlet by a long extension cord and blasting the local country station, as usual. My heart clattered like pebbles in a tin can; I felt about as rattled, too, but forced a normal tone as I asked my sister, "You want to join them?"

Jo shook her head at once. She was too flustered over talking to Blythe at Eddie's just a little earlier. Her cheeks were still pink, her eyes starry and her hands had a slight tremble. God, their mutual attraction was going to eat them alive. I wondered just how long she'd be able to resist him; judging by her expression, not long. Well, I had tried. I told her about my dream, I warned her that she would get hurt. But Blythe wasn't helping matters, being so darn gorgeous and sweet, and so intent on sneaking a minute alone with her; though of course he claimed to have simply bumped into us at Eddie's, I knew for a fact that he'd been dying for just such an opportunity to get Joelle's full attention.

"No, I think I'll head inside," my sister mumbled, and I caught her around the waist for a quick hug. I sat on the bench seat of our ancient golf cart, watching Jo walk away through the darkness, listening to the music and the low din of conversations back at the fire, trying to ratchet up enough nerve to join them—my every nerve ending sizzled with the knowledge that Justin was here at Shore Leave, just a few dozen steps from where I sat just now, exhilarated and terrified, all at once. What was he doing here? What did it mean?

He hadn't dared to show up since the evening we walked along Flicker Trail. I felt all shredded up, aroused and agitated to the extreme; I closed my eyes, still clutching the steering wheel, gathering strength, and when he said, "Jill," I made a sound that was half-shriek, half-gulp, the voice which haunted my thoughts and prowled into my dreams suddenly right beside me. My eyes flew open to find Justin standing on the far side of the golf cart, gripping the wide-set roll bars, one in each hand, closer to me than he'd been in weeks. My heart tried to leap out of my chest. He appeared stone-faced but his eyes burned into mine, hotter than the bonfire that backlit him in a demonic red glow.

"Hey," I managed to breathe. My entire body was galloping.

"I'm sorry I've been avoiding you," he said, blunt and direct, as was his fashion. He looked good, so damn good, that I curled my fingers into my palms to keep from reaching for him. He stood completely still, bending at the waist so that he could meet my gaze beneath the top cover of the cart. His long, lean legs were clad in faded jeans, like always, his t-shirt fitting snuggly over his powerful torso. I imagined all the black hair on his chest, his legs, his forearms, the strength of his body against mine. I swallowed and could do nothing but continue to stare at him.

He said, and his voice was husky, "God, you're beautiful. I miss you, Jills."

No one could see us, hidden from sight by the edge of the garage. But even if they'd all been staring, I could not have stopped myself from sliding across the seat and grasping his shirt in both fists, pulling him roughly to me. He released his grip on the bars and crushed my shoulders in his hands in the next instant, pinning me to him as we kissed with all of the pent-up desire raging between us since we'd made love on the dock—urgent, hungry kisses along my neck, my jaw, his teeth closing over my earlobe as shivers rippled violently over my skin. I felt feverish and dangerous. I released my grip on his shirt and slid my arms around his neck. His hands were all over me, hot and intense, gliding over my hips and thighs, catching me behind the knees and fitting my spread legs around his hips.

I yanked him forward so that I lay on my back on the seat, Justin bent over me. He kissed me with such force, so much passion, bracketing the side of my neck in one hand, curling the other beneath my ass, lifting me firmly against his body—my blood leaped in response, my insides liquid and flowing like molten rock. The red haze descended again. I touched him everywhere, greedy for him, digging my fingers into his thick black hair, over his shoulders and then under his shirt, where his skin was hard and warm. I moaned against his lips, his tongue in my mouth, joined with mine. I had almost reached his jeans when he groaned as though in pain and drew back, breath pelting my face.

"What?" I demanded breathlessly.

He stared down at me with so much intensity that I felt as though I'd just leaped from the high dive and into empty air. Through two layers of denim between us I could feel his hard length and a pulse beat frantically between my legs, the insides of my thighs hot as coals.

Now, tell him now. *Tell him that you're in love with him.*

But some instinct warned me that I would only scare him more. He was so afraid of his feelings, of daring to love someone again, because once you loved someone you could be ripped apart. And anyone with an ounce of sense shied away from that kind of potential pain.

"Jilly," he said, his voice sounding strangled. I squeezed my legs around his hips, curling my hands possessively into his hair.

Justin, just say it, oh God, just tell me what's in your heart.

"What?" I whispered again, almost pleading. His eyes above mine were so serious; he appeared to be in actual pain. And then, to my dismay, he disentangled himself from my grasp and stood up. Turning away, he covered his face in both hands. I went up on my elbows, feeling as though a part of my own body had been torn away. My heartbeat flooded my ears.

He spun back to me and raged, "*Goddammit*, Jillian," as though to blame me for his distress. Which was, technically, fair. His eyes scorched a path through the air between us.

Disappointment and anger battled for the upper hand; I felt as though he'd hit me, or something equivalent, though Justin would never dream of doing such a thing. Though for a moment I wanted to hit *him*, my lips swollen from his kisses, my nipples like spear points, so aroused and wet I was almost afraid to stand up. All of these things contributed to me saying, cruelly, "You're *such a chicken!*"

He moved for me instantly but I scrambled away, furious now, putting the golf cart between us. He practically growled, "You don't understand."

I glared at him, tears sparking into my eyes, even though I never cried. I snapped back, "No, I guess not! I've never been hurt before, right?"

It pained him that I said that, I could tell. The angry tension flowed from him as he said, his voice low, "You *know* I don't mean that."

But I would not be pacified and demanded, "Then what the hell *do* you mean?"

His full lips compressed into a tight line, his jaw bulged, eyes almost unbearable with what he begged me to understand. And deep inside, I knew he loved me and was too afraid to tell me. It was a strange sensation, this heady knowledge swirled together with my current frustration. But I was determined that he tell me first. I needed him to show me that he could muster up that courage. I waited, my chest rising and falling, barely able to restrain the need to fly back into his arms. The air between us crackled.

His eyes never straying once from mine, he said dangerously, "You don't know what you're asking."

"Dammit, Justin," I said, further infuriated as tears swept over my cheeks.

"Aw, Jilly, don't cry," he said, moving swiftly around the golf cart that still separated us, but I wasn't about to accept his pity right now. Instead I shoved his chest, stunned at the force of my fury. Heat leaped back into his eyes and he caught my upper arms in his hands. I tried to pull away while he clung; locked in a grapple, breathing hard, I kicked his shin, though it couldn't have hurt much since I was wearing flip-flops. But I kicked him fiercely and he dropped his hands from me, eyes flashing.

"Go home and *be alone* then," I choked out, turning and storming away, from both the bonfire and him, swiping violently at my tears. I could hear the song "I Can Love You Better" by the Dixie Chicks blaring forth from the radio, which fortified me. I heard him come after me and so I ran.

He caught me around the waist and I would have fallen to the ground if not for his arms around me. I struggled against him, twisting, kicking at him while he tried to hold me still. One of my sandals went flying and then I was clawing at his shirt as though to rip it from his body and he was kissing me, groaning deep in his throat as our mouths crashed together and our heads slanted one way and then the other, frantically, unable to get enough of each other. I commandeered his hand and brought it to my belly, pressing against him, our kisses wet and lush. He groaned and nearly ripped my shorts as he slid his hand into my panties, cupping me, stroking heatedly. My knees went weak and I clung to his shoulders, moaning against him as he sucked my bottom lip into his mouth and closed his teeth over it.

His strong, questing fingers caressed everywhere at once, at last deep inside, where I needed so much to be touched. I pressed my mouth to the cords of muscle that played over his right shoulder as he made me come. *Good with his hands, indeed.* I dug my fingernails into the muscles of his back and bit the side of his neck to stop myself from making enough noise for everyone to come running. He breathed roughly against my hair as I tried to pull myself together, my face buried against his chest. I was shaking and only wanted more of him. But I was angrier than ever, too, despite everything. The air around us energized with the onset of an approaching thunderstorm, echoing the unrest in my heart. I tipped my chin against his chest and looked up at him. He held me tightly. His gorgeous, tortured eyes told me everything he couldn't say.

"I do know what I'm asking," I whispered. "That's why I'm asking it."

I forced myself to move out of his embrace. But this time when I headed for my apartment, he let me go.

Chapter Eleven

It wasn't until Trout Days, four days later, that I saw him again. I knew from Dodge that Justin was out drinking pretty hard core in the past few nights, which only tripled my anger at him. He was anything but a coward when it came to everything but this. I'd sat on the dock for hours every night since Monday, Joelle sometimes joining me for a beer. I knew she was wrapped up in her own problems, enough that she wasn't paying attention to mine.

Then again, Jo wasn't as observant as me, and had never been. I sympathized with her, I truly did. Not only because she was my big sister and I loved her, but because Jackson did her a rotten deal and she deserved to find happiness with someone else. And as much as I liked Bly, I was afraid he couldn't deliver that for her. Jo obviously longed for him, crazy-longed for him, it was as obvious to me as if she waved a glittery banner. But I continued to pretend I did not know how she felt. There were so many secrets swirling around Shore Leave. If I'd been a teenager, I would have been elated with the intrigue; now, it just exhausted me.

I managed to talk Joelle into going into town on Friday, after we'd worked lunch. Before I headed over to my apartment to get ready, I saw Justin's truck pull into the lot. I knew he was stopping out to drop off a canister of gasoline, among other things which Dodge requested over the phone an hour ago. I watched from the safety of the front windows as he climbed from his truck, dirty and sweaty from his day at the filling station, looking so handsome and manly and utterly tempting. I'd never longed so terribly for someone in my life.

"He's a good-looking boy, ain't he?" Gran acknowledged. Somehow she sidled up beside me without me hearing; I'd been too absorbed in studying Justin out the window.

I felt my face flush and Gran rubbed one hand, the one not clutching her cane, over my back. I sighed and then leaned to kiss her wrinkled cheek, soft and delicate as tissue paper beneath my lips. She moved back to the coffeepot without another word, and I untied my apron and lifted my chin, then walked out onto back porch. Justin looked up at me immediately and then went still, pausing in the middle of unlatching the tailgate of his truck. His gaze held mine and heat leaped between us. I walked slowly down the porch steps; his eyes never left me, but he didn't move forward. I tossed my head and looked away from him, with real determination, thinking, *Just you wait. I'll make you so jealous you won't be able to focus.*

That is, if he planned on going to the dance.

Twenty minutes later I'd cleaned up, slipped into my sexiest sundress and even applied a little make-up. My heart was firing on all cylinders as I saw that Justin's truck still sat in the lot, but I gathered together all my willpower, like so many scattered twigs, and played it cool. I saw him out on the dock, arms folded as he chatted with Joelle. I knew he was concerned about her, and Justin knew better than anyone, being Jackson's old best friend, just how much Jo had loved Jackie; Justin knew their history. I drew a fortifying breath and forced myself to go outside, smiling as though I hadn't a care in the world. Justin turned to walk back along the dock to the grass and his footsteps slowed as he caught sight of me. Aware that Jo was watching, I called, "Hi, Justin," offering my sweetest smile.

We weren't more than three car lengths apart and his eyes moved over me slowly, with so much heat that I trembled, but I couldn't allow him to see that. He lifted his right hand in a wave, as though to speak was too difficult for him at the moment. I looked at Joelle, calling over to her with my usual sassy tone, "Come on, Joey, I'm sick of waiting for your ass!"

My sister groaned and grouched, "Oh for the love, Jillian." But she joined me gamely enough; I tried to pretend I wasn't vividly aware of Justin talking to his dad before driving away. I longed to ask Jo if he'd mentioned going to the dance tonight, but reminded myself that would be pitiful.

We walked over to Landon and spent the afternoon eating cheese curds and drinking tap beer while Jo caught up with old friends from school, pretending all the while that she was just fine and responding numerous times that yes, Jackie was joining her later this summer. No one suspected a thing; in her own way, Jo was just as good at pretending as I was. If I found myself covertly sweeping the crowd—though my internal radar remained quiet, which suggested to me that Justin was not yet here—I made even more effort to enjoy the conversation around me. It was a total act. Eventually, in the deepening twilight, we came across Clint and the girls; my son extracted himself and came over to give me a quick squeeze. I hugged him hard, smelling his familiar scent that still called to mind my little boy, even though Clinty was far from little these days. It was just like him to give me a hug in front of everyone; in that way he was just like his dad, all sweetness.

"Hey, Mom," he said, drawing back and letting me ruffle his hair. He added, "Justin was looking for you."

Everything inside of me went instantly on alert. To cover my agitation, I took a long sip from my plastic cup and then asked, as casually as I could manage, "He was?"

Clint caught sight of his buddy Liam and yelled, "Hey, loser, over here!" before responding to me. He said, "Yeah, he caught me just a minute ago and asked if I'd seen you here yet."

Really. My heart fired like a piston, my eyes darting through the crowd. Just a minute ago, Clint said. Justin was here, finally, somewhere in the crowd. I realized my hand was trembling and lowered my cup so I wouldn't spill the contents down the front of my dress. Liam joined Clint and then they both went darting away. And then Mom, Gran, Rich, and Aunt Ellen found us in the crowd, Mom toting a cooler of icy-cold beer on a strap over one shoulder. I noticed Jo doing a quick inventory, looking for Blythe, but he was not to be seen. I wanted to tell her I knew exactly how she felt. I was like a teenager in a *Friday the 13th* movie, jumpy as hell, not knowing from which direction Justin was going to approach. I couldn't help but giggle at the thought, taking another deep drink and waving at Liz, Justin's little sister, as Joelle swept her into a hug. Just down the slope of beach, Flickertail appeared perfectly smooth, enchanting in the dusky evening air, rippling with shades of blue from indigo to violet, lapping at the shore. Kids ran everywhere, shaking sparklers, laughing and dodging adults, while a local guy, Todd Kellen, strummed a few test chords on his guitar and then at last took the mic.

"Evening, everyone, hope you're here for a good time," he said, amid cheers and whoops, and then Untamed, his band, launched into some kick-ass country music, the kind that makes it impossible to sit still. I leaned into Joelle and practically yelled to be heard over the noise, "You having fun?"

She nodded at me, seeming sincere. I could see the almost-visible relaxing of her shoulders as the music played and she observed her girls enjoying themselves. Ruthie sat with Liz's kids, the four of them trading parade candy and giggling, while the adults—it was difficult including Jo and me in that group, even though I was kidding myself if I thought otherwise these days—sipped beer and smoked and chatted. Clint dragged both Camille and Tish to a table full of his friends; I vowed to watch for wayward cans or flasks being passed in that group, although I knew better than anyone how impossible it is to stop teenagers from having a good time.

"Here, let me take some of these to the kids," Jo said, gathering up a few cans of soda and making her way into the crowd. I sat talking to Liz a few minutes later, and didn't realize at first that Joelle was no longer alone. Her face was unusually flushed and I narrowed my eyes to see Blythe right behind her, watching her steadily as they walked. *Shit, shit, shit. Distraction.* The music was pounding and when my sister sat back down I leaned into her and asked, "You wanna go dance?"

She did, and I grabbed Liz, too. Ruthie and the triplets joined us, and Camille, though Tish stayed with the boys at Clint's table. A half hour later I was having a fantastic time, in spite of myself, drenched in sweat. I needed a drink, so I threaded my way back to Mom's cooler, feeling eyes on me as I neared. I lifted my gaze from the ground and was suddenly looking smack at Justin, leaning on his elbows at our table, drinking beer. My breath, already short from dancing, lodged in my throat.

Cool, play it cool, I reminded myself, totally unable to think about anything other than the last night we saw each other, pulling him down over me in the golf cart. I couldn't tell in the fairy lights if his neck still bore my teeth marks.

"Hey, guys," I said faintly and slid opposite Blythe, on Justin's left, smoothing my skirt gently beneath me as I sat. Justin's eyes followed my every move, but I didn't dare look his way.

"Hey, Jills," Blythe responded, his hands curled around a soda can.

Justin sat stubbornly silent.

"Here, Jillian," Mom called from down the table, sliding a beer my way.

"Thanks," I responded, holding it to the side of my neck before cracking the top.

Bly leaned over the table and commented, "You guys look like you're having fun."

I smiled at him, unable to help it; he was so besotted with my sister that I felt a flash of guilt for attempting to drive a wedge between them, however subtly. But it was for both of their own good. With that thought on my mind, I realized the music was switching from fast and frenetic to slow and sweet; Blythe realized the same thing, his gaze instantly sweeping across the crowded dance floor, catching and holding Joelle as she laughed and fanned herself fifty feet away, in a group that was pairing off all around her. Blythe drew a breath, his shoulders lifting, and braced his hands against the table, all set to stand up, stride out there, and ask her to dance.

"Justin," I said, and his name felt so good in my mouth. Our eyes crashed and held. I so badly wanted to say, *Dance with me*, but actually said, "Go dance with Jo."

He narrowed his eyes as though gauging my motive; we hadn't spoken since I'd been wrapped in his arms Monday night. I added, "For old time's sake."

Liz darted up to the table and snagged a couple more beers; Justin studied me hard for one last instant, before rising and following in his sister's footsteps. I stared after him as he walked away and Blythe leaned over the table and asked, "What the hell?"

"What do you mean?" I hedged, braving his irritation, his brows drawn low and jaw squared, and he gave me such a knowing look, such an *I'm calling you on your bullshit* expression that I squirmed with discomfort.

He changed tactics, demanding, "What's with you two?"

"With me and Justin?" I whispered, scanning the crowd to spy Justin looking back my way. Blythe watched them, too, shifting restlessly, hating the sight of Joelle held in someone else's arms. Guilt weighted my shoulders.

Blythe made a sound like steam releasing from a pressure cooker, clearly aggravated by me. He said, all drippy with sarcasm, "No, you and the guy playing drums."

"Mike? He had a crush on me in middle school," I said, eyeing Mikey Mulvey as he wielded his drumsticks. I mused, "He's a cop these days."

"Jilly-*Anne*," Blythe said, interrupting my prattling, stressing my name the way Jo did when she was upset. Slightly more calmly, he said, "Come on."

I relented. "I'm sorry. I really am. I just don't know what to do."

Blythe studied me for a second, somber and intent, like usual. He said, "Well, he really likes you, in case you hadn't realized."

My heart stung—I looked at Justin to find his gaze on me yet again, across the crowded dance floor.

Blythe surprised me by adding, "I'm sure you've realized, since you notice everything."

I looked at him, figuring he intended to punish me a little with those words—he obviously realized at least to some extent that I was trying to keep distance between him and Jo.

I wanted to tell him I was sorry, that I was only attempting to protect my sister. I said quietly, "Not everything." And then I admitted, "I like him, too."

"Then what's the problem?" Blythe pressed. He finished his soda and set aside the can.

"It's complicated," I whispered, restraining the urge to lower my head to my forearms.

Justin was headed back our way now; Blythe said, "It doesn't have to be," and abruptly got to his feet. As Justin reached the table, he said, "I'll see you guys later," and disappeared into the crowd without another word.

I felt terrible, flustered and angry, fully deserving of Blythe's anger; I couldn't blame him. I could no longer bear simply sitting here and jerked to my feet, setting my can on the table with more force than necessary. But I could not let my resolve crumble apart now. Justin and I stared at each other until I was sure a fire would flare to life in the air between us. I was determined to wait him out, let him walk away first, but in the end it was me. I bit my lip, so goddamn frustrated, wanting to shove against his shoulder as I skirted him on my way back to the dance floor. I joined my sister and threw my heart and soul into appearing to be in a good mood, shaking my hips and melding into the dancing crowd. And when I turned back that way, Justin had disappeared.

I dreamed about Chris just before dawn, the first he'd visited me in my sleep in years. In the dream I wandered along the edge of Flickertail under a sky that could only occur in the sleeping world, an inky black palette studded by stars in every glowing jewel-tone imaginable, ruby and topaz, sapphire and peridot. The small, impossibly green stars caught my eyes especially as I ambled along, using a long stick to poke at the water where it met the sandy shore.

When one of the peridots fell from the sky, with a sizzling trailer, and appeared to land just a few hundred yards ahead, I abandoned my stick and hurried after it, desperate to retrieve the treasure. I pushed heavy tree branches from my way, felt the soggy ground leak into my shoes, soaking my feet even as I moved away from the lake. My breath came hard, hurting my chest, but at last I found the fallen star, glinting at me from the grass. I picked it up and cradled it in my right palm, regaining a measure of calm.

And when I straightened, Chris stood there, appearing exactly as he'd looked when I saw him last, age twenty-two, my sweet, gentle husband. My heart expanded and filled my entire chest. He was here in front of me, no longer just a memory.

"Oh, Chris," I whispered, my hands cupped around the pulsing green star, so tiny and fragile. In the sky it appeared so large, so vital, and in my palm it was just a fleck of gemstone. I felt an intense need to protect its light; I wanted to touch my husband, but I couldn't drop the star. I looked up and into his kind, familiar eyes with their woodsy colors mixing like the surface of a pond scattered into ripples. I implored, "Help me, Chris."

He stepped forward without a word and obediently put his hands around the star. Although I could see him touching me, I felt no pressure. He smiled and I tried to speak to him again, to reach for him, but the star suddenly blazed hot against my palms, glowing steadily brighter. I dropped my gaze in wonder, watching as beams of green light burst from between my interlocked fingers. I made a small sound and when I looked up to see what Chris thought, Justin stood there instead, scars and all, his eyes steady on mine. He closed both of his strong hands around mine, warm and solid, and said, "Come on, Jilly."

And then I woke up.

I felt so fragile, as though the lightest touch might shatter me into jagged fragments.

My room was dim and gray, tears hot on my cheeks. I rolled to one side, aching, not knowing what to make of the vividness of the dream. I bunched up the covers and pressed them to my belly, wrapping around the bundle I'd created as though it was a baby, or something that needed protecting. I cried and cried, muffling the sounds, until I eventually fell back asleep.

Hours later Clinty tapped on my door and peeked into my bedroom, dressed and combed, and asked softly, "Mom, you all right?"

My sweet boy. He added, "Everyone's here for breakfast, and Justin just asked me where you are."

My heart hurt. Justin was over at the cafe and he'd asked where I was. I thought, *Justin, oh God, come over here yourself. I need you so much. I need you to crawl into my bed and hold me, just hold me. I need to breathe against your neck. Oh, God.*

I said, forcing cheer into my tone, "Honey, I'll be over later. I'm just tired from our late night."

"K, Mom," he said, dashing back through the house and then outside.

I heard his footsteps pounding down the steps and for a moment was entirely grateful that my only child was a boy; any of Jo's girls would have heard something in my voice that suggested I wasn't telling them the truth, and would have plopped on the bed and demanded to know what was up. But Clinty accepted my words and ran off to eat more of Ellen's caramel rolls, which she'd been prepping yesterday. I groaned and rolled to my other side, burying my face in my pillow.

Because Trout Days was still in full swing in Landon, we closed the cafe after lunch. By early evening the western sky glowed with a rich, creamy pink, the air sweet with the fragrance of the rose bushes beyond the porch. It always seemed to me that dusk lifted fragrances high into the air, made them almost tangible. I leaned against the railing and inhaled with pleasure, catching all of the smells of summer I loved best: the lake, fresh-cut grass, the rose blossoms.

Across the parking lot Milla and Tish were trying to climb into the golf cart, piloted by my laughing son, who kept inching forward so they couldn't quite board. I smiled a little, despite the ache that settled behind my breastbone like a leaded weight, dense as guilt. I was glad the kids were oblivious to anything but themselves, headed for an evening of fun just like Jo and me, once upon a time. The activity from downtown danced across the water in waves of laughter and bursts of firecrackers; the music would get rolling in an hour or so. Just down the shore, my sister sat on the dock with her legs crossed, her gaze also fixed on the kids; her own low mood was practically visible in the air above her head, a gray cloud streaking rain over her shoulders.

Behind me, Ellen fired up the charcoal grill; I turned with a sigh and went to retrieve drinks for everyone. When I came back out, Jo slowly climbed the porch steps. I called over my shoulder, "Ruthann, grab your mom a beer, will you, honey?"

Jo plunked into a chair near Gran, her eyes ringed with shadows, her shoulders drooping. I was exceedingly grateful that it was just us girls for the evening, no menfolk in sight. I slid across from Mom at the table just as Gran piped up, "Jillian told us about the divorce."

Jo glared instantly at me, twisting her long hair over one shoulder. I only tipped my head to the side and asked her with my eyebrows, *What do you expect, it's Gran?* In truth, I'd only commented that Jo better stick around here and not even consider going back to Chicago. I didn't mention divorce, but Gran read between the lines in our conversation earlier today.

"We aren't getting divorced yet," Jo said, a hint of acid in her tone, which she drowned with a long swallow of beer.

Mom's eyes brightened at this news and she patted Jo's knee. She said, "Oh, Jo, I'm glad."

My heart clenched up at my sister's expression. I was just about to say something when Ellen, her back to us as she flipped burgers on the grill, said, "Joan, how is the girl ever supposed to trust Jackson again?" Gran nodded with satisfaction, while I exhaled, relieved beyond measure that Ellen neatly contradicted Mom. Aunt Ellen continued, "Jo, I just don't feel like Jackson deserves you. Not now."

I realized that none of the womenfolk suspected anything about Jo's attraction to Blythe. At least, not yet. They were all so focused upon Jackson, and how Jo was dealing with him, and with her girls, that no one noticed what was right under their noses. Well, maybe Gran. But she hadn't breathed a word to me, not yet.

"Not ever," Gran added, immediately lifting her hand as Jo's eyebrows drew together and her lips parted to respond. Gran hurried on, "Joelle, he was the best-looking boy in Landon, I admit it. Those eyes, and his easy way of talking. I know you loved the boy. But re-examine the man, honey. You are better off without him. You know it."

Jo's eyes sparkled with tears; she realized the truth in Gran's words, and I sent Gran a surreptitious look of relief and gratitude before I turned my expectant gaze back to my sister. Jo studied Ruthie, down the shore playing fetch with the dogs, and her face reflected everything she was grappling with; the decision to leave her children's father was sharp and pointed and potentially painful as the tip of a knife. I pressed my lips together and conveyed a telepathic message to my sister: *You know Gran is right. You know it, Jo.*

At long last Jo released a shuddering breath and said, "I know you're right."

Gran nodded, pleased. I felt the tension in my shoulders ease just a fraction.

Jo added, "But it hurts so fucking much."

"Oh, sweetie," Mom said, patting Jo's knee again. I was pleased that despite Mom's differing opinion about Jackson, she was being supportive.

Jo's lips twisted as though she was trying not to cry, but she managed to say, "Hey, it's Saturday."

Gran winked at me and then added, "Then you and Jillian better get your asses into the kitchen and whip up some margaritas."

A full moon was such a splendid thing. Especially the June full, called the Strawberry Moon. When I was a kid, Dodge told me the name of each month's moon; I thought back then that he'd made them up, but realized eventually that he'd actually lifted them from the *Farmer's Almanac.* I remembered sitting on the top of the tire swing that used to hang from the big oak by the garage, drifting in lazy arcs, twining the rope between my fingers while Dodge used the hedge clippers on the raspberry bushes, his big voice soft as he told me about things like full moons and growing seasons and summertime constellations. Curling low on my spine, nearly thirty years later, I remembered him explaining why the June full was known as the Strawberry.

The music from the street dance rippled over Flickertail; we were into our third pitcher of drinks and I sipped yet again from my goblet, made of clear-blue glass with a long stem and a base curved like the petals of a tulip. Since my teenaged years this glass was mine for our Saturday margarita nights. This evening I clutched it like the old friend it was as the womenfolk talked and laughed, their words flowing and swirling around me like eddies in a busy stream; Ruthie snored on the glider. I lifted my eyes to the silver-dollar orb in the sky, flooding us with its brilliance, casting our shadows, which danced along the porch like the darker parts of our souls set free for this one night.

I was thinking again of Justin with no relief in sight. What was he doing this evening? Certainly he was downtown. What was he thinking? I was still so wounded by his continued avoidance, his fear of daring to acknowledge his feelings. What would it take? Tears stung my eyes and I refocused on the conversation in progress with effort, suddenly recalling that Clint asked me about pictures of my father, his grandpa, whose name was Mick Douglas. I hadn't remembered to question Mom about this request, despite the fact that it was over a month ago, when Clint needed pictures for school. Going through old albums only cemented the fact that we Davis women, as a whole, possessed very few photographs of the men from our pasts, including my own husband.

It's the curse, I heard Great-Aunt Minnie whisper, and shuddered. I thought, *No. I don't believe in it...*

I found my voice and asked, "Mom, Clint wondered once if you had a picture of Mick anywhere? Do you?"

Mom also sat studying the sky and answered dreamily, "I have our engagement picture somewhere, and a few from that summer. He liked to take pictures more than he liked to be in them."

That I already knew. I was drunk, and aching for Justin, and I was afraid that tears were about to fall over my cheeks and then everyone would wonder what the hell was going on. To top it off, I'd realized earlier that tomorrow would have been Chris's thirty-fifth birthday. I heard myself whisper, "I wish I had more of Chris."

From across the table I could sense Jo's surprise at my sudden choice of words. To punish myself, I went on, "He would be turning thirty-five tomorrow." Though it was probably after midnight; I glanced down at the watch I wore when I worked and added, "Today, actually." The thought made me immeasurably sad, but I still felt like a flake, a faker, as I said, "I just can't stop thinking of him tonight, guys, I'm sorry."

Because the man I truly couldn't stop thinking about was Justin Daniel Miller. But my family couldn't know it, not yet. I felt like such a coward, a total jerk, and I turned my chin against my shoulder and pressed my mouth there, wanting so much to give in and weep.

Gran murmured, "It's only natural, love."

Did she know? Her gaze was sharp and shrewd upon me. Maybe she meant that it was only natural to move on, to allow myself to love again. Maybe she was trying to convey that to me with those words, or maybe I was just reading too deeply into her obvious concern.

Jo said softly, "Jilly Bean, we love you. We love you so much."

I nodded in response, swamped with guilt, knowing that was true but wishing at least my sister knew the real reason I was so utterly torn up inside. From across the water the music stopped and I whispered, "I think it's time for bed."

Jo wasn't satisfied with this and asked, the concern in her voice overt, "Do you want to take a walk, Jilly Bean?"

She rose from her chair, stumbling a little as she made her way to me and cupped my head in her hands. Mom and Ellen both stooped to kiss my cheeks, and I sheltered for a moment in their collective love, letting its balm comfort me a little. I caught Jo's hand in both of mine and at that moment I was struck with a Notion, right smack in the gut, of her and Blythe wrapped in each other's arms. *Tonight.* Somehow, some way, it would be tonight, and there was nothing I could do to stop her from taking this path. I didn't even want to anymore. I loved her; I loved Bly in my own way, and they deserved this happiness, fleeting though it may be.

I whispered, "No, thanks though, Jo."

Mom and Ellen flanked Gran on their way back to the house, supporting her, and Jo asked, "Hey, will you help me with Ruthie?"

With difficulty we lifted her, half-asleep and floppy between us. We couldn't help but giggle, hauling her across the dew-damp grass and then up two flights of steps, to the loft the girls were sharing for the time being. Even without turning on the overhead light I could tell it was a wall-to-wall wreck. I scraped mounds of clothes from Ruthie's bed to the floor and then we managed to get her tucked into it, as she murmured something about drums.

Unexpectedly, another flicker of a Notion struck me—about Ruthann, inexplicably. As Jo tucked the covers up to Ruthie's shoulders and kissed her cheek, murmuring to her youngest, I struggled to cling to the wavering image. I could have sworn I just saw Ruthie's body shimmering, as though no longer fully solid, as though light could pass through her.

But as Jo straightened up, the strange sensation blinked away. *You're just drunk, Jillian,* I thought. *Quit this. It's nothing.*

Back outside Jo and I stood under the amazing moon flooding earth and sky with its light; depending on my mood, the moon's face took on varying expressions. Just now it seemed censuring, disapproving. I was drunk enough to shiver slightly. Jo asked quietly, "Are you worried about the kids? Should I head over to town?"

The air around us seemed tense, charged with something I couldn't quite define. I sighed a little and then responded, "Nah, they're fine, Clinty will bring them home now that the music is done."

I turned my face to Jo's at last; she watched me with a slightly wary expression, unsure what my tone actually conveyed. At that moment I longed to spill everything to her. But I had to let her go; I'd seen it. I sighed again and whispered, "Night, Jo."

As I made my way across the grass to my empty apartment, she called good-night, her confusion at my attitude clear in her tone.

Alone in my little house, I curled into bed, wrapping my arms tightly around myself, and finally managed to doze. It wasn't until much later that I was awoken by the buzz of my cell phone, tossed carelessly onto my nightstand. It pulled me from a vague jumble of dreams and I pressed the button to answer without fully acknowledging that someone calling at this time of night always meant no good. But I could sense my son in his room and so fear didn't flash within me like so much lightning; I didn't hear that nausea-inducing hockey buzzer in my head.

"Hello," I murmured into the stillness.

"Jillian," he said softly and my eyes flew open. My heart sprang to life as though electrocuted and I couldn't respond. He whispered, "I miss you so fucking much."

"Justin," I whispered back, longing and desire and all of the wretched hurt he'd caused me these past weeks flowing through my voice. I could tell he'd been drinking, probably way too much, and my heart continued its agitated rhythm against my breastbone.

"I'm so sorry," he said.

I wanted to ask him about which of the many things he definitely owed me an apology regarding, but I held back, finally whispering, "Where are you?"

"My house," he said roughly, and he sounded miserable. Though I hated that he was suffering it was a kind of consolation, knowing it. He knew how to change all of that, but he needed do it; I was more determined than ever. In the silence I could hear his breath and the pulsing thud of my heart.

I wanted to tell him I'd be there in ten minutes. Five, even. But I heard myself say, "Good-night, Justin," and though it just about killed me, I hung up on him.

Morning came on with a dull, heavy sky the gray of concrete blocks. I made my way over the grass in the morning hours, craving coffee and a chat with Gran. But she was still sleeping, as were all of the kids besides Ruthie. Ellen looked me over with a practiced eye, making sure I was truly all right as I poured myself a steaming mug and then drifted outside to sit and drink it, at least until it started raining. Judging from the sky that would be in about ten minutes.

I knew Mom and Ellen continued to worry—today was Chris's birthday, after all. I couldn't help but imagine what we'd have been doing were he still alive and actually turning thirty-five today, and not just in my imagination. I wondered the same things at Christmas, or on Clinty's birthdays. The western edge of the world grumbled with the approaching storm and the humidity in the air stroked all along my limbs. And almost instantly my traitorous thoughts turned to Justin. He'd drunk-called me, which I resented, while another part of my soul thrilled to the fact that he'd said he missed me. God, I missed him.

At that moment I caught sight of Jo making her way across the grass and wondered suddenly how her night had gone with Blythe, a welcome distraction. I couldn't act as though I knew anything, but I watched her watching me oh-so carefully, knowing that if anyone suspected it would be me. For a second I almost smiled at her uncharacteristic wariness. Just to torture her, I called cheerfully, "Good morning!" as she climbed the porch steps. I saw her shoulders relax an inch, and asked, "What time did the kids get back last night?"

She hedged with me, grabbing my coffee cup and taking a sip before saying, "Late."

I followed this with a slightly more pointed question, "How about you?"

I wanted her to tell me what happened and sent her silent messages to confide. She fiddled with my cup and opened her mouth as though to speak when Justin drove up, his truck tires rumbling over the gravel. My heart propelled blood through me hard enough to cut off any words I intended to say. Jo noticed that my gaze snapped away from assessing her and she turned to watch as Dodge climbed out of the passenger side and called, "Hi, girls!"

Justin followed his dad, silent and pale beneath his tan, sunglasses still in place. I couldn't pull my eyes from him, unable to offer a reply to Dodge.

Jo said brightly, "Morning, guys!"

Dodge clacked through the screen door calling cheerful greetings to Ellen and Mom, but Justin stopped near our table without a word. My heart was out of control. Jo teased, "A little under the weather this morning, Mr. Miller?"

He grimaced slightly, the side of his leg braced on the edge of the table closest to me. I was grateful that Jo seemed unaware of my distress. Justin murmured, "Don't ask."

Jo said, "I saw you heading into Eddie's last night, buddy."

I looked at my sister, surprised by this statement; I assumed that Blythe had shown up here at Shore Leave last night. I asked, "You went into town?"

Jo seemed to realize she'd said too much; I could read her thoughts as she backpedaled, groping for an excuse. At last she admitted, "Yeah, I saw the fireworks."

Yeah, I'll bet, I almost teased. But suddenly Ruthann flew through the screen door with the cordless phone from the counter in her hand, effectively cutting off any comment I might make.

"Mom, it's Daddy!" she informed Jo, whose face went slightly green.

I watched in sympathy as Ruthie's eyebrows lifted and she wiggled the phone at her mom, not understanding why Jo wasn't jumping at the chance to speak with Jackson. Justin pushed back his sunglasses and my eyes flashed immediately back to his face, noting that his eyes bore the marks of a sleepless night.

Jo reached for the phone and I forced some cheer into my tone as I addressed my niece, saying, "Ruthie, come with me and let's get another muffin, huh?"

Jo gingerly brought the phone to her ear and then disappeared in the direction of the dock. Ruthie galloped back inside with no further encouragement and left me stranded with Justin. I met his gaze and my heart clobbered my ribs; he watched me in silence, his eyes shadowed with smudges. After a moment he said, "Poor Jo told me when we were dancing that Jackie loves someone else."

"She did?" I asked, and then sighed. "Leave it to Jackson."

Justin's eyes burned into mine. I wanted him to mention that he'd called me last night, though I sensed he was waiting for me to say something first. Neither of us noticed Blythe until he cleared the top step and said, "Hey, guys," by way of greeting. I jumped a little and Justin shifted his gaze to Bly, replying, "Hey."

Blythe sent me a pointed look as the first raindrops spattered the deck boards. He was about to continue into Shore Leave but suddenly changed course, moving swiftly to the porch rail nearest the dock, bracing both hands around it and asking, "What's Joelle doing down there?"

"Talking to Jackson," I tattled to his back, and watched as Bly's huge shoulders squared with tension. Everything about his posture became instantly both threatening and protective. Down below, Jo paced with the phone, her free hand moving as though she intended to punch something. Or someone. Rain flecked the lake with pockmarks, and Blythe pushed himself from the railing, ducked inside the door and re-emerged seconds later with the raincoat from the tree rack.

Lightning flashed like a beacon in the next instant and it must have been some signal to the sky to unleash a downpour. I squeaked a little, jumping up to go and haul my sister out of the storm, but Justin gently caught my elbow and said, "Jills, he's got it," before drawing me closer to the cafe, under the awning of the roof. My skin pulsed where Justin's hand held me. I watched Blythe make his way through the rain, down to where Jo was pacing and obviously shouting, her words drowned out by the thunder. At the last moment I looked up at Justin and he let go of my arm. Our eyes collided and I wanted nothing more than to hurl myself against his chest and hold him, feel his strong arms around me. I almost gulped at the expression in his eyes, before muttering, "Come on," and led the way inside the cafe.

Chapter Twelve

A WEEK PASSED WITH THE USUAL FLUTTER OF JUNE HEAT-
ing into July, both with the weather and with the increase in business as
Landon's busiest tourist season kicked into high gear. And yet despite
the bustle, I found moments to both confess to Joelle that I was in love
with Justin and confront her about Blythe. She was sympathetic about
my feelings for Justin and, by contrast, angry at me for expressing my
fear about her getting hurt. As a result, we were aggravated with each
other for days, playing the silent treatment, until I couldn't take it another moment and vowed to confront her and make amends. I bided
my time, waiting until one late evening after dinner rush. Clinty had
planned a bonfire all week, and invited two of his best friends over to
camp out, and I resolved as I wiped down my porch tables that there
was no better time to talk to Jo. Though I shortly discovered from Mom
that Jo already made plans—to go into town and hang out with Leslie
Gregerson.

I watched Mom as she mixed up a pitcher of lemonade for Ruthie,
whose own buddies, Liz's triplets, were tagging along with Dodge for
our bonfire. Mom's hair hung in a long braid, drawn over one plump
shoulder, her earrings large, neon-yellow hoops. Probably Ruthie picked
them out for her. I studied my mother's familiar face, her sunburned nose
and summer freckles, as she bent over the task, and couldn't help but
think, *Are you serious? You actually believe that Jo is going to meet Leslie?*
But then I reminded myself that Mom, while loving and dear and whose

opinion could always be counted upon, was also less than observant. *A free spirit*, Great-Aunt Minnie always called her. *Joanie the dreamer.*

I could hear Jo and the girls in the bar, over the whine of the blender; Ellen was busy mixing up grasshoppers for the girls. I entered just in time to hear Jo lying about meeting Leslie in town.

"Have fun," I couldn't resist sing-songing, and she turned and met my eyes with a look of such guilt that I relented slightly. No secrets between us anymore, and on one hand, I was truly delighted for her and Blythe; both of them glowed with buoyant happiness, Blythe hardly able to remove his besotted gaze from her at any given second. But I feared so much for the fall that was inevitably coming.

"I will," she said, reassuring me with her tone. Her eyes spoke volumes more, completely silently, apologizing for the past days' tension.

I looked hard into her familiar golden-green irises, telling her that I was sorry, too. I couldn't resist imploring, *Jo, be careful. Shit, please be careful.*

At that moment Dodge banged through the screen door and into the dining room, calling out, "I've got firewood in the truck, heard we were having a bonfire out here tonight! Clint, get out there and help the boy unload."

Of course by *the boy* Dodge meant Justin—I hadn't expected him this evening and my heart was all at once radiant with excitement and hope.

Jo's expression changed markedly, her lips lifting into a teasing, knowing grin. She poked her finger into my ribs, crooking her eyebrows as she said, "You have fun, too, Jilly Bean."

She headed back over to the house to change, while I darted into the bathroom in the bar, my face suddenly hot and my hands all shaky. Justin was here to hang out tonight, whatever that meant. I regarded myself in the small mirror, fishing my lip gloss from the front pocket of my server apron, applying it carefully, fingers trembling through my hair, wishing there was time to run home and shower. But that would look too suspicious, too obvious. I pulled my Shore Leave t-shirt over my head, glad I was wearing my favorite flowered tank beneath it. I tugged the neckline a little lower, smoothed the soft material over my belly and then twisted around to make sure my jean shorts were stain-free after working dinner. They were, and my legs looked tanned and sexy, if I did say so myself. I dabbed again at my lip gloss, ran the tip of my index finger over my lashes, stowed my server apron on the counter and then clamped a determined hold on my nerves.

Out at the bar, the girls all sported green milk mustaches. Ellen was just disappearing out the screen door with a six pack of beer in one hand. Ruthie smiled at me and said admiringly, "Aunt Jilly, you're so pretty."

"Aw, Ruthann," I said, touched at her sincere words. "Did I mention you're my favorite niece?"

Tish giggled and clunked me on the arm with the side of her hand. Camille seemed oblivious to all of us, chewing her thumbnail as she studied the screen door. Clint thundered up the porch steps, yelling for me, his voice cracking. Boy, I couldn't wait for him to outgrow that. He appeared in front of us, sweaty and disheveled, his hair standing on end; I couldn't help but smile at him.

"Ma, where's my dive shoes?"

"Look down on the dock," I said, while Tish leaped up at the mention of going back in the lake.

"Wait, Clint!" she yelped, leaving her mug on the bar. I snatched it and took a long drink of the minty froth.

"Aunt Jilly, do you care if I go with Noah for a little while?" Camille asked, standing abruptly; I saw a car pull into the parking lot, clearly Noah Utley's.

I scrambled to remember if Jo had mentioned anything about not wanting Camille to go anywhere this evening.

"I'll be back early," my niece said, already threading her purse strap over her shoulder.

"Sure, that's fine, honey," I relented, hearing Justin's voice outside. I added, "Back before eleven, all right?"

"Thanks," Camille said with her beaming smile; she disappeared outside as though into thin air.

Justin was inside the cafe then, coming through the dining room. He called, "Ruthie, you in here? The kids are looking for you!"

At his words, Ruthie shrieked in excitement and flew outside, bounding away and subsequently leaving me abandoned. Justin's footsteps advanced to the bar, my heart keeping pace, and he appeared in the arch between the two rooms. He pinned me with his gaze, leaning one shoulder casually against the wall.

He looked amazing. I hadn't been alone with him, hadn't so much as talked with him, since he pulled me out of the rain last Sunday, and my heart insisted that this was way, way too long. His black hair was all shaggy and I wanted to mess it up even more. He wore orange swim trunks and a white t-shirt, sunglasses hanging on a cord around his neck. He looked tan and lanky and sexy and dangerous, and I wanted to leap across the room and directly into those powerful arms. My breath grew sharp, revving me up to do just that. I sensed that things were about to change and my entire body pulsed with anticipation.

I. Love. You, I thought intensely, projecting the words into the air with all my might.

"Hey," he said. His voice was all husky. A smile hovered around his lips and before I could reply, he said, "You've got ice cream on your lip."

Dammit.

He advanced across the bar—two feet away he stopped and drank in the sight of my face, just as I did his. His eyes stroked over my lips and then back up, and then he grinned, slow and steamy.

I squared my shoulders and said with as much attitude as I could muster, daring him, "Well, get it."

His grin deepened and he reached and curled one hand around my upper arm, drawing me close without hesitation. My breath caught. He used his thumb to gently swipe my bottom lip and then leaned back, while my knees almost gave out.

"There," he said, and backed away, turning as though to head outside. I was pleased beyond measure to catch the way his voice shook a little on that word, as cool and calm as he otherwise appeared.

I stood anchored in place, burning up. At the arch he looked over his shoulder and asked, "You coming or what?"

I couldn't let him see how much he affected me and so I said, injecting as much sass into my voice as possible, "I'm coming."

Still, it took me a minute to make my legs move forward. I finished Tish's abandoned drink and then slipped behind the bar to fetch myself a beer, which I held to my forehead before venturing outside, where the air was perfect, the lake crystal blue in the evening light. I felt a shudder of appreciation ripple over me as I reveled in the familiar sight of Flickertail glinting beneath the long beams of setting sun. The trees along the water's edge were backlit in a honey glow; I was just in time to see Mom's station wagon leave the parking lot, my sister behind the wheel on her way to "visit Leslie."

There was intense activity around the fire pit, with Dodge directing operations as usual. I watched from my semi-secret vantage point on the porch; Dodge directed Tish, Clint, and his buddies in setting up two tents while Justin carted more wood from the back of Dodge's truck. Justin's muscular arms bulged as he deposited another armload, and my stomach went hollow just watching. Mom, Ellen, and Gran settled into lawn chairs, sipping from the plastic cups we kept behind the bar. Ruthie and the triplets arranged a blanket and set out food. Gran lit a smoke and caught sight of me, spying from above. She beckoned and I walked slowly down the steps, heading over to help Clint stake out his old tent, setting aside my beer.

"Aunt Jilly, Clint says only *they* get to stay out here," Tish complained, hunkering beside me as I shoved with both palms on a stubborn tent stake.

Only Tish; she truly wanted to be a part of their group, unable to understand why Clint would abandon her for his buddies. I said, "Honey, you don't want to sleep in there with those guys. For one thing, they don't smell all that great by morning."

She giggled a little and Clint said, from ten feet away, "I heard that, Mom."

"You can have a sleepover with me if you want," I told her. Unless of course someone else intended to stay the night. I mentally kicked myself, almost giggling at the thought of trying to smuggle Justin up into my apartment with so many pairs of watchful eyes around here.

"Maybe," she said, slightly mollified, her feather earrings twirling. And then she suddenly tattled, "Hey, Mom told Milla to stay here tonight but she left with Noah."

Shit. I would have to take the blame for this one. Darn that Camille—if Tish knew her big sister was supposed to stick around Shore Leave then of course Camille had been well aware. I asked lamely, "She did?"

"Yeah, they just left. Mom's going to be *so mad.*"

"Well, why didn't somebody say so?" I complained. "I didn't know your mom said that."

Tish huffed a sigh and offered, "I won't tell if you won't."

"I can't lie to my sister!" I said, exasperated. "And you shouldn't be lying to your mother!"

"I don't—" she began to say, but Mom interrupted us, calling, "Tish, honey, can you run inside and grab that bag of pretzels off the counter?"

"Sure, Grandma," Tish said, darting away.

I gave up on the tent stake, wiping my palms on my jean shorts, only to observe that Justin snagged the lawn chair right beside the one he knew was mine, sitting with his feet widespread, forearms braced on his thighs. He was two-thirds of the way into a beer. As I claimed my seat, he shifted just subtly closer to me. We were so aware of each other we might as well have been screaming and gyrating; instead, we sat in silence, while all around us our families carried on in typical summer-night-bonfire fashion.

"Justin!" Clint yelped, barreling over to us, followed by his friends; the boys looked like trouble with a capital T, and Justin grinned a little, likely remembering himself at that age. I could only imagine what they wanted. Clint asked earnestly, "You wanna take us in the motor boat?"

Justin said, "I would but it's getting too dark."

Clint's shoulders slumped a little; immediately he asked, "Can we go swim, Mom?"

I nodded assent, watching as the three boys, Tish on their heels, stampeded down the slope to the lake. Seconds later there were multiple splashes, followed by laughter and various insults.

"Those damn kids said they wanted to learn poker," Gran grumbled.

"Gran, no swearing," Ruthie said, still busy arranging food on the blanket. "Remember, you told me to remind you."

Gran flapped a hand and everyone laughed. I reminded Gran, "Clint knows how to play already. You taught him when he was little."

"Jo's girls don't know how," Gran complained. "And Clint hasn't learned a thing from me. He has too many tells. His face is an open book."

Ellen said, "Dodge, you watch that big log on the top," and he groaned and made a playful swipe at her with his fire stick.

Ruthie told Mom, "Grandma, we're gonna run inside and get more marshmallows." And so saying, she and two of the triplets ran for the cafe. The third, Fern, instead climbed on Justin's lap. He grinned and cuddled his niece, and she requested, "Uncle Justin, tell us about the time when you drove Grandpa's truck into the store."

Justin yelped good-naturedly, "How do you know about that?"

Dodge laughed with a deep rumble, while I watched Justin holding the little one on his lap; I couldn't help but think about what a good father he would be, and how I would be more than happy to give him the opportunity. Then I took a long swallow from my drink and thought, *Holy shit, Jillian, slow down there.*

Mom supplied, "I remember that day. You couldn't have been more than twelve or so."

Dodge explained, "Fern, what happened was I told your uncle that he couldn't do something, which in this case was get behind the wheel of my truck, and of course the first thing he did was get behind the wheel of my truck."

"Hey, you left it running," Justin said, lifting one hand in a defensive gesture. "What did you expect?"

Dodge laughed again, saying, "Sure as hell not my son putting it into gear and then driving it over the curb and into the corner of the god-damn hardware store. Thanks be to Jesus no one was injured."

"Except me!" Justin said. "Later, after you'd strapped my ass until I couldn't sit for a week."

"Uncle Justin, don't say *ass*," Fern reprimanded amid everyone's laughter.

"With a belt!" Justin added.

"Spare the rod," Dodge intoned, but the look he gave his son was affectionate.

Ruthie and the other kids returned and proceeded to roast marshmallows for us, while the fire painted our faces orange and Justin was close enough that if I reached six inches I could have cupped his right knee. I felt whole with him so near, loving every word and laugh and gesture, noticing every detail as though for the first time. His lean, muscled forearms and wrists, dusted with dark hair. His beautiful strong hands, broad palms and long fingers with oil stains that were never fully scrubbed away. His lanky legs and bare feet; he'd kicked off his flip-flops somewhere. His straight nose, his long eyelashes and teasing mouth. His firm jaw and stubborn chin, presently peppered with stubble now that it was evening. His hair was black as ink and hung almost to his shoulders when wet; it was wild and wavy now in the firelight, making my fingers itch to caress it. His deep laugh that I felt deep in my belly. Surely I was resonating with longing, though I laughed and joked every bit as much as usual, feigning nonchalance.

Soon, I assured myself. *Soon.*

Hours later Jo returned home to find us still around the fire, followed almost immediately by Bly; it was clear, at least to me, that they hoped everyone would believe he just showed up coincidentally, and I worried about how transparent my sister had become. I knew it was because she was hoarding her time with Blythe, getting desperate now that summer was rolling along like a reckless child on a scooter, faster and faster, potentially dangerous, on a collision course with the end of the road. We took the canoes for a midnight ride on Flickertail at Tish and Clint's persistent begging; I insisted they help haul all the gear back to the shed before taking off for the house and the promise of food, leaving Justin and I alone to finish cleaning up. Everyone else had long since vanished to bed; the last of the embers smoldered in the fire pit. Joelle headed back to the house as Blythe drove away; I saw them sneak a quick kiss, Blythe leaning out of the driver's side window to grasp the back of her head.

For the first time I thought, *Maybe it could work between them...maybe Blythe will stay around here. Maybe...*

Justin lingered behind with me, taking his time putting away the life jackets. Despite how much we'd flirted while out on the water, me in the bow of the canoe and him steering us along the edge of Flickertail, we hadn't been truly alone since he removed the ice cream from my lip earlier in the evening and I tried to cover my nerves by kicking ashes over the last bit of glowing coal.

"Anything else that needs to go in here, Jills?" he called from inside the shed.

I headed that way to find him stuffing the last life jacket in place. He turned and I swallowed, only a few feet from him. It was dark and the breeze picked up as night advanced, but the shiver that fluttered over me had nothing to do with the chill air. Justin's eyes were hot as coals. I was in his arms in the next instant; I wasn't even sure which of us moved first. He caught me close with one arm, catching the back of my head with the other, tipping me into his kiss, while I clung to his neck and kissed him back with total abandon. His tongue swept into my mouth and he tasted sweet, like the roasted marshmallows we'd been eating all night. We hadn't kissed since the night on the golf cart, far too long ago. Justin took us back into the life jackets piled haphazardly on the cement floor of the shed without breaking our kiss. In fact, it intensified he rolled us to the side, my thighs around his hips. He was angled just above me now and I experienced the fleeting thought that if I died at this moment I would die happy, in his arms at last, my heart bounding with the joy of it.

"You taste so good," he muttered against my mouth, his fingers widespread, gripping my hips. "So damn good."

I curled into him, kissing his chin, his neck, inhaling his scent like an illegal drug that might not always be available to me.

"I can't handle being apart from you anymore," he said, and hope absolutely welled within me. His eyes drove into mine as he asked, with formality, "Will you be my girlfriend?"

I couldn't help but giggle at his choice of words and though I longed to be much more than that to him, I would take this for now. I rested my forearms against his chest and said, "I think I'd like that."

He cupped my jaw in one hand and said softly, "You're right, I have been a total chicken shit this last month and I'm so sorry. Jillian, beautiful woman, will you let me make it up to you?"

"Starting now," I whispered, leaning in and taking his bottom lip between my teeth, lightly biting him.

He made a sound deep in his throat and caught me hard against his chest, moving swiftly over me and kissing me with all of his skill. I gripped his shirt with both fists, considering just how risky it would be to get him out of his swim trunks right here in the shed. But it was that exact instant I heard my son, from a distance, calling, "Mom! Hey, are you still out here?"

I pulled back, desire stalling my movements.

Justin shook his head, coaxing, "Don't go yet...*please...*" He drew me into one more kiss and I clung for a heady moment before duty insistently tugged me away. This time he rose with me, crushing me close and hard, rocking us side to side.

"I'll see you tomorrow," I told him, moving reluctantly from his warm arms. I added, teasing him a little, "My boyfriend."

He grinned widely, running his hand down my bare arm, sending shivers rippling all the way to my toes. Clint was fast approaching, I could hear him, and I hurried around the edge of the shed, hoping I didn't look like I'd just been making out. Justin followed, collecting his keys from the ground near the fire pit.

My son was totally unobservant to nuances; there was no danger of Clinty suspecting anything. He saw me and said urgently, "Mom! We're outta toilet paper!"

Justin laughed, responding, "You're camping, buddy, use a leaf," as he headed for his truck. His teasing words struck me as something Chris would have said to Clint, had he lived to watch his son grow up. I watched Justin go with my heart simultaneously joyous and aching; just before he got to the driver's side he paused and looked back at me, and I felt a deep, lightning-quick flash of what makes life worth living.

Chapter Thirteen

THE NEXT NIGHT, JUSTIN PICKED ME UP FOR OUR FIRST-ever date.

I spent an hour getting ready, my stomach trembling with equal parts excitement and wonder. I listened to the radio while soaking in my tub, using my favorite coconut oil in the water, then shaved my legs and dabbed vanilla-scented perfume lightly between my breasts. I blew out my hair so it would be especially soft; studying my reflection in the mirror, twining short golden strands around my fingers as I wielded the dryer, I thought that maybe I could grow it out again. I wasn't the world's biggest fan of make-up but spent a little time accenting my eyes and applying tinted gloss. Finally I slipped into my sexiest bra and matching thong panties, black and sheer. Over these, my hands growing shaky now as I anticipated Justin removing everything I was currently slipping on my body, I wore a soft red sundress, patterned with tiny cream flowers and a short, swishy skirt.

"Girl, you look like you're headed for trouble," Gran teased as I roamed over to the cafe minutes later, seeking a beer to calm my nerves.

Ellen caught me around the waist for a hug and said, "Sweetie, I'm so happy that you're going on a date with Justin. He's had a crush on you for ages now."

I regarded Ellen with surprise, which she saw on my face and rolled her hazel eyes, adding, "I may not see as much as your grandma, but I'm not blind."

Mom said, "Jilly, you haven't looked so pretty since I don't know when."

I knew she meant this as a compliment and so thanked her. I felt pretty, and desirable, and absolutely giddy with anticipation, waiting for Justin to arrive. As I sat at the counter to sip my beer I found myself thinking about autumn evenings in high school, getting dragged to football games with Jo, who attended to watch Jackie play; he'd been quarterback, after all. I could close my eyes and perfectly picture Justin in his Rebels football uniform, white with blue, his black hair even longer back then, hanging well past his helmet in back. His jersey was number six, I remembered that, too. In high school he'd been even leaner, wiry and fast on the field. Though I hadn't been entirely conscious of it, my eyes had followed Justin even back then; I could acknowledge that now.

I couldn't help but remember Aubrey from those days, too; she'd been a cheerleader, a tall, leggy girl with long auburn hair of which she'd been inordinately vain. Aubrey Pritchard, the kind of girl who got away with almost anything because of her good looks. I hated her in those days; she was arrogant and snobbish, a bragger. But I could also clearly recall Justin pitching his helmet to the side as he darted across the field after the game, sweeping her into his arms and kissing her. And so maybe I'd hated her for a deeper reason; Justin loved her once upon a time, married her right out of high school. I truly believed she was the reason he was scared to acknowledge his feelings for me, and I couldn't blame him. We'd both been hurt, and we both lost a spouse, but Justin was betrayed. And I'd seen only some of the aftermath of that.

"The boy's here," Gran said, jolting me from the past. I beamed at the sight of Justin climbing from his truck, all set to dash out there into his arms, but Gran said decisively, "No, he'll come to the door like any young man taking my granddaughter out."

I tried to inhale slowly, and thereby steady my heart, but then heat flamed over my face and down the rest of my body as I saw that he carried an enormous bouquet of flowers. Lilacs, unbelievably purple, my favorite color. I took one more gulp from my beer before Justin climbed the porch steps, grinning and handsome as hell, decked in jeans and a white polo shirt. The white accentuated his dark tan, his black hair and eyebrows, and although I could tell he'd just shaved, there was still a hint of shadow on his jaw. My entire body pulsated with desire at the sight of him in the evening light. Why had I fought it for so long?

Mom and Ellen sat the porch rolling silverware, and he stopped to chat with them, grinning and teasing them about something; Mom made him laugh and happiness swelled inside of me just hearing the sound of it through the open windows. At last he came in the cafe, his eyes seeking me, and a slow smile lifted his lips. He let his gaze move over me and blinked once, almost in slow motion, his eyes sizzling into mine. I couldn't help myself, I didn't care that there were still a few customers in the bar; I gave in to my instinct and flew to him, throwing my arms around his neck and kissing his jaw as he crushed me close with his free arm, the one not cradling the flowers, aware that interested looks were directed our way.

"Hi," he said, low and soft. "You look amazing."

"So do you," I told him. "And these are beautiful. I love lilacs."

"I know you do," he whispered.

"Oh, for heaven's sake, let me get those flowers in some water," Gran said, coming up behind us, cane thumping over the floorboards.

"Yes, ma'am," Justin said, relinquishing the lilacs to Gran, who momentarily buried her nose in their delicious sweetness.

The she glared at us and ordered, "Have a good time, you kids."

Justin assumed a serious expression, squaring his shoulders, and said formally, "I promise to show Jillian a good time."

I bit the insides of my cheeks to contain a giggle, heat radiating across my lower belly at his words.

Gran snorted and lightly rapped Justin's ankle with her cane before heading for the kitchen to find a suitable vase for such a wealth of blossoms. The second her back was turned, Justin took my hand and kissed it, then hooked his fingers through mine. I almost couldn't believe the wealth of touches I'd been so long without, his warmth and presence that took my breath away. He said, "I picked them myself, just so you know. Well, used a hedge clipper anyway, on that big lilac bush by the station."

"Thank you," I said softly, as Justin led me outside into the mellow, blue-gold evening. Mom and Ellen waved as we headed across the parking lot. At his truck he opened the door and put his hand on the small of my back to help me inside; it felt so good I almost stumbled, wondering how in the hell I would possibly wait until sometime later, maybe even hours, before I could get my arms and legs wrapped around him. It wasn't that I didn't want to have dinner and chat like a civilized person for a little while first…I did, truly, but there was an insistent ache within me that only he could relieve.

Patience, I reminded myself. Besides, I was so happy just to be in his company that I would not have cared if we simply drove around Landon all evening.

"So I was planning to cook dinner for you," he said, climbing behind the wheel. "But I thought you might want something more gourmet than mac and cheese."

I giggled, responding, "Don't lie, you can't even make that."

Justin drove approximately fifty feet, until we cleared the sight of Shore Leave, and then abruptly pulled over on the side of the road and wasted no time sliding across the bench seat and gathering me for a kiss. I murmured in gladness, slipping my arms around his neck as he kissed me deeply and absolutely, before drawing just slightly away. His eyes caressed mine. My heart clattered against his chest.

"God, you look good," he said softly. "I wanted to kiss you right away, but it's a little intimidating with Louisa right there."

I giggled again, a part of me wondering when I'd become such a giggler. He brushed his lips gently over mine, just the faintest of touches, flooding my belly with desire, before moving back to his side of the truck. I bit my bottom lip, still tasting him, lightheaded.

Justin caught my left hand in his right, again curling together our fingers. He said, "But don't worry, I have a plan."

"A plan?" I teased, stroking the back of his wide hand with my thumb. His skin was tough and tanned, his knuckles a firm ridge, such working-man hands. I couldn't have loved them more.

"I thought we could get dinner at that little Italian place in Bemidji and then…well…I do have a carton of ice cream in my freezer. I thought maybe if I was lucky that might entice you back to my house."

"Should I be offended?" I asked, teasing him right back. He knew well that ice cream was my favorite dessert. I added, "I mean, if ice cream is all you think it takes…"

"Jilly-Anne Davis, I would risk life and limb if I thought I might have a chance to get you to come over."

"I don't expect anything *that* drastic," I said, though his easy teasing pleased me immeasurably. "Ice cream works just fine. As long as it's caramel, with pecans."

"Fuck, I bought chocolate," he said, taking the truck through town and then heading for the interstate.

"Then no deal," I said breezily. "Some boyfriend."

"I guess you'll miss out," he said, shrugging.

I turned over his hand and placed it upon my left thigh, bare beneath the short skirt. He inhaled a deep breath, not taking his eyes from the road, and skimmed his palm gently over my flesh.

"That's just playing dirty now, Jilly. Like when we played pool," he said, and then murmured, "You're so damn *soft*."

I shivered at his tone and replied, "You should have bought caramel with pecans. *Dammit*, Justin." As he merged onto the interstate I told him, "I was just thinking about watching you play football back in high school. Jo used to drag me to all the games to watch Jackie. You were number six."

"You know what, I tried to put on that jersey a few years ago and I couldn't get it over my shoulders. I was a skinny little bastard back then."

"You weren't ever skinny," I disagreed. "Well, maybe as a little kid. But 'skinny' isn't the right word. You were sexy as hell in high school. I was just thinking that I noticed way more than I realized."

"I've been thinking about you back then, too. Your long hair." He continued to stroke my thigh, his voice soft as he added, "I think your hair suits you better short, though, Jilly. You are incredibly beautiful. I've always thought so."

"Thank you," I murmured, inexplicably shy at the compliment.

Justin added quietly, "You keep it short because of Chris, don't you?"

If this was a regular first date, as in the couple didn't know much about one another, he'd have never dared or even known to ask. But this wasn't a regular first date, and we knew more about each other than many married couples. And because I was in love with him, even if I hadn't spoken the words yet, I was able to say, "Yeah. He loved my hair so much."

"Aw, Jilly, I could hardly bear to be at his funeral, it was so sad. And what you did, putting your hair into the coffin with him…that moved me so much. I just want you to know that." His voice was husky as he trailed to silence, probably fearing to offend me for real, but I wasn't offended; I took his hand once again into mine, thinking of my dream, when the green star grew hot and pulsing because Justin was near. He sensed my need and held securely. After a moment he said quietly, "I have never forgotten how you looked curled in the snow that day."

"That was such a horrible day," I whispered, but I wasn't in danger of crying. "I wanted to freeze in that snowbank. You carried me inside, but I didn't realize it until later."

Justin tightened his grip on my hand. He nodded.

I said quietly, "Thank you for that."

"You don't need to thank me." His voice took on an almost confessional tone as he said, "God, I was shredded up that day. But I know it wasn't anything close to what you were feeling. I wanted to climb on that bed with you and take you in my arms. I knew I had no right to feel that, but I did. It was so hard to walk away."

I wanted to tell him, everything inside of me ached to tell him that I loved him. But I only said, "Thank God for Jo and my family. Clint wouldn't have managed without them."

"He's a lot like his dad, isn't he?" Justin asked.

"Yeah. He's sweet as could be, never gets upset, just like Chris," I said, but no tears sprang into my eyes. Instead I just felt grateful for my son, that in him the best parts of Chris would live on.

"Chris would love to see how much he's grown. Clint is a good kid. You should be proud of yourself, Jills."

With no false modesty I said, "I am. Clinty is the best thing I've ever done."

"Is it unforgivable for me to be jealous of someone who's dead?" Justin asked a second later, catching me by surprise.

I said, without thinking, "No, because I'm jealous, too." He turned to look at me, the angle of his eyebrows asking me to explain. I added, "Of Aubrey. I told you I was thinking today about high school."

Then I felt small and petty, but Justin said, his voice so serious, "Jillian. She's got nothing on you. Don't get me wrong. I loved her once. Or at least, I thought I did. It's funny how that works."

"That's what Jo said about Jackie," I mused. And then, maybe just to torture my own happiness, I asked, directing my gaze out the passenger window, "Do you still miss her?"

"No," he said, squeezing my hand. "She and I should never have gotten married in the first place."

I dared to look at him, relief flooding me. I confessed, "I always hated her, you know."

Justin laughed. "Yeah, I got that sense pretty strongly the night we talked on the boat landing. Remember when you told me that she was telling everyone that I liked to get spanked?"

I grinned, shaking my head at the memory. We'd covered quite a range of emotion in the last fifteen minutes, now returned to easy laughter. I admitted, "I *totally* lied that day. I just wanted to shock you, or impress you, or something."

"Well you made an impression, all right. I've never told anyone this," he said next, and it was my turn to raise my eyebrows at him, intrigued by his tone. A smile played over his mouth as he said, "The night you said that, the night Jackie and I fell off the train, I dreamed that you, sweet little Jillian Davis, were spanking the hell out of me. So that's what comes when you tell lies."

I made a disbelieving noise that was choked out by another wave of laughter.

"It was a pretty sexual dream, I'm not gonna lie," Justin went on, grinning. He added, "I felt all guilty and shit, like I'd cheated on Aubrey.

How ironic, huh? And then when I saw you at prom that's *all* I could think about. That soft little pink dress you were wearing that night...and then we danced. I felt like you'd punched me in the chest, Jilly."

"*That's* why you were so weird that night," I mused. A little life mystery solved. I pressed, "Was I spanking you with my bare hand or with an implement of some kind?"

He answered so quickly I knew he wasn't pulling my leg, saying, "Some little strap thing. And then...oh my God, Jilly...then you pushed me to my back and straddled me. God, it was *so* real, I could feel you on top of me, and then I woke up before the best part. I almost cried. Seriously, I lay there in bed and almost cried. And I can't believe I just told you that."

"Wow," I marveled. "We had a whole subconscious connection even back then."

"Yeah we did," he agreed. "But you can't tell anyone about the spanking thing."

"I'm not promising," I said. "And if you make me angry, I know *just* how to punish you."

"I'm holding you to that, you little sweet thing," he said.

We ate dinner on the deck of the cozy Italian restaurant, huge plates of pasta, talking so comfortably, laughing about every other thing. I stole meatballs from his plate, while he helped himself to my mushrooms and bread crusts; I liked to pull out the soft white middle of the Italian bread, leaving the outer shell, and Justin grabbed these without asking permission, swirling them through the olive oil. When it was time for dessert, he reminded me, "Ice cream at my house."

We left the restaurant under a sky that was a backdrop for a wealth of glittering stars. In the parking lot, Justin curved his arms around me from behind, letting me lean back against his solid strength to study the heavens.

"Thanks for dinner," I told him, tipping my face to kiss his jaw.

His lips against my temple, he whispered, "Thanks for coming."

I whispered back, "Well, I haven't yet, but I was hoping to a little later."

He didn't miss a beat, replying, "More than once, if I have anything to do with it."

I turned in his arms just enough to nip his chin and he shivered, tightening his grip.

"Let's hurry," I said. "I think that ice cream is starting to melt."

Justin laughed and hauled me into the truck, firing it to life and driving out of the parking lot. He teased, "I love it when you talk dirty."

"Put your hand on me," I ordered, and he cupped his fingers around my thigh and slipped his palm right under my skirt.

"If you tell me you haven't been wearing panties the entire time, you're in trouble," he said, sounding a little strangled. "I will pull over and risk indecent exposure charges right here." His fingers skimmed to the edge of my panties and he exhaled a little. "God, these are so tiny."

I was already so wet and ready for him, and we still had to drive miles back home. I played with the idea of straddling him as he drove, but even with the growing red haze clouding my sensibilities, I knew that was too dangerous to risk.

"Slip these down, *right now*," he commanded.

I lifted my hips and eased the tiny garment down my legs, and then slid my palms softly back up, making a show of caressing my skin, drawing the edge of my skirt just a little higher.

"Holy fucking shit," Justin said passionately.

I couldn't help but smile at his choice of words. "You should be a poet."

He laughed, shaking his head, his hand gliding up my thigh. He said heatedly, "Here's a poem for you. There once was a woman named Jillian…"

His fingers reached the vee of my parted legs and I gasped a little, but demanded, "Go on."

He angled me a blazing-hot look, murmuring, "Whose skin was the softest in all of creation." He caressed inside me, groaning, "Holy *Jesus*, woman…"

"That doesn't…rhyme," I managed to say.

"And who drives me absolutely insanely crazy," he concluded, stroking with conviction now. I curled my fingers around the edge of the seat, my head falling back.

"Oh my God, *Justin*..."

"Shit, I'm gonna drive off the road," he said.

"*Don't stop*," I begged.

"Honey, I'm just getting started," he promised.

In his driveway, he barely put his truck in park before I was in his arms, my panties abandoned on the floor. Justin practically growled into my neck, curling me across his lap, not breaking our kiss as he opened the door, climbed out with me in his arms, and then kicked it shut behind us.

"What will the neighbors think?" I murmured against his lips, digging my hands into his hair.

"I don't give a god*damn*," he said, swinging open the front door and kicking it closed as well.

Once inside, he carried me through his living room, up a flight of steps and then to the second door on the right. I caught a fleeting glimpse of his bed before I was on my knees upon it, tearing off his shirt, his jeans, his boxers, ordering breathlessly, "*Hurry*," and he took me instantly to my back, drawing my thighs around his hips. His eyes were onyx in the dim light, spear points of desire. He was at once inside me, bracing above and thrusting deeply, taking my chin between his teeth before ravaging my mouth. I moaned as our bodies crashed together, tightening around him at the first few strokes, gasping out his name, clinging with arms and legs. Minutes later he groaned and came hard, his mouth open on my left shoulder. He bit down lightly before cuddling me close and collapsing us to the side. From a few inches away, our lower bodies still joined, he grinned into my eyes and whispered, "Sorry, but you had me so revved up in the truck."

"Don't be sorry," I scolded. "That was just what I needed."

"I want you so much," he said, his hands widespread on my back, so warm and strong. "In case you didn't notice that. But I don't want you to think that's all I want from you."

I lazily stroked his thick hair from scalp to full length, over and over.

I said, "I don't think that. And besides, I want you so much it's all I can think about."

"Good," he whispered, smiling with sweet satisfaction, softly kissing my lips. And then, as I slipped my hands from his hair to his shoulders, he implored, "Oh God, please don't stop. You have no idea how good that feels."

I resumed my ministrations; a little later he shifted to one elbow and looked down at me, tracing gently along the edge of my face. He said, "Here's what I want to do right now. I want to get us bowls of ice cream and then take a bath. How's that for the second half of a first date? And then…" And his free hand was busy now, cupping my right breast, stroking over my waist, coming to rest on my belly, fingers angled toward my pelvis. "There's a certain sweet little spot on you that I haven't kissed yet."

I reached and slid my palms across his lower back, gliding over his ass, pulling him all the more tightly into my body. Arching my hips, I whispered, "What spot is that?"

"I'll give you a hint," he said, tonguing my nipples with soft, slow strokes. I moaned and felt him grin against my breasts. He licked a hot path along my neck and reclaimed my lips.

"Another poem?" I whispered, loving how hard he remained.

Justin murmured gamely, "I would climb the tallest mountain, swim the most shark-infested ocean, walk the hottest, sandiest desert…*barefoot*…"

"You should write some of this down, seriously," I teased, quivering in pleasure as he moved within me, my hands guiding his motions.

An hour later we were up to our shoulders in bubbles, in his deep, claw-foot tub. Justin sat behind me, my back neatly against his chest in the slippery, honeysuckle-scented water.

"Here, let me help you," he offered, again soaping my breasts in circles, just under the water.

I giggled and squirmed at his tickling touch. He cupped both in his strong hands, biting the side of my damp neck and making me squeak. I could not resist teasing, "I don't know what's more surprising, that you have bubble bath or that it smells like flowers."

Justin bit me again, then licked the spot and said, "It was from Liz. The kids picked it out for me."

"Well, that's sweet," I murmured, pressing against his wide palms, twitching my shoulders a little in an invitation for him to continue stroking. He did at once, thumbs gliding over my nipples.

"'Sweet' is my middle name," he said against my neck, and his deep, husky voice vibrated in my belly.

"I thought it was Daniel," I said in my best know-it-all tone, scooping handfuls of bubbles and spreading them on the surface of the water, then anchoring my grip around his knees, stroking with both thumbs. His legs were hard and lean with muscle, covered in coarse dark hair, and a ripple of undiluted happiness spread outward from my center, tucked here in the bath with Justin, wet and naked and blissful.

"Ma wanted to call me 'J.D.' Isn't that funny?"

"I've heard Liz and Wordo call you that."

"Jillian Rae," he added, pressing soft, hot kisses along the top of my shoulder.

"That gives me the shivers," I told him, shivering joyously.

"I have a few other things in mind, sweet, sexy, scrumptious woman. If you'll join me."

We dried each other fast, still damp and practically steaming as he swept me back into the bedroom.

Though my son was fifteen years old and thoroughly capable of tucking himself in, I still felt a guilt pang as I crept into my apartment at some time after three in the morning. Justin walked me up the steps that climbed the outside of the garage and we spent lovely, lingering minutes kissing good-night. I couldn't let go of him; when at last he tipped his forehead against mine and said, "I better let you get to bed," I shook my head wordlessly.

His eyes smiled as much as his lips.

"Thank you for the date," I whispered.

"You are so welcome," he said. "I'll see you in the morning, Jills."

I wanted to invite him in so we could wake up together, but certainly couldn't give in to that urge with my son in the same space. At last I conceded, "In the morning, then."

Justin took my right hand and kissed it, first my knuckles and then my palm, closing his eyes. When he opened them everything inside of me surged forward, toward him, wanting him and loving him with such force that I clenched my jaw to hold back the words I longed to say; he would tell me first, I would have it that way. It was there in his eyes, strong and true, and my heart crashed against my ribs.

"In the morning," he promised, and then turned and headed back down to his truck in the parking lot. I leaned over my small railing and watched. Again, he turned and blew me a kiss before driving away.

Chapter Fourteen

THE NEXT EVENING I WORKED DINNER FOR MOM, KNOWING I couldn't get out of it every night, despite my desire to shirk all duties and simply run away with Justin. Anywhere, I didn't care, as long as we could spend the rest of our days and nights tangled up together. He came to Shore Leave for coffee with Dodge right away in the morning and was hardly up the porch steps before I banged out the screen door and he caught me in his arms for a hug. Dodge, just behind him, stopped and watched us, grinning as much as I'm sure the womenfolk were from inside the cafe; we were clearly framed in the wide front windows. But I didn't care.

"High time," Dodge said, as Justin rocked me gently side to side and our kiss continued; Dodge cleared his throat in mock sternness and finally skirted us, making his way inside. He muttered again, "High time."

Justin drew back, keeping me aloft in his arms, and he looked so happy, his eyes lit with joy. He looked gorgeous, and smiley, and like himself. Like the Justin of old. Except that now he was my boyfriend, all mine, and my answering smile could have lit up the entire solar system. Just because I could, I curled my fingers into his thick hair and roughed it up a little.

He said, "Morning, tomboy."

"Morning," I whispered, tucking wayward hair behind his ears. I confessed, "I missed you a little bit."

"Just a little?" he teased.

"Maybe a lot," I murmured, clinging to him. "I wanted ice cream for breakfast."

"God, same here," he said with feeling, grinning at me, pulling me close for one more kiss.

I was moony the rest of the day. Intensely so. I found myself gazing into space or out over Flickertail, pelted by thoughts of him and welcoming this. Making love, what we'd discussed, thinking of how we'd eaten ice cream in his bed. He bought caramel with pecans, which he knew was my favorite, despite all his teasing about chocolate. He knew me so well. I stopped about a thousand times to lean in and smell my lilacs, which Justin picked for me and were now arranged in a tall glass vase on the counter, spilling over and scenting the air with their delicate, delicious fragrance.

"So, how's my little sis today?" Joelle asked at one point. Her tone indicated that she had a pretty damn good idea what I spent half the night doing, her lips curved in a knowing half-smile. Besides that, her own glow emanated at around ten thousand kilowatts, only superseded by Blythe's. He couldn't keep his adoring eyes from her; I was a little worried he would walk into the wall, or burn himself on the grill. The two of them were about as subtle as a field of fireflies at dusk.

"Justin must have gotten past the thinking you were taking pity on him bullshit," she murmured, hooking an arm around my waist. And then, "Any word on the new arrival?"

The Notion struck me the night before last, when Jo and I fell asleep together on the couch in Mom's house—suddenly I'd known, with the bone-deep sense that never yet proved wrong, that someone was coming to us. I didn't know who, or when, just that someone *was*. It was an inexact science, for lack of a better term.

"No, nothing new," I said. "And Justin is…he's…"

"Why, Miz Jilly, I do believe you're blushin'," Jo teased, doing her best Southern belle.

I felt my face absolutely torch and busied myself with wiping down a table.

"*Wow*," Jo said, and I could hear the grin in her voice. "Way to go, Justin."

He came out to Shore Leave around eight, just as I was getting done with dinner rush. He sat and drank a beer with Gran while I flew home to shower and change. This time I wore a short, periwinkle-blue sundress, a delicate, barely-there gold chain, and my favorite red flip-flops, dabbing vanilla perfume on my collarbones and between my breasts. When I reentered the cafe I found Justin situated comfortably between my grandmother and my son, angled so that he could listen to Clinty chatter about something, with Gran looking on; Gran was double-timing her drinks, sipping alternately from her coffee mug and a bottle of beer. Tish leaned on the counter on the far side. Justin turned and sent a grin over his shoulder at me. Clint kept right on talking, trying to command Justin's attention, but Tish called, "Hi, Aunt Jilly! So, Justin's your boyfriend now?"

The Queen of Discreet, that one. But I loved that she was blunt; Tish would never hide something from her mother…not like Camille. I loved all three of my nieces equally, but worried more about Milla than I did about Tish or Ruthie. Camille was secretive this summer, closed off somehow, and I wasn't yet sure how to help her—surely her reticence was directly related to her sudden desire to spend every waking moment with Noah Utley. And if any of Jo's girls were observant enough to catch on to their mother's nocturnal activities, it would for sure be Milla.

"He sure is," Justin answered Tish. I reached them and rubbed my hand over Clinty's back before twining my arms around Justin's broad shoulders, just behind him, and kissing his cheek. He wrapped an arm about my hips, squeezing me gently to his side.

"Hi, guys," I said.

"Hey, Mom," Clint replied with his usual cheer, tilting his head at me in the way that meant he was about to ask for something he figured I would deny. He and Tish both inherited the true-blue eyes bestowed upon me by my errant father, Mick Douglas. I used to tease Jo that the stork truly intended Tish for me, rather than her and Jackie. Clint already knew Justin was my boyfriend since I'd talked with him about it earlier today. He'd said, "Cool, Mom" and I was grateful for the countless time to have such an easygoing child.

"What is it, son?" I asked, reading him the way I would a favorite book.

He asked in a rush, "Can I maybe drive the boat?"

Clint's tone was so hopeful that Justin and I both laughed, while Tish cried, "You get to drive the boat? Can I?"

"Ask Justin," I told them.

Tish turned her gaze to him, folded her hands as though praying and widened her eyes in pleading; that expression had never failed on Jackson, I was sure.

"If your moms say it's all right, I'll teach both of you," he promised.

"All right by me," I said.

"Can we take out the canoe for a while right now?" Tish asked, and this time Gran piped up, "Be sure to grab life jackets first, you two."

Tish and Clint raced out the door and Gran's face wrinkled into a knowing grin. She added, tapping Justin's leg with her cane, "You two kids remember the same thing."

"Did Louisa mean that I should use a condom?" Justin asked a few hours later, his voice drowsy and content, after he'd definitely *not* used one twice since we'd gotten to his house. "Now I'm feeling a little guilty."

I giggled at his teasing, my cheek on his chest, lazy and replete, expecting to hear myself begin to purr any moment as Justin caressed my back with soft, languid stokes.

"I think maybe," I conceded, my eyes closed. I could hear Justin's heartbeat as I lay there, the slow, steady thump of someone who just spent the better part of an hour making love. "But don't listen to her. I love feeling you inside me without that in the way."

"Me, too," he agreed, stroking my hair. And then, "Can you stay the night, Jilly-Anne?"

I felt so good, so warm and satisfied and about to melt into him, but I murmured, "I better not, not yet."

"Soon, though?" he asked, cupping the back of my neck and massaging. "I'm selfish. I want to hold you until morning."

I spread my fingers and curled them lazily into his thick chest hair. "I could sneak you into my place. But you'd have to sneak out in the morning, too."

Justin laughed, his chest vibrating under my cheek. He said, "I could bring a rope and go out the window." His tone became speculative. "That could work…"

I giggled, saying, "It's not as though Clint would be angry or anything. It would just be a little awkward. But he likes you a lot. He always has."

"I like the kid, too," Justin murmured. He shifted a little, curling me more securely against him, and then resumed stroking my back. He said, "When I'd see you around town with him after Chris died it always hit me hard. I've worried about you much longer than you'd think, Jilly. For years."

"I knew you worried," I admitted, nuzzling his chest, my eyes still closed. After a time I whispered, "Did you know you were the first person to make me laugh? That first summer, I mean."

"I was?" he asked. "Well, good."

I kissed him just in the spot where I could feel his heartbeat. I confessed, "Speaking of worry. The day of your accident I wanted to chase right after Dodge. I wanted to fly to the hospital and make sure you were all right. But I knew I couldn't. That was so horrible, waiting to hear, not knowing."

He was silent, no doubt grappling with memories. At last he whispered, "I don't honestly remember much after the battery acid hit my face. It was probably like something out of a horror movie. I was flopping on the garage floor like a hooked fish. God, it burned so bad and I couldn't stop it."

"I was so afraid for you. And afterwards, it was so hard to watch you suffer."

"Jilly," he murmured, tightening his arms around me.

"I've wanted to touch you for so long," I admitted, and he stroked my cheek with his thumb. "That night we sat on the boat landing dock and you were so angry. Even though I yelled at you, I really just wanted to touch your face and show you that I wasn't afraid to. And then I was too chicken, after all."

"God, I wish I'd known that," he said softly. "But maybe I was too angry then. I was so mean to you that night, baby, you didn't deserve that."

"You weren't mean," I contradicted, thrilling at the way he'd called me *baby*. "Besides, I was pretty mean, myself."

"But honest," he said. "I needed someone to be that way. Other than Dad, that is."

"I'm so glad I found you that night. I almost didn't walk that direction."

"That was when you told me to come back to Shore Leave in the mornings," he whispered. "That meant so much to me, Jilly."

I shifted just enough to raise myself to one elbow, our legs braided together. He held me tightly with one arm and I put my fingertips gently on his face. His eyes closed immediately as I traced over his scarring, only a little hesitant, knowing how self-conscious he remained. I wondered how to convince him that it didn't matter to me, that I loved everything about how he looked. Time, I supposed. And satisfaction darted through my belly, a swelling rush of happiness at the thought of time with him. He remained almost motionless as my fingers carefully explored the right side of his face, where the marks were red and created ridges, continuing down his neck where his work shirt would have been open and exposing his skin that day. His skin was olive-toned, darkly tanned, and the scars had become less intense over the years. I shifted over his chest to put my lips on him and he shivered just slightly, eyes still closed, his wide shoulders hunching in an almost instinctive defense.

"Let me," I implored in a whisper, pressing soft kisses along the same route my fingers had just taken. I kissed his forehead and eyebrow, the outer edge of his right eye, his cheek and jaw and then his neck, where I paused and inhaled against him, imagining all too vividly what he described just few minutes ago, about writhing on the floor of the shop, unable to stop the burning acid from destroying his skin. My heart constricted and I shifted to kiss his temple. In the dimness of his bedroom I might not have noticed, but I felt the warm wetness against my lips, as tears trailed down the side of his face. He made a sound deep in his throat.

"Justin," I breathed, my heart clanging with love and concern. I was so in love with him, so head over heels over tail over teakettle. I rolled instantly on top of him and hugged him as hard as I could. He turned us to the side and wrapped his arms around my waist. I held his head against my breasts, stroking his hair, pressing my lips to him while he sobbed. Terrible, chest-wrenching sobs that I knew had been buried inside of him for years. He clung to my waist, his strong arms like bands of iron around me. I murmured to him, wordless sounds of love, holding just as fiercely. And when morning came tiptoeing across the bed on sunny feet, we were still wrapped around each other.

Just a few nights later, the womenfolk held our annual Fourth of July Eve party at the cafe. Jo and I shared my apartment bathroom to get ready, just like the old days when we fought for space in the mirror. She was wearing a drop-dead-gorgeous green dress that made the jade in her eyes absolutely sparkle. Bly would be speechless when he saw her. I was pretty proud of my own dress, a deep blue number with a tiny skirt and ruffles over my breasts, absolutely designed to make my man fall to his knees. Though I had to make quite a show of enjoying myself, playing eye games with him on the sidelines, before he drummed up enough nerve to brave the dance floor.

"Come here and dance with me, woman. God, you're making me crazy," Justin said, as a slow song began, holding out his arms.

I moved into them with joy, nagging, "It's about time you got your ass out here."

"You look insanely gorgeous," he said, his eyes caressing me in the candy-glow of the lanterns as his hands curved around my waist.

"You're forgiven," I replied primly.

"This color matches your eyes almost exactly," he went on, smoothing the material over my hips in a deliberate, seductive stroke. I curled my fingers into his hair, smiling up into his eyes.

"I'm glad you like it," I murmured.

"I love it," he said, his eyes so intense that my heart jolted. He added, "And when can we get out of here without offending anyone?"

"Now," I decided instantly. "Let's go now."

Fifteen minutes later we were in his bedroom and the air was supercharged. Even more so than usual. We rode in complete silence on the way to his house, though the space between us crackled with nearly perceptible sparks. When he pulled into his driveway my knees were almost too jittery to allow for climbing down. But I needn't have worried; Justin came around the hood like a man on a mission, hauling me by the hand as he led us into the house and up the stairs. Something had shifted and I was clanging with the energy of it. In the darkness of the bedroom he took my shoulders in both hands. We hadn't spoken a word since sneaking away from Shore Leave.

"Justin…" I implored. Need and want spilled through me, pulsing in my blood.

"Jilly," he said. He took my hand and pressed it to his chest; his heart pounded fiercely beneath my palm. He said hoarsely, "I'm so scared."

Tenderness rocked me. I curled my hand around his t-shirt, just over his thundering heart. I said, "Don't be scared, not of this. Never of this." He closed his eyes and gritted his teeth, almost unconsciously, but I insisted, wanting to shake the truth of this into him, "You are an incredible man, Justin Daniel Miller, and beautiful. You always have been, inside and out. You have to believe me when I tell you that. Don't you know—"

His eyes opened and burned into mine and I was so close to telling him that I loved him, it would have been the next thing out of my mouth, but he said, his voice harsh with pain, "Jillian, God, oh my God, you don't know. You don't know how dark I can be, how terrible my thoughts are sometimes. I thought about killing myself for a while after the accident. I didn't think I could go on another day."

I wrapped my arms around his waist, holding fast, wishing I could bring him even closer to me, into me. I demanded, "You think I don't know? You think I didn't have those feelings once, too? But I had Clint and he needed me, and so I couldn't kill myself and leave him alone. Justin, sweetheart, you can tell me these things. I understand."

He closed his eyes and rocked against me, burying his face in my hair. I said, "You can tell me anything," desperate to comfort him, as I had the other night.

His words spilled out in a passionate rush, "Do you know that I wish Clint was my son? I wish I'd shared that with you, Jillian. You and I should have been together all these years. I don't mean to insult Chris's memory, I swear to God, but that night we danced at your wedding all I could think was that I'd married the wrong woman and that you'd just promised yourself to the wrong man. But then I told myself I was drunk and forced that out of my head for good. But I know I was right that night, and we wasted so many years apart."

I vividly recalled that night, dancing with Justin at my wedding, though I would never have dreamed that he felt these things in that moment.

"Then let's not waste another second," I whispered. "Not one more second, Justin."

He exhaled in a rush, as though he'd expected me to shove him away and run for the door. He whispered, "I need you, Jillian."

"I'm here, I'm right here."

"Now, you're here *now*. But what about next month, next year? What about when you can't take me anymore?" He felt me shift in protest, about to contradict his words, and drew back, taking my face in his left hand, his eyes pouring into mine as he said the words I'd been aching to hear. "Jillian, oh God, you have to know that I love you. I'm *in love* with you and it's more real than anything I've ever felt. I've never been so happy, but I'm so fucking scared. I can't count on anything anymore."

Tears spilled over my face and the back of his hand as it cupped my jaw. My voice caught as I whispered his name, "*Justin*. I've been in love with you for so long now. And I'm not letting you go."

He thumbed away my tears and claimed my lips, possessive and passionate. I arched against him, joy shuddering over me like the aftermath of an earthquake, one he caused in my soul. He said, "I'm so sorry I said we made a mistake the day after we made love. I didn't know what else to do. I couldn't imagine that you could love me when I look this way. Jilly, making love with you is so incredible, so many million times better than in my fantasies."

"I love everything about how you look," I told him sternly, and then I couldn't help but tease a little, digging my fingers into his ribs as I questioned, "Fantasies?"

He choked a laugh against my neck and admitted, "Yes, hell yes, I told you that you drive me crazy. I've loved you for *so damn long*."

"Well good," I said then, softly, immeasurably pleased, and he tumbled us onto the bed in one smooth motion, angling over me on one elbow. I reached up to caress his face. His precious face that I wanted near me from here on out.

"I've wanted to tell you for so long now," he whispered.

"You have told me, in a million different ways," I whispered. "The way you'd tease me, or call me all those nicknames, or ask how I was doing. Just you *being* there at Shore Leave. I looked forward to all those mornings just because I knew I'd see you, even back when you were still married, and I felt so guilty. I longed for you even then. I could hardly admit it to myself."

"It was the same for me," he said, with quiet passion. "My day never felt right, or complete, until Dad and I would get to the cafe. I could have had coffee at home, but then I wouldn't have seen *you*. What a hypocrite I am—furious at Aubrey for cheating on me, when I turned away from her long before that."

"Justin," I whispered, overcome. I said intently, "I love your scars because without them, you might still be married to her."

Justin looked deeply into my eyes.

"Come here," he ordered, and kissed me, open-mouthed, his tongue playing with mine, stroking my lips. Without breaking contact, he slipped down the straps of my dress, baring my skin and then unhooking my bra; he separated our mouths only to remove his own shirt and toss it to the edge of the room, before pinning my wrists to the mattress, lightly rubbing his chest against my breasts. I murmured wordless sounds of pleasure that made his smile deepen and sent him traveling down my center, trailing hot kisses along my collarbones, my nipples, teasing my belly button, making me squirm and giggle, before he moved lower and all laughter fell from my throat. I threaded my fingers into his hair as he lifted my skirt with slow, calculated movements, building my need for him to a feverish pitch.

"Jilly," he whispered, his fingers warm on my thighs as he slipped off my panties. I gasped and clutched the bedspread. His voice was husky with desire as he ordered, "My beautiful woman, I want you to come all over me." I couldn't manage to answer with words as he bent his head between my legs and proceeded to make me do just that.

"Oh my God," he panted. I was drenched in sweat, barely able to recall my own name, but I clutched his shoulders and curved my thighs around him. He moved with fluid grace, grasping my hips and driving deeply into me, just like I needed. He was everything that I needed.

"I won't be able to walk...for a week," I murmured much later, after he collapsed above me and then tilted us gently sideways.

His chest rumbled with a laugh and I propped myself lazily onto one elbow, studying him in the dim glow of the streetlight outside. His eyes were closed, the hand not clutching me resting palm-down on his hairy chest. Again I marveled at his manliness, admiring him in repose. I loved the line of dark hair that extended from his chest hair, down over his flat belly. I felt the urge to run my tongue along that length, but held back, busy relishing in being here beside him like this. His jaw was shadowed with thick stubble, pirate-like, giving him a menacing, totally sexy appearance that made me shiver with desire, despite the fact that he'd just left my body and I was already a little sore. His lean, hairy legs extended far past mine on the mattress. His lashes fanned his cheeks, his lips soft and just slightly parted. I couldn't resist and planted a single kiss on them, feeling the pulse in my vitals expand outward.

He'd told me, finally.

I burrowed against him with a small happy sigh. He kissed my hair, inhaling like he always did. He whispered, "Jilly, tell me you can stay 'til morning, sweetheart."

"There's nowhere I'd rather be," I whispered back, hooking my right leg over his thighs.

Chapter Fifteen

I woke on my belly and found Justin propped on one elbow, studying me in the soft morning light. His bedroom faced east, bathing the space in the glow of an amber sunrise. His eyes were so warm, crinkling at the corners as he smiled. I tipped my face against the pillow and snuggled closer to him.

"Good morning, baby," he said, kissing my shoulder.

And then in the next second I couldn't contain myself, moving swiftly on top of him, fitting our bodies together, getting my arms around his neck and covering him with kisses. He laughed and rolled me along the bed, kissing my lips and chin and collarbones, ending with me angled just under him. I clutched his wide shoulders as he slid one hand over my belly and clarified, "*Damn* good morning, if I do say so myself."

An hour later we'd showered and dressed, and Justin drove me back to Shore Leave under a sky as cloudless and clear-blue as a polished gem. Dodge was either already or still here, and Justin parked next to his dad's car. The yard and the porch were strewn with the remnants of the party last night; we walked beneath strings of lanterns that bobbed merrily in a gentle breeze, holding hands. Just at the edge of the porch I said, "Let me run home and change quick."

Justin said, "I'll be in here."

I hurried up my steps and into my familiar little kitchen, pit-stopping to peek in at Clinty, snoring like a ripsaw, one long leg sticking out from under his covers. I couldn't resist creeping over his carpet and shifting his leg back underneath. As I did, he blinked sleepily, knuckling his eyes and croaking, "Hi, Mom."

"Hi, honey," I murmured, perching on the edge of his bed. "You have fun last night?"

"Yeah, it was great. Did you leave with Justin?"

There wasn't a disingenuous bone in my son's body; he asked this with sincere curiosity and I cupped his freckled cheek for a tender moment, like he was still my little boy. I said, "Yeah. I really, really like him. Is that okay with you?"

So I oversimplified a bit with that statement. Clint regarded me seriously, before smiling and saying, "Of course, Mom. *Jeez.* He's a good guy. And I can tell he makes you happy."

"You can?" I asked, feeling tears sting the back of my nose.

Clint stretched and propped himself on one elbow. He'd grown so tall, slim as a string bean, his face all planes and angles and his hands all knuckles. But he was utterly composed, adult-like, as he said, "For sure. You smile so much around him. I'm glad for that, Mom."

My tears spilled over as I hugged him against me, rocking him side to side as I whispered, "Thanks, son."

It was Friday but also the Fourth of July, so we closed the cafe directly after lunch. Jo and I helped finish cleaning the yard and the porch, wiping down the tables and stowing party decorations.

"You're glowing again, Jilly Bean," Jo observed as we hauled the last of the lawn chairs into the garage. Despite the melting heat outside it was always damp and cool in the garage, where no one ever parked except in deepest winter. Years' worth of tools, equipment, junk, broken furniture, and cast-off belongings occupied the space, along with cobwebs, dust and the scent of lawn clippings. Dodge used the old rider mower every few days to trim the grass around the parking lot and porch. I smiled, recalling how happy he was about Justin and me; he'd told me last night at the dance.

I wrapped my arms around my sister's waist, hugging tightly. She snuggled me right back, smoothing my hair almost like a mother as she whispered, "I'm so happy for you."

"How about you?" I asked, looking up into her beautiful golden-green eyes. Her hair was twisted into a graceful knot, strands drifting down her neck, her cheeks flushed. I warned, "You two aren't fooling anyone anymore, I hope you know. Well, maybe Tish."

Jo cupped her forehead and whispered, "Oh God, Jilly, I love Blythe so much. I need him. And I can't have him, can I?"

My heart twisted at her words; this was exactly what I'd feared, precisely why I'd tried so valiantly to keep them apart. But it was a monumentally worthless effort. Their attraction was practically gravitational and I could see plain as spilled sugar on the speckled counter at the cafe that Blythe loved my sister, too. A whole lot. But then, I'd known that from the beginning.

"Jo," I said softly. "I can't answer that."

She closed her eyes, pressing her knuckle to her lashes, refusing to let tears fall. She straightened up and collected herself, whispering, "But not yet. Not yet." She attempted a smile, asking, "You and Justin going to the fireworks later?"

"Yeah, he's stopping out after work. Clinty and I talked about him this morning. Clint told me he can see that Justin makes me happy."

"Even Chief and Chester can see that," Jo teased. "And they're dogs."

I giggled a little, swiping hair from my eyes and certainly leaving behind a streak of grime. I wondered aloud, "Do you think you and I will be capable of partying this way when we're Mom and Ellen's age?"

Jo snorted and amended, "Shit, even when we're *Gran's* age."

The Landon Township fireworks were always detonated over Flickertail; our tradition was to load up on the pontoon that Dodge kept moored over at the filling station, taking it out to the middle of the lake. Everyone in town with any form of watercraft elected to view the show from the water, though the beach was always just as crowded, often with tourists. This year we were too great in number to allow for everyone to board the pontoon; Dodge, Ellen, Mom and Gran were joined by Liz, Wordo, Ruthie, and the triplets. Jo was faking a headache and didn't seem to notice that Camille had disappeared with Noah Utley. Justin and I took Tish, Clint, and Liam with us on the motor boat. Justin's boat was one he'd purchased for a song and subsequently fixed up good as new, a snazzy Siemens outboard he mainly used for fishing. But it could certainly drag water skiers and got my son all excited with visions of surpassing forty miles an hour on the water.

I always loved the rebel spirit that seemed to permeate the air on the Fourth. Justin picked us up on the end of the dock at dusk, Flickertail alive and glowing with watercraft of all kinds; colored lanterns and lightbulbs indicating port and starboard bobbing from boat decks like misplaced red and green Christmas lights. People shouted and laughed, drinking beer and soda; most of the pontoons were equipped with grills, which sent the spicy aroma of roasting meat dancing across the water. Small fireworks burst in crackling, sparkling arrays from every direction, snaps and sharp bangs bouncing almost visibly. The kids were literally jumping with excitement; Tish and Clint leaped into the boat behind Justin, while gentlemanly Liam lent me an arm before boarding.

"Wow, can we light these off?" my son demanded, on his knees and rooting like a puppy through the cardboard box containing Justin's stash of fireworks. Clint's voice cracked as he yelped, "Roman candles! *Sweet!*"

Justin laughed, catching me in a hug and kissing me on the lips, but discreetly. It was enough to send my heart cartwheeling, his scent and taste and presence filled me with such buoyancy. He smiled into my eyes, his hair all wild from driving the boat over, his shoulders so broad and strong in his t-shirt. Over that he wore an unzipped white hoodie, along with his orange swimming trunks; his feet were bare, as were mine, and I curled my toes against the forest-green outdoor carpet beneath them.

The boys freaked out over the box of goodies; Tish grabbed a package of sparklers and asked, "Aunt Jilly, do you have your lighter?"

Justin tossed one to her and then reclaimed the steering wheel, calling to the kids, "Here we go, guys, hang on." The motor growled as he backed out and eased the bow around, before revving it a little, taking us left and out onto the lake. I sat in the front seat to the left of Justin, curling up my legs and wrapping both arms around them, drinking in the marvelous view as we left behind the dock. The air out here was chilly; I'd worn cut-offs and a bright red t-shirt and just as I considered grabbing the sweatshirt I'd brought, Justin said, "Here, baby," and immediately shrugged out of his own. I snuggled into its delicious warmth, the kids laughing and chattering behind us, their voices carrying along in the wind created by our rapid movement. They lit sparklers, in the light of which their excited faces glinted gold and magenta. I curved my shoulders and drew up the neck of Justin's sweatshirt, just to better inhale the scent of him clinging to the soft cloth.

He angled me a grin and gripped my right knee in one hand. Moments later he slowed the boat to a crawl, piloting around dozens of other boats. The mood was pure circus under the darkening sky, where streaks of violet-tinted clouds drifted along the western edge of the world, a pale yellow in the last of the sunset. Stars were beginning to glint, spangling the sky with diamonds, and I thought for a moment of my dream and the green star I cupped in my hands. I slid my palm over Justin's hand on my leg, and he flipped it over to thread his fingers through mine, his hand so warm and strong, holding me tightly.

"There's everybody!" Clint yelped, pointing his sparkler like a magic wand, and we caught sight of the pontoon. Justin effortlessly maneuvered the boat to them, where he killed the engine and Dodge tossed a lead rope over, which Justin expertly knotted around the railing, keeping us tethered together. He was so good at so many things, so capable. That in itself was so totally sexy. Good with his hands—and now I knew for a fact how very true that was; my cheeks kindled at just the thought. Ten feet away, on the deck of the pontoon, the womenfolk passed out chips and hot dog buns, sodas and plastic forks. Gran, a blanket drawn over her knees and her floppy-brimmed straw hat on her head, sat in a lawn chair holding her yellow can coolie; she blew us a kiss. Dodge manned the grill, joking with his son-in-law, Wordo, who was busy lighting sparklers as fast as the kids burned them out. A radio from someone's nearby boat played the local country station out of Bemidji.

"Hey, guys!" Liz called, grinning, waving at us with her free hand, the other clutching a beer bottle. I knew just how much she loved her older brother, and worried for him, and that he was happy was probably almost as heartening to her as it was to me. She moved over to the railing nearest us and said, "Jilly, you look beautiful." And then, "Clint, you're getting so damn tall. What in the hell? You're supposed to be a little kid." Liz was pretty and petite, with the same long-lashed, pecan-brown eyes as Justin and a mouth like a sailor.

Without missing a beat, my son said, "Hey, shit happens."

"J.D! This is your fault!" Liz yelped, as everyone laughed.

Over his shoulder Justin added, "Heya, sis."

Tish called, "Grandma, can we please get some hot dogs over here?"

Justin, finished with the knot, grasped my hands and pulled me to my feet, then neatly enfolded me in his arms and sat us back down, this time with me on his lap. He leaned back comfortably into the chair, which curved up like the seat of a car, and fit his arms around my waist. Again I thought I might begin purring. He was so warm behind me; I snuggled against him and linked our fingers over my belly. His chin was just at my temple.

"Jilly, Justin, you two want hot dogs?" Mom called over, smiling our way. She wore a bandana printed with an American flag tied over her braided hair, and red feather earrings. She looked a little like a biker's girlfriend and I suppressed a giggle at the thought.

"No thanks, Joanie," Justin told her, and I agreed. "Maybe later, though."

I was soaked in happiness, drenched in it, and let myself feel that. It had been so long, so very long since I'd felt this way. Truly, maybe never. Justin Daniel Miller, who I'd known my entire life. Whose name I was linking with my own in my thoughts these days—Jillian Rae Miller. *Mr. and Mrs. Justin Miller*. But I was too superstitious for much of that. I couldn't get ahead of myself; I would simply enjoy this moment in time to the depths of my soul. Justin, holding me against him like I was the most precious thing in his world. Feeling his heartbeat against me, remembering how I held him as he sobbed, as he let go of some of the ancient hurt. My heart thumped with pure gladness. I let the excited chatter of the people I loved, both of our families, permeate me as I relaxed against him.

"It's too bad Mom has a headache," Tish said as she fished another soda from the cooler behind the front seats. "That sucks."

I knew for a fact that right now Jo was tangled up in Blythe's arms, with anything but a headache—that had been a total ruse. But I didn't blame her; I understood completely. In a month she was supposed to pack up her girls and head back to Chicago; I was quietly sure she would not make this decision, ever since the night a Notion came to me in a dream, one which I'd kept absolutely to myself. I knew Jo and the girls would stay here, but it would be at the price of my sister's heart breaking. I'd seen that, too. *Dammit.* And I hated the thought of Blythe leaving Landon; I adored him and would miss him. Though I knew my pangs of missing him were nothing compared to the way Jo would feel.

If only...

"Mom, can we let off a Roman candle?" Clint pleaded from the stern of the boat.

"Ask Justin," I said, in the same tone I would have said, *Ask your dad.*

Behind me, Justin said, "Sure, but let me help you."

"No, don't move," I complained, and he kissed the side of my neck.

"I'll be right back," he promised.

The Roman candles were pretty awesome, I had to admit. I curled my legs under myself and laughed with as much delight as the kids as Justin launched the fireworks off the end of the boat, amid the cheers of everyone in the vicinity. Clint and Liam crowded him, getting in the way, but he was patient and let them do some of the fuse lighting. Tish joined me instead, bundled in a hooded sweatshirt that I recognized as one of Jackson's old ones, tucking her arm through mine. It always touched me when Tish showed affection, and I held her arm tightly against my side.

"Justin's so cool," she said. And then, her voice soft and wistful, "I miss my dad."

At that I looked over at my niece; the sky was almost totally dark and the real fireworks would begin any moment. There was still plenty of illumination from lanterns and mini-explosions, and in those tinted lights I studied her with concern. Tish, who looked more like me than Joelle; Tish, who I sometimes pretended was my own daughter. She was hurting, but I didn't want to placate her. For all his failings, Jackie was a good dad, and I knew the girls loved him and couldn't see his faults. And Jo was mature enough to keep her more uncharitable thoughts about Jackson to herself.

"Aw, Tish," I said at last. "He misses you guys, too. I know he does."

"Does he?" she asked, with a cynical edge. "He hasn't come up here like he said he would. And he has a new girlfriend."

"But he still misses you and your sisters," I told her firmly. "No matter what. You know that, right, Tisha?"

She shrugged, but I was heartened when she bent her head to my shoulder for a second. Before she could move, I kissed her temple. With unknowingly perfect timing, Justin looked back at us and called, "Tish, you want to light the last one?"

She beamed and leaped to her feet to do the honors. In the next minute the first low-pitched boom sounded, announcing the beginning of the show. Justin tossed the remnants of the candles into the box, brushed off his hands and left the stern seats to the kids. He rejoined me; I held out my arms and he grinned, his eyes flashing into mine as he swept me into his embrace and tucked me against his chest. The crowd quieted with almost reverent silence, other than the collective *ooohs* and *aaahs*. My happiness was so overpowering that I trembled a little; Justin reached and grabbed a blanket from beneath the seat, swirling it over us and snuggling me close. I kissed his jaw, whispering with passion, "I fucking love you so much."

His chest bounced with a laugh. He whispered back, "I told you I love it when you talk dirty."

"What's your favorite kind of firework? You like those really loud ones that sound like mortar fire, don't you?" I asked, braiding the fingers of our right hands together. With his free hand, Justin stroked the length of my bare thigh, safely hidden beneath the blanket; I shivered more at his touch.

He kissed my hair and said, "Yeah, I like those. And the gold ones that look like weeping willows after they explode. What about you?"

"I like when they try to make a shape. Remember the star from last year?"

"That was pretty cool," he agreed. I lifted my chin as the next one exploded, watching the colors paint his face with green and silver. He lowered his lashes and looked down at me, then tightened his arms around my waist, kissing me with so much feeling that I made an inadvertent sound in my throat and turned in his arms, threading my fingers into his hair. Everyone was looking at the sky; no one paid us any mind in the darkness. But I wouldn't have cared anyway, as the fireworks that mattered most in the world were happening right here, between us.

Chapter Sixteen

"Jillian, you mean to tell me this kid has no behind the wheel experience?" Justin teased, a few weeks later on a lazy Saturday evening after dinner rush. He leaned over the chair to my right; I was busy rolling silverware and Clint, on my left, begged me to take him driving.

"Well, not much," I admitted. "It scares me to let my little baby boy drive."

"Mom!" yelped Clint in protest, his voice racing through an entire octave.

I laughed, shaking my head. "Just kidding. But it does scare me a little. Why, are you offering to take him?" I raised my right eyebrow at Justin, who winked.

"For sure. This kid needs to know how to drive a manual. Shit, I was driving one by eleven."

"And crashing into hardware stores by twelve," I teased, and Clint hee-hawed a laugh while Justin's dark eyes told me he'd like nothing better than to bend me over his knee. I wanted him to bend me over the table, but that would have to wait until later.

"Can we go right now?" Clint begged. "Please?"

Justin said, "As long as it's all right with you, Jilly."

"Of course," I said. "Clint, listen to Justin though. No fooling around."

"Who, me?" Clint wondered aloud.

"He did a great job, actually," Justin told me later as we snuggled in his bed. I'd stayed through the night two times now, but otherwise I felt compelled to return to my own apartment, for Clint's sake. Justin understood; though I longed to stay with him, he dutifully drove me back around the lake every night that I didn't drive Mom's old station wagon. We'd make out like teenagers in his truck in the parking lot, and then again on my landing before finally saying good-night. We had spent just about every free minute with each other in the last month, and sometimes my happiness was so complete that fear nudged at the back of my neck and along my ribs. I knew exactly what Justin meant when he told me he couldn't count on anything anymore, but I forced myself not to dwell on those kinds of thoughts.

"And he listened to you?" I asked.

"He's so polite," Justin marveled. "I was such a shit at that age, so mouthy to Dad. And I would bet that you never so much as laid a hand on Clint when he was naughty."

"No, but he's never really been naughty," I admitted. "It's like he sensed that I had a rougher time because his dad was gone and didn't give me trouble." Justin's arms tightened around me. I went on, softly, "I'm not feeling sorry for myself, truly. Moving back in with Mom and Ellen and Gran was the best thing I could have done. They helped me so much. It wasn't like I was ever truly alone."

"But you were hurting so bad," Justin said, his voice just above a whisper. "I remember those days. I remember how you looked that first summer, Jilly. It was heartbreaking."

"But you were there and you made me laugh, brought me back to life," I reminded him.

"I'm so glad I helped you, even indirectly. I would have done more, so much more. Oh God, Jilly, I wanted to so bad. I thought about you all the time, but I couldn't dare acknowledge it, hardly even to myself."

"You were married," I whispered, lifting to one elbow to better see his eyes. He stroked my cheekbone with the pad of his thumb, his expression one of absolute tenderness.

"But I still longed for you," he said, soft and husky. "I would catch myself watching you, worrying over you. You and Clint would be at the co-op, or you'd be at the cafe, and I'd have to bite down on the urge to get your attention. I tried to be your friend…I wanted that, but I wanted so much more. And there would be times when I'd catch you looking back at me…like you felt it, too, but didn't know how to express it, either. And then I'd feel guilty as hell."

"Oh, sweetheart," I whispered. "You're right. I did look at you, and long for you. Like crazy I longed for you, and I felt so guilty because I knew I had no right to want those things. Even if I never liked Aubrey…"

I could hear the humor in his tone as he said, "Yeah, I finally understood that."

"It wasn't my place to say anything," I said, latching one leg over both of his, possessively. "But she was *so* wrong for you. Dodge knew it, too. Did he ever tell you he felt that way?"

Justin nodded, hooking my knee in his hand and drawing it higher up his body, to his hip. He ran his palm gently over my thigh, up and down, skimming my skin. "Yeah, he told me before I even married her. But I was so young. I thought I loved her. I couldn't see past her face, not back then. It's shameful, is what it is. It took me almost as long to admit what a shallow person she is."

I smiled a little, voicing my uncharitable thought as I said, "It's almost like her and Jackie should have been a couple in high school."

Amusement rolled over his face as he nodded agreement, saying, "They're very much alike, that's God's truth."

"Gran never liked Jackie," I remembered. I took Justin's chin between my fingers and caressed it with my thumb, delighting in the feel of his skin, so completely besotted with him. I said, teasing with my tone, "Now *you*, she always liked. Great-Aunt Minnie, too, the both of them absolutely loved you."

Justin's smile became a grin. "That's about the best endorsement a man could get." He smoothed both hands around my ass and hauled me closer. He said, suddenly no longer teasing, "You know, I remember Minnie telling me something once. Shit, it was ages ago. I was probably about eight or nine." He looked up at the ceiling, back into time, his face growing even more animated as he recalled. "Liz and me were at Shore

Leave with Dad, and I had been fishing and ran back up to the cafe for a glass of water, or something…" His eyes came back to mine, and wonderment was in his voice. "I swear I haven't thought of this since the day it happened, Jills…"

I felt a strange chill, a momentary pressure on my spine. I could have sworn that a hand other than Justin's just touched my flesh. I whispered, "What did she say?" That Minnie spoke of a Notion to Justin, for certainly that was what it had been, all those years ago, was of great importance to me. I needed to know what she'd told him—what she'd seen. With an edge of desperation that I tried hard to control, I repeated, "What was it?"

Justin saw my agitation. He knew something of Great-Aunt Minnie's abilities, as talk always occurred among the Landon locals; I'd only just begun to tell him more. He shifted and brought me more fully into his arms, turning us to the side so that I was sheltered protectively against his chest. He kissed my nose and assured, "It wasn't bad, sweetheart. In fact, I think she meant it as a good thing. She said, 'There's a storm, boy, but you'll weather it.' Wow, it's all coming back to me like it happened yesterday."

I drew a slow breath and held it, wishing for the countless time since she'd passed that I could talk to my great-aunt. Justin's remembrance of these words didn't scare me as I'd feared they might—he was right, Minnie's statement came across as fairly optimistic. I speculated quietly, "Do you think she meant the accident?"

He nodded, catching my hand into his and kissing my palm, then laying it against his scars. Tenderness moved through me as swiftly as my blood—and love, endlessly my love flowed for him. As much as I knew he craved my touch, he had never purposely put my fingers on the evidence of the accident. It was a sweet, outward expression of his trust in me.

"Justin," I whispered.

"She knew," he said.

I thought of Minnie telling me that I would be all right. She had known that, too.

"There is so much I wish I could have asked her before she died," I whispered. "Minnie knew so many things. She was so wise. There are so many stories I don't know."

"In your family?" Justin asked, keeping his hand atop mine, twining our fingers.

I nodded. "There was supposedly a Davis ancestor who used to be a prostitute. A saloon girl! Minnie insisted," I said, at Justin's surprised laugh. "But I don't know anything more. And Minnie and Gran's grandma had some terrible sadness associated with her...but I don't know anything else about her."

"I'm still stuck on the saloon girl bit," Justin teased, tickling me now. I squirmed and giggled, and he rolled me beneath him to nuzzle my neck. "That's kinda sexy. Those corset get-ups they wear in western movies, and all that..."

"*Men*," I chastised, maneuvering so that I could get my fingertip into his belly button, which drove him insane. I reached my destination, and he yelped and pinned me to the mattress; we were unable to keep from grinning at each other.

"So what do you want for your birthday?" Justin asked. "It's coming up in a few weeks here."

"Just you," I whispered.

"You've got me," he assured, kissing away a tear as it rolled over my temple. He said, "I mean something you don't have already."

"Clinty was just asking me about what I wanted, too," I said, luxuriating in the strength of his body against mine. "I honestly have everything I want."

"Jilly, quit with that. You get spoiled on your birthday in my book."

"I think I did give you extra coffee on yours," I said, curling a hank of his thick hair around my index finger. "But that was back in May, when I was so attracted to you I could hardly be near you."

"Oh, really?" he asked, brows lifting; his lips curved into a satisfied grin even as he confessed, "Same goes for me, with you."

"That morning you stretched right in front of me when you were sitting at the counter. That was just cruel," I complained, reaching to glide my hands over the firm bulges and valleys of his powerful biceps, just because I could. I shivered again, with delight.

Justin snorted a laugh, saying, "Yes, I've always thought of myself as a cruel man."

"You are," I insisted. "With your work shirt that's always unbuttoned and showing your chest hair. It drives me crazy..."

He laughed in earnest at this statement, rolling from atop me. I poked his ribs, which made him grab for my tickling hands. "My ch... chest hair?" he managed to gasp, catching both my hands before I lit into his sides again.

"It's *sexy*," I informed him, wrestling to free my wrists from his iron grip. He used his considerable size advantage and pinned me again upon the mattress.

"Well, I'm glad you think so," he said, and his shoulders shook with laughter. "God knows I have plenty."

"I love it," I said, glaring up at him, pretending to be angry at his teasing. "Now let me up!"

He shook his head wordlessly.

"I mean it," I said, squirming to free myself, hampered by my breathless giggles. "I can't breathe!"

"Oh, that's the oldest trick in the book," he said, keeping my wrists held out to the sides, one leg braced over both of mine. "No way am I falling for that."

"You are in trouble," I pronounced; though my efforts were clearly futile, I still struggled.

"I'm not the one flat on my back," he said, then laughed again at my expression.

"Justin Daniel Miller," I threatened. "I will...withhold sex from you!"

In response he secured my wrists even more firmly before bending down and kissing my neck, softly, the kind of tender kiss that caused shivers to flutter all along my belly.

"I will not...fall for that," I whispered, but his eyes were both amused and confident. Slowly he kissed the other side of my neck, warm and sensual.

Willpower, Jillian, I told myself.

But I was no match.

He exhaled against my skin and kissed my lower lip, softly as a passing feather. A butterfly's wing grazing my mouth. My nipples swelled hard as gemstones against his bare chest and I arched upward, making a small sound in my throat. He grinned lazily and then fell for my trap, releasing my wrists to cup my breasts in both hands. As he freed me I twisted to the side and shimmied away, shrieking and laughing as he lunged and caught me around the waist, the sheet hampering my escape.

"Nice try," he murmured, this time pinning me flat on my belly with his weight, forearms braced around my shoulders. He bit my shoulder and ordered, "Now, tell me what you want for your birthday and I'll let you up."

"I'll scream!"

He laughed heartlessly. "No one to hear you," he whispered, and kissed my back, tracing his stubbled chin between my shoulder blades. I felt feverish, trembling and heated, as he stroked along my thighs, easing them apart.

"Too bad you're holding out on me," he murmured against the nape of my neck, caressing in earnest.

"Don't stop," I demanded breathlessly, curling my fingers around the sheets. "Oh my God, Justin, don't stop."

He smiled against my skin and muttered, "I wasn't planning to, baby. Now come here."

Much later we lay tangled in languid satisfaction—when, like a bucket of ice water upended over the bed, a vision of Joelle struck at me. It was so sudden that I muffled a gasp, both hands flying to my forehead as if to stop something tangible from leaping forth and into existence.

"Jilly, what's wrong?" Justin demanded, real fear rife in his voice. He sat up at once, running both hands frantically over me in the darkness, as if checking for damage.

"It's Jo," I said, with certainty, as a picture of her weeping ripped through my mind.

"Jesus, you scared me," he said, exhaling in a rush. "I had a dream you were hurt the other night, and it scared the shit out of me; I didn't remember it until just now—"

"I'm fine," I assured him, sitting up and getting my arms about his waist, pressing close; I could feel the urgent pounding of his heart against my right cheek. Justin had known about my ability to sense things since we were kids, but he'd never actually witnessed me experience it. Worry continued to flow from him and I said again, "I'm just fine, sweetheart, I promise. But Jo needs me right now."

"Blythe, you think?" Justin asked quietly. I had told him all about my sister and Bly, even though nearly everyone who'd attended the Fourth of July Eve party at Shore Leave probably had a good idea, too; Jo wasn't exactly keeping their relationship under wraps these days. But tonight something had changed.

The curse, I thought, without intending, and shivered violently.

Stop it. There is no goddamn curse!

"Jillian," he said, concerned anew, having felt me shiver. "I don't want you to leave."

I clung to him, finally insisting in a whisper, "I don't want to leave, but she needs me."

I dressed quickly while Justin pulled on his jeans and shrugged back into his t-shirt. At the cafe ten minutes later, Justin held me close in the cab of his truck and asked, "Should I stay? I worry about you out here all alone."

The last thing I wanted was for him to go back home without me. Joelle wasn't here yet, I could sense immediately, but she would be soon. And she needed me. I tipped my face against Justin's neck and inhaled. Eyes closed, I murmured, "I'm just going to wait for her on the dock."

"I know, but you're mine and I worry about everything," he said against my hair. "What if you fall asleep down there and get kidnapped?"

At that I did giggle, knowing he was half-kidding. I teased, "By a pirate ship that pulls up to the dock? Or maybe the mosquitoes?"

He laughed a little, too, but said, "Not funny. Call me later, all right? I don't care how late."

I stood in the parking lot and watched his taillights head back around

the lake, sensing his reluctance. But he understood. And my sister needed me right now. Or would, very shortly; no more than twenty minutes
later I sat smoking my third cigarette (after appropriating the pack on
the windowsill) when I heard Blythe's truck pull into the lot, just up the
incline from the dock. I tensed, waiting, but heard nothing other than
the quiet click of a truck door closing; a minute later Jo was alone, walking out onto the dock where she knew I would be, as Bly drove slowly
away. I turned to her and said without preamble, "I'm sorry, Joelle, I am
so sorry."

"Oh, Jill," she moaned, sinking to the glider beside me, her voice ravaged by tears. Immediately she bent forward and hid her face, sobbing
wretchedly.

I had known this would happen. I wanted to ask for details but wisely
kept my mouth shut, rubbing her back and projecting my love for her
into my touch. She kept repeating, her voice cracked and choked, "I love
him, Jillian, I love him so much."

But again I remained silent, letting her cry, letting her know I'd be
here, no matter what.

Chapter Seventeen

August, 2003

"Aunt Jilly, you have a minute?"

I set aside the list I'd been making, at once, reaching a hand to beckon my niece closer. I said, "Of course, honey. More than a minute, in fact."

Camille joined me in the booth, sliding gracefully over the smooth vinyl, sighing even as she settled her elbows upon the familiar old plastic-covered tabletop, lacing her fingers the way kids did in elementary school. She'd twisted her walnut-brown curls into a loose knot in the August heat, strands drifting gracefully along her neck. Camille had always reminded me of a girl from one of those old-time, sepia-tinted photos; the word *fetching* was a perfect descriptor for her. And it tugged my heart to catch glimpses of Joelle so clearly in her face, the same delicate contours of chin and nose, long-lashed eyes of rich golden-green, those Davis family eyes. I also saw hints of Jackson—the olive tone of Camille's skin, her dark, wavy hair. Her mouth was Jackie's, too, with the same curve like that of a plump willow leaf.

And now she was pregnant with Noah Utley's child—and had not seen nor heard from Noah in the past month.

"I know it's yours and Mom's birthday party tonight and I don't mean to make this about me," Camille began, lifting her thumbnail as though to chew it, then thinking better and re-lacing her fingers.

"Milla," I said as sternly as I was able; her rueful, half-anxious gaze held mine, her shoulders curling inward in defense. I added quickly,

"Don't apologize. I'm here for you, anytime. Birthday, Christmas, Valentine's…President's Day…what have you."

A reluctant smile tugged at her mouth. I waited patiently, with no further prompting. At last she said as though thinking aloud, "I feel like you can see right into my thoughts."

"I used to think that about Great-Aunt Minnie," I admitted. "The secret is that I'm just really observant."

"But you know things, it's not just about being observant," she insisted. She leaned slightly away, cupping her belly as she whispered, "Like how she's a girl."

I smiled at these words, nodding agreement; her child was indeed a girl, and a beat of love for the unborn baby nudged at my heart. I was gladdened to see the flush of pride bloom along my niece's cheekbones.

"I know it, too," she whispered, with unmistakable reverence.

"Have you dreamed about her yet?"

"Not yet, but I can't wait."

"Soon," I predicted. "Once she starts moving around and you can feel her, she'll visit you in your dreams."

"I love her already," Camille declared, with quiet passion. Tears splashed her cheeks and I clenched my jaw to keep from offering comfort, which I knew she did not seek or wish for, not just now; she hated feeling as though anyone pitied her. She continued in a painful rush, "It just hurts so much, Aunt Jilly, that *Noah* doesn't love her. He doesn't know she's a girl…he wouldn't care, anyway…"

Her throat closed off and she bit down on her lower lip, savagely.

"He's scared," I said. "I'm not making excuses for the little prick, I swear, but he's scared out of his mind."

"Like I'm not?" she demanded in a hoarse whisper. The cafe was late-afternoon quiet, but even still Camille's gaze skittered around the dining room as though expecting someone to be listening to us. Sunbeams filtered through the leaves outside and painted wavering lacy patterns over the table, breaking at right angles before spilling golden to the floor. We could hear Gran and Ruthie back in the kitchen, Gran mixing up cake batter, explaining her methods to Ruthann.

"That's not my point," I said, considering my next words with care. "But women deal with their fear of pregnancy a little differently, if not to say worlds better. For one thing, it's not like you can outrun it."

Camille scrubbed at the tears on her face. Her belly remained flat— no one could tell by looking that she carried a child; she just appeared curvier than usual. She finally said, "I don't want to come to the party tonight." She paused before confessing, "I'm worried Mom will be mad. Will you talk to her?"

"I will," I said. "But I think you should come, honey."

"I just can't face everyone," she admitted. "It sounds exhausting." Her chest rose with a sigh as she said, "And Tish told me Mom was thinking of inviting our neighbor, the one who stares at me like he has no manners whatsoever…"

"Jake McCall," I recognized at once. I said gently, "It's just because the poor guy has a monster-sized crush on you."

Camille all but cringed at my words. She said with sarcastic gravel in her tone, "That's just great. He *knows* that I'm pregnant, thanks to Tish's gigantic mouth. But he still likes me, it's like nothing deters him. God, Aunt Jilly, it's probably just because he thinks I'm easy."

"Camille," I groaned, releasing a laugh that had more to do with shock than any kind of humor. I reached over the table to grasp her fidgeting hands. Squeezing them in mine, I said, "I've met Jake plenty of times and he is not that type, not one bit. He likes you because you're *you*, no other reason. You're pretty likeable, you know."

"Like any guy my age wants to date a girl with a baby," Camille muttered bitterly. "And besides, everyone *else* thinks I'm easy."

"Has anyone said that to you?" I demanded, anger streaking my chest. I knew from talking to Jo that Camille suspected this sort of cruel gossip.

"No one directly to my face," Camille admitted. "But all the girls I hung out with earlier this summer won't call me and don't come out to Shore Leave. And Clinty told me this one girl in particular, Mandy Pearson, was telling people that I'm some…*slut* from Chicago." She spit out the word like a mouthful of spoiled milk.

"Mandy used to date Noah, I think," I said, riffling through the local gossip stored in my memory. "And that would explain her saying that sort of bullshit thing. She's jealous as hell."

"But what if people believe her?" Camille asked, almost a moan. "What if people think that about me? It's so untrue. I'd never even had sex before Noah, not with anyone. I'd barely even gotten to second base, Aunt Jilly." More tears now, gushing her face, dripping from her chin. She begged, "Oh God, please don't let Mom make me go to Landon High. I'll do anything."

My heart seized anew at the sincerity of her impassioned words. I said, "Camille. Listen to me." When she didn't seem inclined to do so, I lowered my chin and fixed my gaze on her, this time really attempting to peer into her thoughts. I said, "You aren't thinking clearly right now, I promise. It's the stress, and the hormones, and the shock of it all. We all hate Noah for ditching out, for being such a goddamn coward. But we're here, all of us. And we'll help you take it a day at a time. There isn't any other way, honey."

"That's what Mom said," she admitted, dabbing at the wetness on her face with a napkin she plucked from the holder situated beneath the window. She whispered, "Oh, Aunt Jilly, it's so hard."

"I know," I said, wanting to get up and hug her close, even knowing she would not allow it. Her eyes were heartbreaking in that instant, bereft and lonely, despite my assurance that we were here for her, unequivocally. And I could not help but think again, a sinister whisper in the back of my mind, of the curse. The Davis women were cursed to lose the men they loved.

I squared my shoulders against such terrible thoughts and said on inspiration, "Hey, the Carters are going to be out here tonight. Bull will talk your ear off about history, especially once he gets into the keg." Camille had been dying to get over to White Oaks Lodge earlier this summer, a lovely local establishment just around Flickertail, with a wealth of history associated with its builders. It was still owned by the Carter family, whose ancestors had constructed the original structure back in the nineteenth century.

Camille closed her eyes and drew a breath through her nose. Then she opened her eyes and directed her wistful gaze over the lake. Seeing somewhere well beyond the far edge of Flickertail, she murmured, "That's all gone now, Aunt Jilly, don't you see? I'll never be a history teacher now. I'll never do anything I meant to."

"That is not true," I disagreed. "Not one bit. In fact, that's a shitty attitude and not like you at all." I meant to shock her a little with my words, concerned at the hopelessness in her tone.

Her lips twisted as she whispered, "I don't know what I'm like anymore."

Before I could reply, Ruthann appeared from the pass-through door, beaming at us as she dashed across the dining room carrying a beater from Gran's electric mixer.

"You have to try some!" Ruthie enthused as she reached us, offering her prize—the beater, thickly coated with Gran's delectable chocolate frosting. "It's for the cake."

Camille swallowed away her bitter words and managed a smile for her littlest sister. She said, "Hey, thanks. This looks delicious."

Taking advantage of her full mouth, I said firmly, "And I want you to show up tonight. It wouldn't be a party without you."

I found Gran back in the kitchen a minute later, the entire cafe permeated by the scent of the chocolate cake that was now baking in all its glory. She gave me a grin and allowed me to snag a fingertip of the decadent, creamy concoction in the ancient yellow bowl used for frosting-making for all of my life.

"Ruthie said it was done," I admitted, stealing a second taste.

"You excited for tonight, doll?" Gran asked.

"Of course," I replied. "It's been a long time since Jo and I have had a birthday party like this."

"It's so good to see you so darn happy," Gran observed, and I leaned over onto my elbows and smiled into my grandma's familiar golden-green eyes.

"I am," I said, though I was usually the last person to make such bold statements; at some level they scared me too much, as though to speak aloud your good fortune was just begging for it to be snatched away. But for this moment, in the warm kitchen where I had spent at least half of my life, I allowed myself to acknowledge that I was happy.

"When Great-Aunt Minnie told me I'd be all right all those years ago, did she mean about Chris?" I asked softly, thinking of what Justin and I had talked about a few weeks ago. Each of us, Justin and me, had weathered a storm in our own way; it took those storms for us to reach each other. I understood that now, and I could never be grateful enough.

Gran pursed her lips and I could almost see the play of her thoughts, back through time. Finally she said, "I don't honestly know. Minnie told me some things and kept others entirely to herself. She knew it was too much a burden for most people to bear. I don't know how she did it. Or how you do it, doll. The Notions strike you hard sometimes, don't they?"

I nodded, and then tried to explain, "But not the way you make it seem. I can't imagine *not* having them. Minnie used to tell me that I would never see more than I could handle."

"Have you ever?" Gran regarded me somberly.

"No...but there've been times when it deserted me, and I didn't know why. Like with Christopher," I whispered.

"It's because Justin has been for you all along," Gran said, her voice likewise soft. "That's why."

I felt tears spring into my eyes at the truth of these words. It was on the tip of my tongue to ask Gran about the curse—even though I never spoke of it—but my conversation with Camille burned in my mind. But Gran spoke before I could, snapping, "Now, you go and get yourself fixed up, honey. I've gotta finish this cake before you eat all of the frosting," all traces of sentimentality vanishing.

Despite the fact that affection normally got Gran all bristly, I said, "I love you, Gran. With all my heart."

"I love you, too, fool girl. Now get!"

By evening's light, Shore Leave was transformed into a birthday wonderland. The air was beautiful, clear and crisp with approaching autumn.

The lake gleamed indigo, glass-smooth as dusk advanced, the yard decorated with lanterns and Christmas lights, the picnic tables laden with food, the cake taking center stage, a gooey chocolate masterpiece. Eddie Sorensen and Jim Olson were busy playing up a storm with their guitar-and-banjo combo as usual, and everyone was laughing and dancing, even Jo. I was glad to see my sister smiling; I knew she'd been unable to talk to Blythe for at least a week. But I felt a rush of relief as I observed her dancing with Dodge.

Justin had been giddy with excitement all evening, like a little boy with a secret. No matter how much I pestered and teased and threatened, he wouldn't tell me what was up his sleeve. Clint was likewise smiley and kept shooting little looks my way. I'd been in Justin's arms all evening; he'd braved the dance floor since the music began. When Dodge came to cut in, he teased, "Sorry, she's taken," to which Dodge responded by simply wrapping his arms around both of us and proceeding to waltz us in circles.

Clinty came to dance with me after the cake pictures, and I marveled anew at my sweet, handsome son. One of the younger Henry girls had been shyly trying to get his attention, all evening. Her name was Claire and she'd been in Clinty's class since kindergarten. Clint, however, was apparently oblivious to these attempts.

"Happy birthday, Mom," he said, grinning down at me.

"Thanks, sweetie," I said, and poked him in the ribs. I demanded, "Hey, what's Justin's secret tonight?"

Clint's blue eyes glinted and he said, "Oh, no. It's a secret for a *reason*, Mom."

"You know? Tell me!" I nagged, but he only shook his head, grinning.

"There's a girl with her eye on you," I couldn't help but tease, and giggled to observe my son's eyebrows lift and jaw all but drop. He became instantly wary, looking around the crowd as though she was a spy, or perhaps armed.

"Nuh-*uh*," he disagreed. His voice cracked as he demanded, "Who?"

"Oh, no," I responded gaily. "That you've got to figure out on your own. Unless you tell me a secret…"

Clint yelped, "I can't believe I almost fell for that!"

The music ended and Clinty ran off to grab Liam in a headlock and speculate who might possibly be checking him out. I navigated my way through the crowd, extremely pleased to notice Camille—who braved attending the party—engrossed in conversation with Bull and Diana Carter, sitting with them near the fire. Bull was Dodge's cousin and a complete chatterbox, the type to put anyone at ease because all that was required was good listening—he'd talk until he was blue in the face, especially when the conversation encompassed his favorite topic—his family and their importance to the history of the area. I grinned at my niece as she caught my eye, offering me a little wave and a sincere smile.

I found Justin sitting with his Wordo, his dad, and a couple of other husbands reluctant to dance, all of them holding beer bottles and paper plates of cake.

"Here, sweetheart, I've got room," Justin said, angling his knee for me to perch upon, which I did, swiping my finger through his frosting. He hooked one arm around my waist, his beer bottle near my hip. I appropriated it for a sip.

"Happy birthday, little Jilly," Wordo said, grinning widely. "Has Justin given you your birthday spankings yet?"

"Not yet," I replied primly, stealing more frosting while Justin grinned devilishly at me at the mere mention of spankings of any kind, and Dodge whooped with laughter. I added, "He hasn't even given me my present yet."

"Soon," Justin promised.

"You'll love it," Wordo said, full of excitement. "You shoulda heard Liz—" But his words were abruptly cut off as Justin smacked his brother-in-law on the shoulder.

"Don't give it away!" Justin yelped, and Wordo shrugged apologetically and rejoined the conversation in progress; Dodge was in the middle of a fishing story, go figure.

"How soon?" I pestered, resting my hands on Justin's broad chest, then sliding my palms deliberately over his ribs. His hands were full and I said smugly, "I'll tickle the shit out of you."

His eyes crinkled at the corners as he grinned at me. He bent forward and murmured into my ear, "As soon as we can sneak out of here, baby."

For good measure I did tickle him then.

A half an hour later the party had that low-key, end-of-the-evening feel. Eddie was still plunking out slow melodies on his guitar; a handful of couples remained on the dance floor, swaying gently to the music. Gran and a few of her friends lingered over last pieces of cake and coffee, situated comfortably on the porch. My son and my nieces, and about ten other kids, lounged around the leaping flames in the fire pit, laughing and joking. Jo had disappeared, probably to try to call Rich; he was due to bring Blythe home from his thirty-day stint in jail back in Oklahoma, as early as tomorrow. I remained on Justin's lap; he'd set aside both his beer bottle and cake plate and tucked me close as we murmured to each other. When Dodge got up to go and mess with the fire, I tipped my nose against Justin's jaw and whispered, "Let's go," and he nodded adamant agreement.

No one seemed to be paying close attention as we skirted the edge of the activity. In his bedroom ten minutes later he clicked on the lamp. I sensed the nervous energy holding him taut in its grip, waiting for him to speak. He said softly, "Jillian," and his eyes were almost fierce, as he looked down at me. Then with one smooth motion, he dropped to his right knee, taking my left hand into his, pressing it to his lips and then holding it to his cheek. He said with quiet passion, "Jillian Rae Davis, I want you to be my wife. I want to hold you close to me every night of my life. I want to kiss your sweet mouth and I want to hear you tell me you love me. I want you to tell me what you dream at night and I want to make you laugh, and feel your hands on me. I need you, Jilly, and I love you like I've never loved anyone before. I want to be there for you, always."

Joy blossomed outward from my heart, sending tears over my face. I cupped his jaw, smoothing my fingers over his warm, scarred skin. Somehow I'd known this was my birthday present, all along. I whispered, "Yes. Oh, Justin, *yes*."

His answering smile took my breath away. He said, "Wait, I have a ring, sweetheart, I almost forgot," and reached into his pocket, presenting not a ring box but the ring itself, held carefully between his index finger and thumb. His dark eyes were tender as he kissed my left hand and then slipped the band over my third finger. Tears clouded my vision and I dropped to my knees to be closer to him. He whispered, "Do you like it?"

I inspected the golden band he'd placed on my hand. It was beautiful, slim and delicate, with a round solitaire sparkling in the copper glint of the lamplight. I whispered, "Of course I love it. It fits perfectly."

"I asked Joan and Ellen for your ring size," he explained, thumbing away my tears and then kissing my cheeks, first one and then the other, with infinite gentleness. "I asked them, and Louisa, and Clint all for permission to marry you, just so you know, which they gave. And we can set the date for whenever you want. Like this weekend. Outside, at the cafe, if you want. At sunset, maybe?"

I giggled a little despite the depth of my emotion, getting my arms around his neck. I explained, "I'm supposed to be the mind-reader, not you."

Justin kissed me, then teased, "Don't be too sure I don't have a few powers in that department, baby."

"You've had this in your pocket all evening?" I marveled, again inspecting my ring at close range. "You sweetheart."

"I checked that it was there about a hundred times," he said. "But I didn't want to leave it here. I couldn't wait to get it on your finger. I almost asked you at the party, but I thought you might prefer a little privacy."

I said, "You could have asked me anywhere. This is the most beautiful birthday present I've ever gotten. Oh, Justin, I love you." I kissed his chin, his jaw, ending on his lips. "I love you so much. You don't even know."

"I know," he assured me. "I know every second."

With a smooth motion, he scooped me into his arms and placed me on the bed. Poised above me, he marveled, "We're engaged."

I smiled at him with every ounce of my considerable happiness. I said, "Next weekend, right?"

"Hell yes, baby."

I teased, "Shit, we better hold off until the wedding night then. You know, out of propriety."

Justin played along, saying, "Yeah, that's a good idea, sweetheart. Propriety." He traced my bottom lip lightly with his thumb, then kissed me deeply, busying himself sliding the straps of my dress over both shoulders and down my body, murmuring, "What was that you were saying?"

"Next weekend…" I muttered, busy unbuttoning and unzipping his jeans, yanking them down. "Don't listen to me. I only fantasize day and night about you kissing me…and touching me…"

"And making you cry out my name, don't forget that," Justin added, grinning at me, and I squeaked a little in protest, even knowing it was true. He laughed, skimming off my panties and tossing them across the room before shifting fluidly and settling me astride him. I rocked my hips and straddled his hard length; his resultant gasp made me grin wickedly.

"We'll see who's crying out what," I challenged.

An hour later I was no longer speculating but certain I wouldn't be able to walk tomorrow. The covers were not on the bed. Neither were the pillows. We'd just energetically plowed through about every position I knew and a few I didn't, and I was at present sprawled sideways, my legs tangled with Justin's, his hand curved over the back of my thigh. My hair was plastered to my temples with sweat. I craved water.

He mumbled, "Did I mention that you're my soul mate, Jilly-Anne?"

I giggled, the sound muffled by the mattress; I was too exhausted to pick up my head. I tilted my face and managed to say, "You said something to that effect."

"Never leave me," he ordered, tightening his hand around my leg, and was snoring a second later.

I wiggled over to him and smoothed his hair with my left hand, admiring the sparkle of the ring he placed there. Then I kissed his temple, promising in his ear, "I won't." And then I slept.

Chapter Eighteen

September, 2003

I SAT UP FAST, ON THE EDGE OF PANICKING, KNOWING IN my gut that something was terribly wrong. My fingers shook and I couldn't press the right numbers on my cell phone. Blythe put his hands on my shoulders, steadying me.

"Joelle, what's the matter, sweetheart? What is it?"

I babbled, "Camille just left me a message. It's Jilly. Bly, something's wrong."

Tears already obscured my vision but I saw how my words affected him—fear and concern crossed paths over his face. He took my phone, because it was apparent I was unable, and dialed. Seconds later I heard my mother's voice as she answered, and she was weeping—my heart burst, sending shrapnel through my veins. Gran, my dear grandmother, had died only a few days ago; we were all still reeling from the pain and shock of her passing; but the tears Mom cried right now were for my sister.

Something had happened to Jillian.

Oh God, oh God.

From upstairs came sudden, frantic knocking on the front door. Sitting on the bed beside me, both of us naked, the covers still tucked around our hips, Blythe was asking Mom, "Joan, what's going on?"

Like someone in a horror movie, I couldn't move normally or think straight, as though enclosed in a cage, mired in thick, sticky tar. The knocking upstairs grew ever agitated, and I shook myself together, grabbing my robe from the floor, stumbling up the steps. I unlocked and flung open the door to see my girls standing there; I scanned them with an instant, involuntary inventory, noting that they all appeared physically fine. But they were sobbing and my heart crumpled. Tish pitched into my arms and I sought Camille's eyes, knowing I must remain calm and find out what was happening.

Blythe appeared behind me, clutching my shoulders. He pressed his face to my hair and his voice was harsh with pain as he said, "Jilly's in the hospital, Joelle."

Camille cried, "Mom, they don't...*they don't know*..."

A roaring in my skull. Tish and Ruthie clung to me, sobbing. Camille stood apart, her eyes locked on mine. Her beautiful eyes that were begging me to tell her this wasn't really happening.

"She was in a car accident," Blythe said hoarsely, his huge chest bracketing all three of us, my two younger girls and me. He bear-hugged us, holding securely. "Oh God, Joelle, she's hurt bad. They don't know if she's...if she's..." No one could bear to say it.

This wasn't right, somehow we had all deviated from the correct path, and someone was going to tell me this was nothing more than a stupid fucking joke. I pictured my sister as I'd just seen her, yesterday evening on the porch, sitting on Justin's lap, wrapped in his arms, drinking a root beer float, the two of them planning their wedding. In the intervening hours, how could she have been in a car accident? *What in the fucking hell?*

I found a shred of control and exercised it, demanding, "Girls, what happened?"

Tish and Ruthie drew back, swiping at tears, gulping, and Blythe led them to the couch, where he sat and kept one arm around each. Camille faced me, swallowing hard and finally explaining, "She was driving home from Justin's early this morning and..." My daughter, my oldest, who'd only recently informed me that she was pregnant, heaved a shuddering breath and I put my hands on her shoulders; she felt so slim and slight beneath my palms. She managed, "When she was coming home a truck hit her broadside, on Fisherman's Street. It just happened an hour ago, Mom. Some tourist guy was driving and he called 911, and they took her into Bemidji right away. We all just found out..." And her voice trailed away into a gasping breath.

"Where're Mom and Ellen?" I asked immediately. "And Clint? Oh God, where's Justin?"

"Joan and Ellen are on the way to the hospital, sweetheart, and they've got Clint," Blythe told me from the couch. "Joan said Jillian is in surgery right now. Dodge went to tell Justin just a little bit ago. I'd imagine they'll head there right away."

I could barely ask, but I needed to know, "How bad?"

"She got hit hard," Blythe said, his voice rough. "Her collarbone and ribs are broken...Joan didn't know anything else."

I felt my knees growing weak and reached out to cling to Camille. She caught me around the waist and I hugged her hard, smelling her hair, breathing against her for strength.

Oh God, Jillian. Fight, you have to fight like you've never fought before. We need you so much. You can't possibly even think of leaving us. Oh, dear God.

I sent my sister all of the strength of my silent plea, knowing somehow she'd hear. She had to; there was no other option. My stomach lurched and I knew I needed to act, to move—I could not just stand here or I would lose complete control.

"I'll get dressed and we'll go," I ordered.

Five minutes later we loaded into the Toyota, the girls clinging to each other in the backseat; I clutched Blythe's right hand in both of mine as he steered us onto the highway, and he squeezed me tightly, silently communicating his concern. I knew he longed to tell me that it would be all right, but he didn't dare. We rode in silence to the hospital in Bemidji.

I felt as though I entered into a nightmare as we crossed the hospital parking lot under blinding sun. I saw Dodge's car, and Rich's, but no station wagon.

"Where's Mom?" I whispered, scanning the vehicles.

"Jilly was driving the wagon," Blythe said quietly.

The ancient shitty wagon, which would have offered no protection in a crash. My blood swam with desperate fear as we rode the elevator to the fourth floor at the direction of a nurse. The elevator doors slid open upon a waiting room awash with placid morning sunlight. Despair, however, radiated from everyone within. Mom and Ellen sat on either side of Justin, who was bent over his knees, clutching his head. Their hands were on his back, offering what solace they could. My heart flew into my throat, thinking the worst. But Dodge's big hands caught my shoulders and he pulled me close, saying in my ear, "She's in surgery, Jo, she's alive."

I looked up into his devastated eyes, knowing he'd tell me the truth. The girls flooded to Clint, who was crumpled in a chair near Rich, Clinty leaning against the older man's chest. My girls descended like a flock of maternal birds.

"How is she?" I whispered. I felt like I was choking, but could not clear away the terrible sensation.

Dodge said, "She'll make it, Jo, she has to." But his eyes were scared. He looked back at Justin and whispered painfully, "My boy can't handle this."

"Did you tell him?" I asked, letting Dodge lead me to a chair. He sat near, keeping one arm around me, while Blythe sat on my other side. Between him and Dodge, I felt a measure of security, and I clung to that.

Dodge nodded, his eyes crinkling at the corners as tears flooded. He wiped his eyes roughly, saying, "He thinks it's his fault since he didn't drive her home like he usually does."

"Aw, Justin, dammit," I muttered, aching for him. His passion was intense, I knew from Jillian, but when misdirected it was potentially devastating. Of course he would blame himself.

Somehow the morning passed. Blythe and Rich went to get breakfast for all of us, though only the kids were able to nibble anything. Justin pulled himself together, though the sight of his face just about killed me. He'd been weeping, and appeared haunted, the shadows beneath his eyes heavy and bruise-like. The moment Justin stood up, Clinty went to him, his own eyes red-rimmed and sorrowful. Without a word he curled into Justin's arms and clung. Justin held him tightly, tipping his cheek against Clinty's hair. It was so fatherly, so endearing, that tears filled my eyes yet again.

"I'm here," I heard him murmur to Clinty.

It was late afternoon before a slim, balding doctor spoke to us; Jillian's left shoulder, upper arm, and collarbones were broken. In addition she'd suffered three cracked ribs on her left side, a punctured lung and multiple lacerations. At the moment she was considered in critical condition, heavily sedated and hooked to several life-giving tubes.

"Can we see her?" Mom whispered, holding fast to Ellen's arm. For the first time I realized that today was Wednesday, and that we'd planned to scatter Gran's ashes off the dock.

Oh Gran, what I wouldn't give to have you here now. I miss you so much, we all miss you so much.

I went immediately to Mom's other side and bolstered her, willing myself to stay dry-eyed despite what the doctor just described about my baby sister, my Jilly Bean.

The doctor nodded. "But just for a minute. And not everyone, I'm sorry."

Mom looked to Ellen for guidance and my aunt said decisively, "Joan, you take Jo and Justin with you. And Clint."

I held Mom's elbow to my side as we followed the doctor down a long, sterile hallway, Justin and Clint just behind us. Clinty, sweet boy, clutched Justin's arm like a little kid. The room we entered was on the right, small and containing a single twin bed and a frightening array of electronic machinery. I made an inadvertent sound at the sight of Jillian in among all that medical equipment, so tiny and frail, her eyes closed and a tube protruding from her mouth. Mom's knees sagged but I held her, then reached my arm for my nephew, as Justin went to the bedside and sank to his knees, gripping the metal bars and pressing his forehead against the topmost. Clint cried almost soundlessly and I held him as best I could with one arm, but Mom said, "Clinty, come here, sweetheart."

I moved to stand beside Justin, whose breathing was harsh. I could find no words, so I sent Jilly another telepathic message, forcing myself to examine her pale face, which appeared at present so lifeless that my heart shrank to the size of a pebble. Her long lashes lay like dark petals on her cheeks. I would have given just about anything to see the incredible blue of her irises.

Jillian, Jilly Rae. Don't leave us. Oh God, don't even think of it. Jilly, we love you so much. We need you so much.

Justin lifted his face and his expression was one of a man being tortured to death. With infinite gentleness he touched the edge of Jilly's hand, limp upon the white bed sheet and palm up, her slim, delicate fingers curled slightly inward. Her engagement ring glinted in the light.

"Sweetheart, I'm here," he said, looking intently into her face. Tears washed over his cheeks almost as though he didn't realize. His voice was ragged. "Jillian, I love you. I'm right here. I'll stay right here until you wake up."

Hear him, please hear him, I begged her, letting my fingertips graze the blanket over her leg; so gently, as though she was a baby bird in danger of being crushed. I was reminded uneasily of the cloth that covered Gran just a few days ago when Cal Price, whose family ran the funeral home in Landon, took her away, but I forced that from my mind at once.

"Mr. Henriksen, may we have a moment?" the doctor was asking.

Justin looked up in confusion and I realized—the mental equivalent of a step behind—that the doctor assumed Justin was Jilly's husband. And Jilly's last name was, of course, Henriksen.

Justin nodded wordlessly, caressing Jilly's hair before following the doctor into the hall. Mom and Clint moved to my side, and Mom smoothed the blanket over Jilly's leg as though tucking her in, echoing Justin's words, "Sweetie, we'll be here the whole time."

Clint whispered, "Mom, I love you. Please hear me. Please hear that, Mom. I love you."

"Oh, Clinty, she hears you," I reassured him, concentrating all of my love toward my sister. "She knows."

There seemed to be a small commotion in the hallway. I heard someone say, "He's fainted."

I said, "I'll be right back," and hurried to see what was happening;

sure enough, Justin lay on the floor, though his eyelids fluttered even as a nurse swooped in to take his pulse. He sat up and yanked his hand away. I knelt near him, asking fearfully, "What's—"

"She's pregnant, Jo," Justin said before I could even ask what was wrong. "Jilly's pregnant."

My eyes flew to the doctor's face, and he confirmed, "According to the hCG levels in her blood, probably no more than a few weeks."

"Is the baby alive?" I demanded breathlessly, gripping Justin's forearm.

"There's no reason to think not, despite everything," the doctor said. "We'll be able to tell more in a few days."

Justin would not be moved from Jilly's bedside. He became feral if anyone suggested he go home for a rest, even Dodge. For the next three days Jillian remained unchanged, floating in darkness while we waited. We all took turns sitting with Justin, who talked to her constantly. Blythe and I stayed late each of the nights; Justin's darker side emerged as the sun went down and the bustle of daytime routine in the hospital quieted, and I was so incredibly grateful for Blythe, who took things in stride, and who seemed to know just what to say when Justin grew utterly despondent.

"I can't bear this," Justin said harshly the second night, near one in the morning. He sat with his head in his hands, fingers plunged into his hair. "If anything happens to her I'll fucking die. I will shoot myself."

My heart clenched at the gritty determination in his tone and I couldn't help but admonish, "*Justin*," but Blythe shook his head just slightly at me, hooking a hand over Justin's shoulder and squeezing him.

"God, I love her so much. I have never loved anyone like this," Justin went on, punishing himself, his voice low and ragged, punctuated by harsh breaths. "I should have known that the moment I found happiness I'd get knocked down again, get kicked in the teeth. *Jillian...*"

"Justin," I pleaded, so worried for him, wanting him to stop talking that way; Jilly would hate that he was saying such things. I looked at my little sister, so very still on the bed, begging her to wake up, to be all right. None of us would be able to bear it, but I didn't say that to Justin. I couldn't bear to even think it.

Blythe kept his hand steady and after a moment, from behind his palms, his voice still shaking, Justin whispered, "I'm sorry, don't listen to me. I'm just so goddamn scared…"

"Don't be sorry," Blythe said. "You love her, and she loves you. Remember that night we went to Eddie's and you two played pool? God, if I could have bottled the attraction between you two that night. You should have seen the way Jilly lit up whenever anyone talked about you, back last spring when I first got to Shore Leave. I'd tease her about how much she liked you and she'd get all mad at me."

I turned from the bedside and sent a grateful look at Blythe. I whispered, "I can just imagine."

Justin lifted his face—he looked so exhausted, so depleted, but he managed a small smile. He whispered, "She did?"

Blythe grinned a little, warming to the topic. He said, "I felt like Jilly was my little sister from the first, and we played this game. She pretended not to see how much I'd fallen for Joelle, if I pretended not to notice how much she liked you, Miller. But it was so obvious."

Justin made a harsh sound and said, "I'd give anything to hear her voice right now. I miss her so fucking much."

I moved and hugged him, rubbing his back. He loved my sister and I loved him for that. I whispered, "She'll be all right," attempting to reassure myself, too. "She will, Justin."

Later, in his truck, Blythe held me as I sobbed. We hadn't left the hospital parking lot, and all of the tears that I hadn't allowed to fall in front of Justin now gushed over my face. I clung to my man, my face pressed against his chest. The driver's side window was lowered about two inches, allowing the scent of early morning into the truck.

"I can't handle this, I try to be strong for Justin's sake, but I'm so scared," I choked out. "Blythe, *what if…*"

"Baby, don't," he murmured, interrupting my desperate words, stroking my hair, rocking me side to side. "She's gonna be all right. Justin is just scared, honey."

"But he said…"

"I can't imagine what I'd be feeling if that was you in Jillian's place," Blythe said. He drew back enough to cup my face, gently smoothing my hair and then touching his forehead to mine. "Joelle, I would be feeling all of those same things."

My throat ached, my nose was plugged. I whispered, "I know."

"I can't imagine thinking it would be worth it to go on without you," Blythe went on, his voice soft and deep. "Joelle, I love you with all my heart. You are everything to me. And Jillian is everything to Justin."

I threaded my arms around his neck and hugged him as tightly as I could; only days ago he'd been in Oklahoma, in jail far away from me, and I'd been crazy with missing him. I kissed the cleft in his chin and whispered, "I love you, Blythe Edward Tilson."

"Let's go home, sweetheart," he said. "I want to hold you while we sleep."

Shore Leave was closed for the time being. Saturday evening found me on the porch with my two younger girls. Blythe was making us dinner in the kitchen; through the open window we could hear him as he worked, the radio atop the fridge tuned to the country station we liked. I rocked on the porch swing with Tish and Ruthie tucked against my sides; the three of us watched a magenta sun sink into the orange sky beyond the trees across the street. The sunset was just slightly earlier every night, the air tinged with the first hints of the autumn to come. My feet were bare and I would have been chilly if not for my girls.

"Mama, I can't think about going to school," Ruthie said. Her cheek rested on my right shoulder and I could smell the scent of her shampoo, comfortingly familiar.

"Me, neither, Mom, not at all. Not when Aunt Jilly is in the hospital. You won't make us, will you?" Tish asked.

"You guys," I said, with gentle admonishment. "I understand that you feel that way. But you have to go to school."

"But, Mom…" Tish began, though at that moment Jake McCall, the neighbor boy who would be a senior this year, called over from his porch, "Evening, ladies," conveniently interrupting her.

The girls shifted position to look over at him; he was their friend, a sort of replacement for Clinty, now that we lived away from the cafe and Clint's constant presence. With far less than her usual enthusiasm, Tish called back, "Hey, Jake."

"Everything all right?" he questioned; he was so polite, and seconds later jogged through the dusk, over to our porch, eyebrows lifted with concern.

Tish explained, "Our Aunt Jilly is in the hospital."

Jake sank to sit on the top step, hooking one arm around his bent knees. He said, "I'm so sorry, you guys. Mom said something about her car accident. Is there anything I can do?"

"That's very kind of you," I told him, truly appreciative. I knew he actually meant his words; how many boys his age would even offer?

"We were just saying that we didn't want school to start," Tish added. "Convince Mom not to make us go!"

Jake looked at me and smiled a little, almost shyly. He clarified, "I meant more like bake you a casserole or something. Besides, school will be great. I'm excited for senior year." He wore a Landon Rebels sweatshirt, I suddenly noticed, white with indigo lettering, our school colors.

"Camille isn't excited," Tish tattled. "She doesn't want to go to school any more than we do."

"But only because of the baby," Ruthie chimed in. "And Aunt Jilly."

"Girls," I scolded; we'd been over this, obviously to no avail. I reminded them, "It's your sister's business."

Jake sat in respectful silence, though I knew that he'd already long since been informed about Camille's pregnancy by my big-mouthed younger daughters. I also knew that he harbored a very big crush on my oldest. I didn't have the heart to tell him that Camille thought he was irritating and avoided him whenever possible.

"Dinner in fifteen minutes," Blythe said, coming out the screen door. "Hey, Jake. You want to join us?"

"Sure," Jake said, and I refrained from rolling my eyes, not in the mood for company. But I supposed he would be a good distraction for the girls. He added, "Mom is working tonight. Thanks."

"Why don't you guys go set the table for your mom?" Blythe asked the girls.

"I'll help," Jake said, and scampered after them.

I held out my arms to Blythe and whispered, "Come here."

He grinned at me, despite everything, and sat on the swing, gathering me close against his warm side. I stroked my fingers through his hair. He'd agreed to grow it out again, if for no other reason than me being able to sink my hands into its length. I ran my nails over his scalp, making him shiver, before my hands sank to rest on his wide shoulders. He kissed my forehead, lingering with his lips against my skin.

I whispered, "I missed you so much this summer. You don't know how glad I am that you're here."

"Joelle," he murmured, and kissed me again, this time aiming for my lips. Holding my face in his hands, he said, "I could never be grateful enough for your love. I don't know how I deserve it, but I cherish it. I cherish it and I will never take it for granted, and that you can count on, sweetheart, my sweet woman. I'm so sorry for everything that's happened this week, with Gran, and with Jillian...but please know that I'm here. I am never going anywhere again."

And for that moment I let myself be grateful for everything I did have.

Mom called a few hours later to see if we wanted to drive over to the cafe for some dessert; she said Clint wanted to see the girls and that Camille had been crying on and off all day. I could tell Mom was nearing her wit's end.

"We'll be there in ten minutes," I said. "Should I bring anything?"

"Just yourselves," Mom told me.

I'd been on the extension in our downstairs bedroom; as I came up the steps I could hear Blythe, the girls, and Jake at the kitchen table, playing poker. I studied them with wordless gratitude, glad for Jake's easygoing personality and for giving Tish and Ruthie something else to focus upon. He leaned over on the table opposite Tish, perusing his cards, and again he reminded me of Clint, possessed of the same amiable sincerity. In some ways he filled the void created by Camille's sudden, forced advent into the world of motherhood. Ruthie and Tish floundered in her absence, and Jake was just the big brother they needed. What other seventeen-year-old boy would be willing to play cards with two younger girls and their stepdad on a Saturday evening just before the school year started?

My gaze moved next to Blythe, who sat facing away from me, his huge shoulders curved forward as he too leaned over the table, cards fanned in his big hands. My fingers tingled to touch him and so I did, sliding my arms around his neck and hugging him from behind, resting my chin on his head. He reached with his free hand to curl his fingers around my left wrist. The kids all looked up at me.

"You want to play, Mom?" Tish invited, even though she knew I was terrible at poker; I had far too many tells.

"Grandma wants to know if you guys want dessert at the cafe," I explained. "Jake, you want to join us?"

"Sure, thanks!" he said.

And minutes later we pulled into the parking lot at Shore Leave. The porch lights glimmered for us, beacon-like, mini lighthouses. In times of trouble we gathered. Rich was already there, and Dodge, hanging around table three with Clinty. I could tell Mom and Ellen were trying to keep things as normal as possible, despite the fact that Jilly's absence from the cafe was equivalent to a gaping, jagged-edged hole a meteor might leave behind. The radio in the bar was tuned to the country station, and Mom and Ellen were just dishing out pieces of Clint's favorite cake, yellow with chocolate-fudge frosting. Justin was of course at the hospital; Dodge already told me he was joining him there later tonight.

Camille sat at the counter, dressed in light blue cotton pants and a tattered old AC/DC t-shirt, formerly her dad's, her long hair in a messy knot on the top of her head. She shot me a look of frustration when she noticed that Jake had accompanied us, her eyebrows knitting.

Sorry, I mouthed discreetly, and Camille turned back to the lemonade she was sipping; I noticed that the calendar image of White Oaks Lodge was again in her hands. Jake studied her back with undisguised lovesickness before quickly looking away; he'd been a goner for her since the afternoon they met, despite the fact that she hardly gave him the time of day. But that was something into which I was absolutely *not* getting involved, and so pretended not to notice a thing.

"Kids, join us," Rich welcomed, snuggling Ruthie with one arm as she went at once to his side. Tish and Ruthie claimed chairs, while Blythe and Jake drew two from an adjacent table and Dodge dealt them all into the next round. Ellen passed out cake and Mom untied her apron and pitched it over the counter, requesting, "Walk with me, Jo?"

"Of course," I said.

Out under the stars, Mom hooked her arm through mine as we made our way onto the dock. She was just a little shorter than me, her freckled arm soft and plump against my side; the scent of the butter cake she baked earlier still clung to her hair. We sat on the glider and I kicked it into gentle motion, keeping Mom's arm close. I finally whispered, "Gran."

"I know," Mom sighed. "God, I wish she was here."

"Me, too," I murmured. A jagged lump seemed to have taken up permanent residence in my throat since last weekend. Too much happened and we were all reeling.

"We'll scatter her ashes when Jillian is home," Mom added decisively, in response to the question I hadn't asked.

"Over Flickertail, just like she wanted," I agreed. "And then we'll have Justin and Jilly's wedding."

"Yes, that sounds perfect. But it breaks my heart that Gran won't be here for that," Mom said softly. "Or for yours. And for Camille's baby, and Jillian and Justin's. Oh, Joelle. I wish I was as strong as her. Ma always knew how to take things in stride. I'm a wreck. I've depended on my mother for so many years." She turned to me, tears streaking over her cheeks; she used her free hand to swipe impatiently at them. "Joelle, I'm so sorry about everything with Jackson. I was wrong. I admit it. Blythe is the man for you, just like Justin is for Jilly. I've been feeling so guilty, honey."

"Oh, Mom," I said, resting my head on her shoulder, and I felt like her little girl, for the first time in a very long time. "Don't feel guilty."

"I do. You and I have always butted heads, Jo, and Jilly has always been so easy for me to get along with. An easier child all around. I'm sorry to say that, but you know. Any mother knows that about her children. But I love you so, Joelle, don't ever think I don't. I admire your courage, and I admire how much you've changed this summer."

"Oh, Mom," I said again, about to give in to full-scale weeping. I turned into my mother's arms and let her hold me, let her comfort me as I hadn't in too many years to count. I knew exactly what she meant; didn't I secretly acknowledge the same thing about Ruthie? My sweetest daughter, the one who gave me the least trouble? It wasn't a matter of loving one child more than another, it was a matter of the ability to get along day to day with the least possible stress. And I knew I'd caused my mother enough stress for a lifetime.

"Your hair is just like Gran's was," Mom observed after a while, gently combing her fingers through it. "You and Jillian both have that Davis cornsilk hair. Comes from some lovely ancestor."

"The prostitute, right?" I whispered against Mom's lap, where my head ended up.

"Maybe so," Mom said; Great-Aunt Minnie always insisted that one of her great-something grandmothers was a saloon girl. We all played along for the notoriety of such a claim.

But reality caught up with me too soon, and I moaned, "I'm so scared, Mom."

Mom's hand stilled its motion through my hair. She whispered, "She'll be all right, Jo. She has to be. For all of us."

"Thank you for apologizing," I whispered, at last managing to sit up, swiping at my wet cheeks with the base of my palms. "That means a lot to me."

Later, we rejoined everyone inside, where the action sounded rather boisterous. I was relieved to see that Camille joined them; she was even smiling a little, elbowing Tish about something as they bickered like the good old days. Blythe looked over instantly as Mom and I came through the screen door, asking with his eyes if I was all right, and I went immediately to him, where he scooted out his chair so I could sit on his lap; I did so with no self-consciousness, recalling how last weekend he'd still been in jail in Oklahoma. To have him here was so incredibly good and I kissed his temple as he curved one arm around my waist, whispering into my ear, "I love you," under the cover of everyone else chattering as Rich dealt yet another round.

We played for another hour, Blythe and I continuously being accused of cheating since we were playing as a "team," Tish proving to be a fabulous little bluffer, though Jake seemed to know every time and called her out. After a second piece of cake and cup of coffee, Dodge finally said, "I better get going. The boy's expecting me."

"Can I come with you?" Clint asked. He appeared exhausted, his blue eyes puffy from lack of sleep, but Dodge said immediately, "Of course."

"I'll come with," I offered. "I haven't been over since this morning."

Blythe hugged me tightly and said, "I'll get everyone home, don't you worry, baby."

At the hospital thirty minutes later we found Justin dozing, his right arm bent under his head, propped on the bed by Jilly's side. He stirred only slightly as we came into the room, so out of it that he probably couldn't see straight, and so I ordered as firmly as I was able, "Justin, Jilly would be furious at me for letting you get away with not sleeping or eating. Lie down on the cot, right now."

Justin blinked and looked for a moment like a little boy, despite some pretty serious five o'clock shadow. He muttered, "Okay, Jo," as though I was an annoying big sister, and let Dodge lead him to the small cot on the side of the room. I tossed over a pillow while Dodge found a blanket and covered his son, who was snoring lightly within a minute. I clicked out the bedside lamp, hoping he'd sleep for at least a few hours. I let Clint take the chair Justin had been using, standing instead so I could stroke my sister's face. She needed someone to bathe her, to wash out her hair. She'd been limp here in this bed since Wednesday.

Goddammit, Jillian, come on, I thought, though anger was totally unjustified—but it was far less frightening than hopelessness. *Wake up. Pull out of this.*

I touched her hair as gingerly as if feeling a baby's soft spot.

Clint said softly, "Aunt Joey, do you think she can feel you doing that?"

"I hope so," I whispered back. Dodge settled on the orange vinyl armchair positioned at a right angle to the bed, folded his arms and let his chin sink toward his chest, clearly prepared to spend the night.

"Mom's having a baby," Clint said, with a certain amount of awe, bracing his chin on the metal railing of the bed. "Just like Camille."

"You'll finally be a big brother," I whispered. The dimness of the room seemed to inspire confidences. I added, "You'll be such a good one. Your dad always wanted a big family, you know, since he didn't have any brothers or sisters of his own."

"I wish I had more memories of my dad," Clint said. "I've seen all the pictures, and Grandma talks about him, and Granny Elaine does, too, but I don't remember anything about him really."

I reached and feathered Clinty's hair, saying, "Well, he looked just like you. Except his eyes were light brown, not blue. He was always smiling and teasing your mom, and never seemed to get angry. Just like you, too." Clint shifted to lean against my side, just like he used to when he was small. I bent to kiss the top of his head. "He loved winter. It was his favorite season. Your grandpa and your dad were carpenters and built all sorts of things, including your crib, the one that Camille is going to use for her baby next spring."

"I wish I could build stuff," Clint mused. "I don't know how to do any of that stuff."

"But you can change oil and work on a car engine," I said.

"Dodge taught me that," Clint said. "And Justin's teaching me to drive a five-speed. It's totally kick-ass. And he's teaching me to drive the motorboat."

"Justin's a good guy," I affirmed, cupping the back of Clint's head, patting him.

"He makes Mom really happy."

"He sure does."

"After they get married, do you think it would be weird if I called him 'Dad'?"

"You know what, Clinty? I think that would make him the happiest guy in the world."

At that very moment Jilly's fingers flickered inward. For a second I thought I might just be seeing things, but then her left hand made a loose fist. I leaned closer to her face and demanded quietly, "Jilly! Can you hear me?"

I touched her face and her eyelids fluttered. Clint leaped to his feet, knocking over his chair in the process, and cried, "Mom!"

And Jilly's blue eyes opened.

"Jilly!" I rejoiced, but then gasped, "No!" as Clint moved as though to throw himself onto her for a hug.

Justin shoved us out of the way to get to the bedside, but I understood the intensity of his desire to see her awake; Clint and I crowded back against him as Jilly blinked and then blinked again, a more welcome sight than anything I could imagine. Clint sobbed and I held him, my tears falling onto my nephew's hair.

"Jillian," Justin breathed, touching her face, tears flowing over his cheeks, dripping from his jaw. "Oh thank God. You're going to be all right, do you hear me?"

Relief swamped through us like rain over cracked earth.

"Oh my God, we've been so scared," Justin said, his words gushing forth, his voice hoarse. "Jilly, sweetheart, we love you so much."

She tried to say something but her throat was too rough, a ventilator covering her nose, a tube between her lips. She closed her eyes and shook her head gently on the pillow. Justin curved his hand around hers and asked, "What is it, sweetheart? What do you need?"

Jilly implored us with her eyes, seeking mine. I leaned in close and whispered, "What is it, honey?"

She managed to utter a whisper, which I understood. I straightened and said, "She said, 'she's okay.'" Though I was not by any shake of the stick as gifted as my sister in the art of mind-reading, I knew in my heart exactly what she meant, and I explained, "The baby, she means." Jilly's eyes held mine and she nodded incrementally, in clear satisfaction.

"She?" Justin whispered, awestruck, stroking Jilly's face, and her eyes caressed him as she nodded again. "Our baby is a little girl? Oh, Jillian, oh my God."

Justin turned and hugged Clint, rocking the boy side to side, and then all of us were bear-hugged by Dodge. He roared with typical good-nature, "For the love of God, someone call Shore Leave!"

Chapter Nineteen

June, 2006

FROM THE MOMENT SHE WAS BORN, RAE WAS HER DADDY'S girl. She knew his voice of course, as he spent hours talking to her while she grew inside me, his palms curved on either side as my belly expanded with each month. I would never forget Justin's expression as the doctor placed Rae in his arms moments after birth. Happy tears gathered in my eyes even now, just remembering. She had been fussing, but Justin kissed her forehead and murmured, "Hi, sweet girl, my sweet baby girl," and almost instantly she quieted and gazed up at her daddy, and thereby claimed his heart, for always. We named her Louisa Rae, but from nearly the first moment we called her by her middle name, which better suited our wild girl. She was now two years old, our little stick of dynamite, with dimples in her round cheeks and Justin's beautiful, pecan-brown eyes. Clinty was practically a slave to her, and Justin was a total goner. At times my heart ached with happiness.

By September, Justin and I would have another baby. A boy this time, and Justin was beside himself with excitement. He, Clint, and Rae all spent plenty of time talking to him, patting and kissing my belly; Rae came up with a new name for her brother every day, names that sounded more suitable for pets than siblings, this morning's being Scamp. I'd spent the afternoon at Shore Leave, lounging on the porch, relaxing after a day of mostly relaxing. For one thing, Justin was insistent that I take it easy; my morning sickness finally dissipated, but only just last week. It was so lovely to feel hungry again; Jo offered to drive into town to buy the fixings for bacon cheeseburgers, at my rather insistent urging. It was Monday, so the cafe was closed, and I was relieved at the relative quiet.

The bell above the porch door tinkled as Blythe came outside, little Matthew on his arm. Matty was fussing, one chubby finger hooked in his mouth, and I immediately reached for him, saying, "Come here to Aunt Jilly, honey-bunny."

Blythe deposited his son in my arms and I grinned at my brother-in-law, whose hair was long and wavy again, falling past his shoulders, the way Jo liked it; both she and I had a thing for being able to sink our hands into our men's hair, obviously genetic. Bly had also grown a goatee; we all teased him that he just needed to learn to play acoustic guitar now to complete the overall look.

To explain Matty's tears, Blythe said, "He wanted a banana, so I got him one and then he cried when I peeled it."

"Of course you did, didn't you, baby?" I asked Matty, bouncing him on my lap; Blythe was still getting used to the contradictory nature of toddlers. I bent to kiss Matty's downy cheeks and he offered an engaging grin, showcasing his newest tooth.

"You little sweetie," I adored.

Bly plunked onto the chair at a right angle to mine and regarded his boy with a fond smile. He complained, "Sure, he smiles for *you*." He reached to pat my belly, the same way you might rub a genie's lamp for luck, asking, "You want anything, Jilly-billy? Wow, I remember when Joelle felt like this, like there was a beach ball under her shirt."

"That's just what a girl in her third trimester likes to hear," I said, elbowing teasingly at his hand.

"Aw, you know what I mean," Bly said, sitting back and stretching out his long legs. He added, "I can't wait to get Joelle pregnant again, I love watching Matty grow." And he had loved every minute, no exaggeration there, much to Jo's only-slightly-amused delight. Blythe was about the sweetest man alive, other than Rich, and I knew he would be thrilled if he and Jo had a dozen kids.

"Better add another addition to your cabin," I said. "Ooh, and I'd love some lemonade."

"You got it," Blythe said, hopping right back up to grab one from the kitchen; I planned, with no guilt, to continue taking total advantage of being pregnant and allowing others to wait on me.

At that moment I heard my husband's truck and my heart clattered with anticipation; I hadn't seen him since early this morning. Justin climbed out of the truck and strode across the parking lot, looking so damn good that I wanted to jump him right on a porch table; his utter masculinity never failed to make my belly go weightless with longing. He saw the look in my eyes as he climbed the porch steps and then leaned his forearms over the back of the chair to my right, which accentuated his wide shoulders.

"Hello there, wife of mine," he said, eyes dancing with a half-wicked grin. "Miss me a little today?"

Instead of answering, I sent a detailed message with my eyes that made him shift position a little, his smile broadening to a smoldering grin.

"Looks like I better get you home, and soon," he understood.

Matty said then, "Hi-hi, Unco Justin!"

Justin refocused on his nephew and said, "Hi there, little guy. You taking care of your Aunt Jilly?"

Matty nodded solemnly and I explained, "Jo took the girls into town for groceries. We were thinking burgers tonight."

Blythe came back outside carrying a frosty lemonade. He said, "Here, sis," as he set it on the table, and then, "Justin, you're just in time to help unload the truck."

"No problem," Justin responded, stepping closer to me and curving one hand around my jaw, bending to softly kiss my lips.

Blythe cleared his throat with mock sternness and teased, "Not in front of the kid, you guys."

Matty giggled, bouncing on my lap, kicking his chubby legs.

Justin straightened and gently tucked a strand of hair behind my ear. I'd let my hair grow out again; it fell past my shoulders these days. I smiled up at my husband with a promise for later, and then turned to demand of Blythe, "So…that *wasn't* you and Jo down on the dock the other night? I must have been imagining things."

Bly flushed, ducking his head.

Justin mused, "The dock…one of my favorite places on the face of this earth," and a scorching flush lit my cheeks; he and I still crept down there sometimes in the hot summer darkness to make love, for old times' sake.

"No one's supposed to know about that," I complained.

Bly said smugly, "Yeah, not fooling anyone, you two."

Joelle pulled into the parking lot driving Blythe's old black truck, Camille in the passenger seat and Rae and Millie Jo in back, the little girls waving out the window. Jo parked and Camille extracted the girls from their car seats, holding their hands to walk them across to the porch.

Rae broke free, yelling, "Daddy!" and Justin hopped down the steps.

"Hi, teddy bear," he said, catching her close for a squeeze before tossing her high into the air. Millie Jo tugged on his arm, begging to be thrown next, and Blythe bounded over to the truck to help Jo unload groceries. I spied him cup the back of her neck and pull her close for a kiss, before slipping his hand down the side of her waist. At the same moment Matty began crying again, stretching out his chubby arms and wailing, "Mama!" as though Jo had been gone for weeks.

Bly took all of the bags while Jo, her long hair arranged in a French braid, hurried up to snag her baby from my lap, covering his face in kisses.

"Hiya, sweetie," she said, swinging him onto her hip. "Hi, Jills."

"Did you get tortilla chips?" I pestered, which I'd been craving all day.

"Aunt Jilly, can we go swimming?" Millie Jo asked, leaning over my knees and regarding me with her solemn, golden-green eyes. She was the spitting image of Camille, and just as serious in demeanor.

"Maybe after supper. Where're the big kids?" I asked the girls, referring to Tish, Ruthie, and Clinty.

Camille sank gracefully onto a chair near mine and said, "Out on the lake."

"Yeah, I got your chips," Jo said, letting Matty slide to the porch and snagging her husband around the waist. "Wait up there, handsome. I need to grab something."

Blythe leaned down and whispered in her ear and she smacked his ass, laughing as she dug out a yellow bag and tossed it to me. Justin came up the steps, Rae clinging to his right arm as he held it extended straight out.

"Lookit, Mama," she said. "Isn't Daddy strong?"

"He sure is," I agreed, sending Justin another extremely heated telepathic message.

Justin let Rae swing to the floor, where she took off after Millie Jo. Matty tried to chase them and got about as far as Jo's knees before getting swept up. Justin winked at me, leaning against the railing, and then Blythe came back outside to snag him for chores. Life at Shore Leave, going on. And at that moment, Camille's man pulled into the parking lot; channeling Great-Aunt Minnie, I said, "There's your fella, doll," and Camille beamed with near-heartbreaking joy, jumping up to meet him as he parked and hurried across the blacktop to scoop her close. I was so happy for her...the past few years had been pretty damn tough on my niece.

But then, that was entirely another story.

...THE STORY CONTINUES IN *Winter at the White Oaks Lodge*

Excerpt from Winter at the White Oaks Lodge

"ANY DAY NOW, SWEETIE, ANY DAY." GRANDMA'S WORDS were accompanied by her hand on my back, patting me between the shoulder blades as I leaned on my palms against the edge of the kitchen sink and attempted to draw a deep breath.

It wasn't that I was trying to melodramatic; I truly could not get enough air into my lungs, courtesy of the enormous pregnancy that belled out my stomach.

"I keep reminding myself that." I grumbled, "It's not fair. Aunt Jilly looks adorable, and she's as pregnant as me. But she never complains."

Grandma said, "That's not true. Everyone complains at this stage of a pregnancy. It comes with the territory. Just be glad it isn't summer."

I smiled at her over my shoulder, my grandma Joan, who'd lived in this same house since her own childhood. The walls here surely witnessed their share of pregnant women. As long as I could remember, we came to Landon from Chicago for summer break; never in my wildest imaginings had I pictured myself living here as a pregnant and single teenager. On the old timeline, I would be finishing up my senior year of high school, at home in Chicago. I closed my eyes, unwittingly dragged to the afternoon I'd sat trembling on the edge of the tub in the bathroom upstairs, gingerly clutching the end of the world as I'd known it—a plastic pregnancy tester with a purple plus sign on the indicator.

"That's right," I whispered. "Mom and Aunt Jilly were both born in August. But at least you didn't have to worry about slipping on the ice."

I lived in mortal fear of falling since the first frost at the end of last

October, warily traversing the slippery sidewalks of Landon as my belly finally outpaced my breasts in size. It seemed to me that the high school was the last place in town that was plowed or de-iced. At least I was done with school for now; Landon High was a study in small-town bias against the "slut who got Noah Utley in trouble."

It was irony of the worst sort, as I was truly the least slutty girl I knew. Of course evidence would suggest otherwise, as here I stood, eighteen years old and well into my eighth month of pregnancy. It was a poor excuse, I understood this, but last June and July, under the magic of the hot summer moon, I believed that Noah Utley loved me. Thinking back on it now, I compared myself to a puppy seeking affection; when Noah complimented me, I all but wriggled with the pleasure of it, believing every word he spoke, without any question. He may as well have scratched behind my ears. And, as anyone besides me could have predicted, here I was without him and carrying our baby. I had not heard a word since he returned to college last autumn.

"Good morning," said Aunt Ellen smiling as she joined us, reaching for the coffee pot. "Camille, what's the story? Is she coming today?"

"Who knows?" I asked, a note of cynicism in my tone. It seemed my daughter was planning a permanent residence in my uterus. But then I was assaulted anew, with pure terror, at the thought of having a tiny living person who would be solely dependent upon me. Grandma sensed as its impact struck my face, as she resumed patting my back.

"It's all right, sweetie, we'll be here to help. You won't be alone," she assured me for the countless time. Probably it was better to have two women with decades of experience in child-rearing at my side, rather than Noah Utley, who'd primarily been an expert at getting me out of my jean shorts.

"I know, Gram," I said. Grandma's familiar eyes were a perfect blending of golden and green, the Davis family eyes, as Mom always said.

According to Aunt Jilly, I'm having a girl. Everyone in our family knows to take Aunt Jilly's Notions for truth. So at night, I curl around my belly on the twin bed made up with the same flowered sheets that my mom used in high school, and contemplate holding a little bundle wrapped in pink. No matter how much I picture her, I know she won't exactly resemble my imaginings, though in my mind she looks like me.

"Besides, she'd be early if she came today," I reminded them.

"Jo and Jilly both came early," Grandma said. "And you're so close to forty weeks now, there's nothing to worry about." She leaned to kiss my cheek before reminding Aunt Ellen, "Don't forget we have the whole crew tonight, for Valentine's. And Liz and Wordo are joining them."

"We'll be a full house. I better get baking."

"I don't know why I'm crying," I moaned, tipping forward. The baby performed what felt like a series of donkey kicks, as though in response. I felt so cumbersome, bloated as a milking cow, my ankles swollen along with just about every part of my formerly slim, agile body. Two huge pimples bloomed on my forehead, which was a pasty, midwinter white, my summer tan long since faded. I looked like something straight out of a birth-control manual: Thinking about having sex? Well take a gander at what pregnancy really looks like and see if you feel the same!

"Camille," Grandma said gently, and she rested her cheek to my shoulder, rubbing my back in small, comforting circles.

"I know," I sobbed, my throat full of shards. How could I admit that if I allowed myself, I would probably cry from dawn until dusk on a daily basis, and then the whole night through, plagued with guilty misery. I loved my baby already, there was no question, but I was so disoriented, disillusioned in all other regards, so often assaulted by thoughts of what my old friends from my former life were doing, back home in Chicago. How at this point in that life I should be writing college entrance letters and polishing my resume, with no more pressing decisions than which campus I might visit over spring break. On the current time line, in which my life sharply deviated from its intended path, I was learning about how it's difficult to go more than an hour or so without needing to find the nearest bathroom, how difficult it is to monkey an infant car seat into place, and that mothers absolutely find it necessary to inform a pregnant girl about how painful their own labors were—and how long.

I was a full forty pounds heavier than I'd been last summer, other than my sisters I was friendless, and my future seemed bleak, gray and peppered with uncertainty. College was out of the question, at least for the next foreseeable five years, surely more. Last spring I spent time contemplating if I would rather teach English or history at the high school level. I'd always been intrigued with the little details that make up a series of events, the primary history found in letters and journals and old photographs. The Civil War was my favorite era, and once upon a time I envisioned myself as that cool, easygoing sort of teacher, my curly hair tied up into a bun and semi-sexy horn-rimmed glasses perched on my nose, creating meaningful and interesting lessons for an avid group of students who hung on my every word. This plan seemed within reach back then.

You're a smart young woman, Camille Gordon, were the words of nearly every teacher in my past. *You'll go places.*

Yes, I thought now. Like the grocery store for another box of diapers.

"Why don't I make you some of that hot chocolate you like?" Aunt Ellen asked, as though I was a little girl, but it comforted me deeply.

Grandma tapped her lips with an index finger. "Remember, there's that old trunk in the attic. Camille, you wanted to look through it."

I brightened at this reminder. Not long ago Grandma came across a little leather trunk in the attic, full of Davis family mementos.

"I put it in my room. Why don't you go have a look?"

I hugged both of them before climbing carefully up to the second floor. Grandma's room was dim in the early morning light, so I clicked on the bedside lamp. This space was comforting in the same way that smelling the scent of my mom's robe would be, familiar way down deep in my soul. A word from eighth-grade vocabulary suddenly flashed across my memory.

Unflappable. The ability to maintain composure in all circumstances. This word perfectly described all the women in my family.

I saw the trunk near the foot of the bed, centered on the braided rag rug adorning the otherwise bare wood floor. A beat of anticipation rippled through me; the trunk looked old, full of intriguing secrets, and I lowered myself with care, settling so that my lower back didn't ache too terribly. My baby pressed outward with her heels. As I watched, I could see the tiny points under my skin, moving along as though she meant to break free. I would never get over how incredible it was to feel a living person inside of me; I pushed gently upon the little protrusion, easing it into a more comfortable position, then patted the spot.

"Look here," I murmured to her, as I liked to do, but only if no one else was around. "It says 'Davis' on this trunk. That's our family's name."

I ran my fingertips over the word, which someone had long ago carved into the leather buckling strap as though with a knifepoint. The hinges creaked and once the lid was open the scent of leather was released. With a growing sense of wonder I studied the contents. There were several small frames, one lying upside down, the backing cracked with age. I was drawn to that one in particular for whatever reason, and when I lifted it and parted the sides of the old hinged frame, a shiver climbed my spine. Immediately, I turned the frame over, searching for a way to free the photograph. I released the tiny metal clasps and slid loose the image, slightly alarmed at my haste. I only knew that I wanted to see it again as fast as possible. There was a date scrawled on the back, and the words Me & Aces. Beneath that, Carter and 1875 were written with the same strong hand.

"This is so old," I said to the baby.

I flipped over the fragile picture. I would be sure to find a dictionary or some other equally weighty book in which to press it tonight, see if I couldn't flatten it out a little. And then I studied the image at close range, with complete absorption. I felt an unexpected rush of excited anticipation, the way I used to feel as a little girl when Tish and I were into mysteries, and tried to find crimes to solve every other second.

"Is Carter your first name, or last?" I wondered softly, tracing his face.

The picture was almost haunting in its simple beauty, sunset somewhere in 1875. Here? Near here? It was tough to pinpoint a location, only that I was certain it was evening, as the long beams of a gorgeous mellow sun backlit both man and horse. Something about his face, captured in a half-grin, made my heart simultaneously pulse and ache, with something I could not begin to articulate.

Printed in the United States
by Baker & Taylor Publisher Services